F
ADL

Adler, Elizabeth.

Please don't tell

Also by Elizabeth Adler

Elizabeth Adler

PLEASE DON'T TELL

Minotaur Books New York

This is a work of fiction. All of the characters, organizations, and events portrayed in this novel are either products of the author's imagination or are used fictitiously.

www.minotaurbooks.com

Design by Kathryn Parise

Library of Congress Cataloging-in-Publication Data

Adler, Elizabeth (Elizabeth A.)
    Please don't tell / Elizabeth Adler. — First U.S. edition.
        pages cm
    ISBN 978-1-250-01989-9 (hardcover)
    ISBN 978-1-250-01990-5 (e-book)
  1. Middle-aged women—Fiction.   2. Granddaughters—Fiction.   3. Serial
murder investigation—Fiction.   4. Suspense fiction gsafd   I. Title.
    PR6051.D56P64 2013
    823'.914—dc23

                                                            2013009812

Minotaur books may be purchased for educational, business, or promotional use. For information on bulk purchases, please contact Macmillan Corporate and Premium Sales Department at 1-800-221-7945, extension 5442, or write specialmarkets@macmillan.com.

First Edition: July 2013

10 9 8 7 6 5 4 3 2 1

For Anabelle Adler Avery and Eric Avery

Prologue

It was a winter afternoon, and a stormy sky was looming. The man was waiting in the black Range Rover, parked in the darkest part of the coffee shop lot away from the lights, when he felt the pain again. A pressure in his chest, a floating sensation in his head, only a few seconds, though. The first time he'd felt that was when he'd lifted a table to move it to a more prominent position. Fool; he should have known better. He must have pulled a shoulder muscle and now it was acting up, just when he needed to be at his best. His brain cleared, the pain left. He forgot about it and concentrated on the work at hand.

The lot was almost empty, just a couple of vehicles belonging, he knew, to the kitchen staff. Customers always parked round the front. It was one of a popular chain in California, right off Highway 1, south of San Francisco. He knew exactly what time the girl's shift finished, knew how she would burst out of the staff door, bubbling with laughter and relief at getting out of there, sometimes with others, but more often on her own. He knew her car was the ten-year-old Chevy Blazer that often broke down and for which she had no insurance, and which she always left in the same spot in back of the café so no nosy cop, dropping in for a cup of coffee and pancakes with phony maple syrup, would take notice of and maybe ask questions about a vehicle that looked as crappy as that.

He knew exactly where she lived. In fact he knew exactly what her small studio apartment looked like. He had been there, easily forcing the cheap lock when she was at work, looking round, touching her things, inspecting the tiny bathroom and the plastic shower stall with the plastic curtain that must have stuck to her naked body when she took her shower. He had run his tongue over her toothbrush, sniffed the underpants she'd left on the floor with the rest of her clothing, exactly where she'd stepped out of them the previous night. He had lain down on her unmade bed, rested his head on her pillow, surprised to find the sheets were clean. She was not a dirty girl, just sloppy and untidy and careless.

He'd marked her as his victim when he had gone into the coffee shop and she had made eye contact, ready to flirt with a customer in the hope of a good tip, though any tip she'd get was probably negligible. He'd liked her fresh clean skin, the pinkness of her cheeks, flushed from rushing between the customer and the kitchen. She worked hard, she was willing. Her name was Elaine. It said so on the badge pinned to her shirt and she was pretty enough to qualify. He had even chatted to her, learned she had quit community college where she had been studying, of all things, biology. She'd said cheerfully she would go back there when she could afford it, which both he and she knew meant never. Still, he liked her plumpness, her long brown hair, her brown eyes and pink cheeks and her jolly girl demeanor. He always liked the nice girls best.

Now he saw her come bursting out the staff door. Alone. She was wearing a black skirt, a too-thin black jacket. He put on his fine, supple latex gloves, got quickly out of his car, called her name. "Elaine." She turned, surprised. He knew she couldn't make out who he was, in the shade.

"My door seems to have stuck, could you help me?" he called, just loud enough, that, thinking she must know him, she came.

He liked the hurried way she walked, half-running.

Her long brown hair swung over her face as she neared. In one smooth move he grabbed it in his fist and slammed the side of his hand hard on the carotid. She went limp and he pushed her into the car, flung her handbag in after her. In seconds he was out of the lot and onto the highway.

He looked at her in the mirror, facedown on the plastic cover he had carefully arranged so that his leather seat would not get stained. She was not moving. At the next exit, he pulled off the road into a quiet place, got out and checked her. She was still breathing. Low hurting breaths. He'd hit her exactly hard enough. He knew what he was doing. He'd done it all before. He stuck a needle in her arm; a quick shot to make sure she would not wake suddenly and surprise him. Her erratic breathing slowed.

He got back into the car and drove on. He'd already picked out the place he was taking her, on the edge of some woods. When he got there he sat for a moment or two, anticipating what was to come. No rain yet, only the harsh sound of the wind gusting in the trees, presaging a storm and sending a shower of leaves over him and the car, and over the girl as he opened the back door. It was still light out but dark in the woods.

He took out the lightweight black messenger bag containing the small video camera, its tripod and his night-vision binoculars—his "equipment" he called it—and slung it round his neck. He pulled the girl out of the car and carried her into the woods . . . not too far, no need . . . nobody ever came here. His heart gave a little bump again: she was heavier than he'd thought.

There was a method to these things, a ritual he had to respect. Everything must be in sequence. He spread-eagled her on a pile of rotting leaves. Nice and soft. He thought she would like that. Next, he took the tripod and the video camera from the messenger bag and set them up next to her, making sure to get her properly in focus. He pulled on the black woolen ski mask, covering his face. Now, he was ready. It was the work of moments to undress her, tugging off her skirt, her white shirt, her underwear. She was not wearing a bra and her small breasts looked very white in the dense blackness.

He pulled the knife from its custom-made leather sheath that he wore strapped to his leg. It was a slim fileting knife, around eight inches long, the kind used by chefs. Pure, hard gleaming steel. Power in the hands of a man who knew exactly how to use it.

Kneeling over her, with surgical precision he slit each of her wrists, then sat back watching the blood ooze, her life begin to drift slowly away. She had not opened her eyes. The supreme moment was almost here. All it would take was one more cut, soft as butter, across her throat. She was limp, unresisting as he raped her, the knife at her throat, just the first small incision . . . waiting . . . waiting . . . he groaned in triumph, slid the knife across her throat, saw the blood spill though she wasn't dead yet . . .

He sat back exhausted. There was nothing to equal that moment, that feeling. The sheer sexual power of it. There was one last thing though; something else he was compelled to do. He took the green Post-it pad from his pocket and using his left hand, printed out a message.

He checked her again. Her mouth hung open. He snapped her jaw shut, then he stuck the green Post-it over her closed lips, added a strip of duct tape, just to make sure it didn't fall off. He had the knife on her neck again; he knew where the carotid was.

He thought he heard something, sat back startled. He had not finished yet . . . A car stopped, then started up again. Unnerved, he grabbed the camera and the bag, crouched low, made a run for it . . . The pain hit his chest and his heart thundered so loud he could hear it, a million beats a minute . . . he was falling into blackness with the pain . . . and the fear that he was caught . . . fear won . . .

He concentrated all his being on driving. It was raining now . . . the pain hit again, lesser this time, not really his heart, more his shoulder . . . exactly where he'd pulled the muscle yesterday, shifting that table.

Should he go to the emergency room? Why? He was fine now, breathing, okay, heart steady as a rock. It was a minor mishap and a spoiled "event." He checked the bag on the seat next to him, felt for the camera. It was there. His knife was there. Everything was okay, but it had been a close call. He would be more careful, find somewhere more remote next time.

He already had his next girl picked out. It made him feel secure, knowing the future, his plans. He'd been watching Dr. Vivian for weeks. Now though, he'd get out of here, fast, get a drink and something to eat. He was always hungry after his little "experiences." He would avoid the freeway, stick to the side roads. He hadn't reckoned on a storm, though, on the bad visibility, the sudden slickness. And then he hit something.

Big Sur, California

It had started out as an ordinary morning for Fen Dexter. She had gotten up late—nineish, something like that. It was Hector who woke her, putting his big paw on the bed, giving her a nudge and drooling on her arm. Labradors always drooled, and they always had to be let out first thing before they burst. Nine was late for Hector too. She opened the door for him, then, when he'd finished, let him in again and went back to bed, feeling lazy, just lying there listening to the boom of the waves hitting the rocks at the base of the cliffs.

Cliff Cottage, Fen's small California house, stood in what Fen had always termed "isolated splendor," on a bluff between Big Sur and the village of Carmel. The "isolated splendor" was meant as a joke since the road was a mere hundred yards away and the "cottage" was far from "splendid." It wasn't even "grand" *and* it was pale blue stucco.

It had been her home for twelve years, bought on an impulse after her husband died suddenly and to her, inexplicably because he was such a fit man, always exercising, running, he even played a three-hour game of tennis the day before. Then, after a morning cup of tea, he looked at her, surprised, she thought, and quite simply crumpled to the ground. And life as Fen knew it ended.

Greg, the "all-American boy" as she always called him teasingly, was in fact her third husband. The first had been the Frenchman, when she was twenty and making a somewhat precarious living in Paris as a dancer, on stage in stilettos and a minimal amount of sequins and wearing the short Sassoon bob wigs all the girls wore. It wasn't what she'd hoped for after all those years of ballet and training but not everyone could be a star, and she met so many people. Including the husband she only ever referred to now as "the Frenchman," the hand-holder, the gentle kisser, the leaver of romantic messages, the donator of generous bouquets of white roses. They were not her favorite flower but soon became so. He was older, thirty-five to her twenty, divorced and with baggage but he wanted to marry her and who was she to say no to a life of romance and kisses. It lasted a year. And then he was on to someone new. That's just the way he was.

The second husband was Italian-Jewish. Who knew there was such a combo? Certainly not Fen, but without any family of her own, she had fallen in love with *his* big gregarious in-your-face family that took over their lives and before she knew it she was trying to decide between a Catholic Italian ceremony or a Jewish wedding with all the trimmings. In the end they sneaked off and got married in a civil ceremony and that was that. And finally when, to their great disappointment, the expected children did not appear, the family decided it was all her fault. Fen knew from their silent looks across the table, the sudden diminishing of jolly family meals, that was what they thought, and when she finally was worried enough to get checked out, to her horror, she found they were right.

Since it was a civil marriage divorce was easy but it left Fen brokenhearted and lonely. She was alone in the world. Again.

On an impulse she flew to California, went to stay with an old friend at her small vineyard in Sonoma County. Her name was Millie, and Millie produced a Chardonnay that was just coming into fashion in the way certain wines did. Fen invested her small savings plus the money she had been awarded in her two divorces (in both of which she was the innocent party) and ultimately financially it was the saving of her. It was also where later, she met her third husband. The American.

Greg was thirty-eight, Fen was twenty-seven. She was living in San Francisco in a small pastel-color Victorian in the Mission District that was only just starting to come into its own and still had rough edges. Too rough, Fen worried sometimes, for a woman living alone. But then she didn't live alone for long. She had a part-time job at the university teaching her specialty, the evolution of dance to its modern form, while also donating her services free to an animal rescue charity, when she got the call from a Mr. Herman Wright, attorney-at-law, asking her to please come to see him. It was very important, he told her and no he could not discuss it on the phone.

Oh shit, she remembered thinking as she dressed in her most respectable outfit, black slim pants (she had good long legs) a soft white linen shirt and an Hermès orange cable cashmere sweater, a long-ago expensive gift from husband number one, when he was still courting her, that is. She powdered her nose, a daring slash of fire-engine red over her full lips, a quick flick of the brush through her golden blond hair. She took a final look in the mirror, wondering if she looked respectable enough for Mr. Herman Wright attorney-at-law and his secret message. She grinned as she waved herself good-bye. Fuck Mr. Attorney at Law. Nobody was suing her. Maybe she had come into a fabulous inheritance from some long-lost relative. Yeah. Right. A kiss for the ginger cat named Maurice who hated to be left, and she was on her way.

She took a taxi to the lawyer's, not wanting to get all mussed up on public transportation, even though she could really not afford it. Mr. Wright's offices were imposing, three floors in a good building downtown. Mr. Wright himself was not so imposing, small, square and ginger as the cat. But what he had to tell her was. It shocked her to her very core, more than anything else in her entire life.

That's what she said to him, then. "But I'm too young!"

Mr. Wright shrugged a shoulder, smoothed his floral silk tie, looked kindly at her over the breadth of his oak desk. "Many women have several children by your age, Miss Dexter." Fen had reverted to her own name after the last divorce. "Surely it can be no hardship for a healthy young woman like you to bring up two girls."

"But they are not *my* girls," she cried, shocked. "I don't have a husband! How could they do this to me!"

The "this" she was talking about and that had come at her like a bolt from the blue—not just any old bolt but a *thunderbolt*—was that a remote cousin Fen did not at first remember having, though they had met once when she was dancing in Paris (the cousin and the husband had come backstage and introduced themselves, had a glass of Champagne then smiled their goodbyes . . .), had perished in a plane crash, flying a small Cessna over a mountainous area where they'd been caught in a lethal downdraft. Their two children were still at their home in Manhattan.

"Of course with the children comes the wherewithal to keep

them, there's certainly enough to see them through childhood and college."

"*College?*" What was he talking about? *She* had not been to college!

He said, "The two girls are ages six and four. Their names are Vivian and Jane Cecilia. Ms. Dixon, I cannot emphasize enough that they have no one else to turn to. Without you it will be foster homes. I'm afraid they are rather too old to be popular for adoption."

He sat back looking at her stunned face. "I know, I know," he said gently. "It is a great shock and a terrible responsibility, but your cousin mentioned you specifically in the will, said you were her only relative and therefore she would leave you her most treasured possessions in the hope that, should you be needed, you would know what to do."

Fen said nothing.

Then, "Here are their pictures." He slid a few photos across the desk.

Fen did not pick them up. She simply stared down at them, at the two young faces of her distant relatives, one dark haired, stony-eyed, kicking the grass with a sandaled toe, unwilling to smile for the camera; the other a blond blue-eyed angel beaming for all she was worth.

"That kid's a natural," she heard herself saying. And then quite suddenly she was crying, sitting there in the lawyer's smart office looking at pictures of two little kids who had no one. They were so innocent. She had been alone herself from the age of eighteen. She thought what she was being asked to do was not a lot different from the work she did with abandoned and abused animals, it all came from the same love source.

"I could love these girls," she said finally, collecting the photos and putting them in her bag. "When can I have them?"

11

And that was how she, Fen—short for Fenalla, a name she'd always hated because she thought it sounded like a stripper—became "aunt," never "mom," to "her girls." Who now, after all the growing up—Fen as well as them—through all the schools and ballet classes, the childhood illnesses, the terrible teens, high school, college, boyfriends, lovers, had become a family.

Vivi the oldest was thirty, an emergency room doctor in San Francisco. JC at twenty-eight was out there somewhere, still trying to become a "star," singing in small clubs and in Fen's opinion, going exactly nowhere. Both girls had their own lives and Fen had decided to let them get on with it. She had probably interfered enough over the years.

. . .

Another hour passed before Fen finally got out of bed and walked downstairs. The kitchen's dark planked floor felt cold under her bare feet. It was going to be a chilly one today. She put on the coffee—how she loved that morning coffee smell—then showered, and got herself generally together in jeans and a gray V-necked sweater, first brushing off the dog hairs. She checked the weather again—also gray and with a cold buffeting wind she didn't like. Nor did the dog. Fen had considered naming him Hercules because he was strong, a survivor, but Hector had seemed to fit the bill better. And now here they were, twelve years on. Alone, together.

Then the phone rang. "Fen," she heard Vivi say urgently, "I need to see you. Tonight. I have something I must tell you."

Fen recognized the sound of trouble when she heard it but refrained from asking what was up on the phone; she would save the questions for later. Vivi was a third-year resident at a San Francisco hospital's emergency department. She worked long hours and she and Fen didn't get to see much of each other anymore. Now, though, Vivi said she would stay the night. Which meant Fen had better drive to Carmel and get in some supplies.

She put on her old dark blue peacoat, bundled Hector in the back of the Mini Cooper—no mean feat since the dog weighed in at a hundred pounds. The dog usually preferred to stick his head out the window and sniff the passing scenery but today was too cold.

Twelve years ago Fen had found Hector abandoned at the top of her driveway. When she first saw the brown paper bag she thought, irritated, somebody had littered her property. She got out of the car intending to pick the bag up and dispose of it properly. Instead, there was tiny Hector, gazing mournfully up at her with his big brown eyes. I mean, what could she do?

In Carmel she got lucky, a Range Rover slid out of a parking spot just as she arrived, giving her plenty of room. It was spitting rain and Fen wished she was not wearing her new suede boots. Suede and rain did not go together. She'd worn them because they were flats and she never could manage Carmel's cobbled streets in heels. In fact there used to be a Carmel ordinance that only flat shoes could be worn in the village, since there were so many accidents.

She eased Hector out of the car and dashed to buy a newspaper, then thinking of Vivi's supper, picked up a crusty loaf, some good aged Manchego and a silky goat cheese, as well as a chunk of Parmesan to be grated onto the salad. Two bottles of the Napa Pinot Noir she liked, plus of course she had a couple of cases of her friend Millie's Sonoma Chardonnay. She was pleased when she also managed to find the nice rosemary-raisin crackers which went so well with the cheese.

She had already made a *daube,* her French-style beef stew (she used filet steak and about a gallon of good red wine and let it brew

13

down for long slow hours, adding tiny pearl onions and fresh carrots when the original ones turned to mush) a few weeks ago with Beethoven's Fifth blasting from the stereo, completely drowning out the boom of the waves on the rocks below. She made so much she had to freeze it in separate batches, which meant that tonight she could unfreeze some and serve up a spontaneous meal without any effort.

By the time she finished her shopping the rain was coming down hard. The wind pushed at her back as she shoved Hector into the car, along with the groceries, and when she turned off the road and into the gravel drive to the cottage, it was bending the Monterey pines sideways. Below the house the gray Pacific roared over the rocks even louder than the wind. Still, she was home now. Safe and sound.

· · ·

By seven o'clock, the fire was lit, the beef daube was simmering on a low light, the kitchen table was set with the knives and forks with the aquamarine plastic handles that Fen had bought in Leclerc, an inexpensive French maxi-market, and which were still a favorite. She'd put out the plates with the pictures of parrots on them and the decent wineglasses. The crusty loaf sat on a wooden board, cheeses warming to room temperature next to it while the rain hurled itself with gale-force ferocity at her big windows, which opened onto the small ocean-view terrace.

In fact the weather had turned so bad Fen began to worry. She tried calling Vivi on her mobile to advise her to turn back but could not get through. She went and looked out of the window; all she could see was her own reflection against the black of the night. She put another log on the fire, shifting Hector with her toe and making

14

him grumble. Hector liked his warm spot. Actually, so did she; she was glad not to be out there herself on a night like this.

Restless, she paced back into her bedroom and checked her appearance in the long mirror on the closet door: jeans; the new suede boots that pinched her toes; the gray V-neck that almost matched her silvery hair, cut in a shortish bob to her chin.

For fifty-eight she wasn't half bad, though not nearly as good as she would have liked. Were those new lines, there, above her nose? Wasn't that what Botox was for? She must ask Dr. Vivi about that when she got here. *If* Vivi ever got here was more like it, which Fen doubted, the way the wind was howling now. Gale force was increasing to hurricane, here on her little spit of a cliff, with the waves boiling on the rocks below and rain that had turned into a deluge.

She went to the pantry cupboard and found the hurricane lamp, just in case, trimmed the wick, checked the oil, carried it into the sitting room and put it on the glass coffee table. She turned up the stereo to combat the growl of the wind and sat there, sipping her wine and listening to Beethoven turned up loud, belting out over the rattle of the rain against her windows. She never closed her curtains because the view of the Pacific in all its moods, with its passing gray whales and sporting dolphins, was what had brought her to this place anyway. Seeking solitude, she had found it. And then she had found Hector. And together, they had found "aloneness."

Tonight though, there was something unnerving in the power of the storm. The sheer ferocity of it rocked around her little house. Windows rattled, beams creaked, doors shuddered on their hinges. Even Hector seemed worried, lifting his head and looking inquiringly at her, as though she should stop it or something.

"I wish I could, Hector," she said, interpreting his look. She and Hector always knew what the other was thinking.

15

She picked up the phone to call Vivi but her line was dead. Of course it was; the phone was always the first thing to go in bad weather. She tried her mobile but there was no reception. Now there was no way to contact anyone.

Frowning, she sat back against the sofa cushions, hoping against hope that Vivi had had the sense to turn back. Surely, whatever it was she needed so urgently to talk about could wait till tomorrow.

She'd finished her wine and had just gotten up to pour a little more when the lights went out. Everything went out: the stereo, the refrigerator, the TV.

Fen froze, glass still in hand. There was a thickness to the darkness, a *texture* to the sudden silence. Even the usual almost imperceptible hum of household gadgets was gone.

She felt Hector standing next to her. She said quickly, reassuring herself as well as him, "It's okay, Hector," pulled herself together, clicked on the lighter and lit the hurricane lamp, relieved she had thought of it earlier because she surely would not have been able to find it now in that cupboard in the dark. She lit the stubby green candles on the kitchen table where dinner was set, then went round lighting up the votives she kept around, mostly as decoration, but now happy to have their small light also.

There was nothing else to be done. She went and sat with the dog in front of the fire, welcoming its flickering glow and thanking heaven it wasn't electric. The wind seemed even louder. Or was it because she was so aware of the house's overwhelming silence? She walked over to the window again. Rain sluiced down the glass in sheets.

She went back and sat near the fire. The dog put his head on her knee, drooled on her jeans. A log slipped in the grate. Fen could even hear herself sipping the wine from the glass.

The sudden knock at the door sent her leaping up, heart jumping

16

in her throat. Her wine slopped all over Hector. Hackles raised, ears pricked, the dog stared toward the kitchen door. There it was again. Someone knocking. *Of course, it must be Vivi. She had made it after all.*

"I'm coming," Fen yelled, shoving Hector out of the way, battling the wind to get the door open. A gust snatched it out of her hand, slammed it back against the wall. Beside her, Hector's lip rose in a snarl.

A man stood on her porch. His wet dark hair was plastered to his skull. Blood trickled down his forehead. And in his hand he held a knife.

2

*F*en froze . . . nothing in her head . . . no fight-or-flee adrenaline rush sending her running from danger; she just stood
there, a scream caught in her throat, then her mind took over, telling her there were no neighbors to hear her even if she did scream,
that Hector could not protect her, he was twelve years old and
overweight, and even though he snarled, his tail was wagging too
as if, like her, he didn't quite know what was expected of him.
What was she supposed to do? When a bleeding man leaned up
against her door on the "dark and stormy night" of legend, holding a knife and staring deep into her eyes . . .

Blood flowed again in Fen's veins. She grabbed the door handle
and, fighting the wind, slammed it in his face. Trembling, she turned
and leaned against it. She had to lock it. Her hands shook. The key
wouldn't turn. She whacked it with the flat of her hand. Gasped.
That hurt like hell. But the man was still on the outside of her door.
And, oh my God. So was Hector!

Hector was in danger . . . she would die if anything happened to him . . . if Hector attacked, the man would stab him . . . oh Hector . . . Hector . . . she must call the cops . . . but how could she, there was no phone connection . . .

She opened the door. The man was still there, leaning against the wall, a hand up to his bleeding head.

"*Get out!*" Fen screamed at him. "*Get away from here, the cops are on their way* . . . Hector," she called the dog . . . *Hector . . .*

"*Help me*," the man said. "*Please.*" He pushed roughly past her into the kitchen.

Fen pressed her back against the still-open door, watching as he lowered himself into the chair meant for Vivi at the nice table she had set with the parrot plates and the decent wineglasses and the aquamarine-handled knives and forks.

She ran to the table, snatched up a knife . . . *if he made one move she would stab him. Could you stab someone with a serrated table knife? Didn't they say you must go for the eyes first? But he wasn't making any moves, just sitting there, head lowered. He seemed to be trying to gather himself together . . .*

Oh God she was all alone here, except for Hector . . . where was Hector anyway, he should be here, protecting her . . .

The door was still open and a sudden gust swept through the kitchen. The candles died. The hurricane lamp flickered and the logs burned redder in the grate.

She must make a run for it . . . but where would she go? There were no neighbors . . . Oh my God . . . she was here with a bleeding man holding a knife sitting at her kitchen table and the storm was wrecking her house and Hector had disappeared and she didn't know what to do . . .

The man sat very still, at her kitchen table, head still lowered,

20

knife still gripped in his left hand. Blood seeped from the cut on his forehead.

Was that cut enough to disable him? Could she simply run away after all . . . hide out there in the trees? Hide until when? Who would ever come to look for her . . . ?

With the knife held before him like a gun, Fen took a nervous step toward him. She stared hard at him; she would need a description for the police later—if she survived that is. She realized she was trembling.

Suddenly Hector dashed back in, bringing with her the smell of the ocean and of rain and wet dog to mingle with the still simmering aroma of the forgotten beef daube.

Another gust sent the wineglasses crashing. The pale silvery rug lifted at the corners and the fire leapt higher, galvanizing Fen back into life. *Her home was being wrecked.* She ran for the door and with all her strength slammed it shut. She spun round. *Idiot! She'd cut off her escape route, she was alone with the killer with the knife.*

He leaned forward, put his head in his hands. Blood seeped through his fingers.

"I had to cut my way out of the seat belt." He spoke suddenly.

She stared at him, disbelieving.

"A gust of wind blew my car off the road, I couldn't see in the rain, I think I must have hit a tree . . ."

He was lying . . . "What tree? What car? Where is it?"

"Whatever tree is near the top of your drive."

"What make is your car?" She was getting all the info for the cops when she got to tell her story . . .

"A Range Rover. Black."

Of course: men always drove black cars.

"I need to see it."

He shrugged. Blood trickled down his face. "If you go out there in this you're braver than I am."

"I might be brave just staying here."

"I'm sorry." He looked her squarely in the eyes. "I hadn't realized how this must look. I frightened you."

She was edging backward to the door, keeping her eye on him . . . *he might still be capable of making a fast unexpected move . . . he might still kill her . . .*

"I'm going to check your car out," she warned, opening the door and tripping over the threshold as Hector shot past her into the blackest night she had ever seen.

Fen stared terrified into all that blackness . . . not a light, not even a star, and the rain falling, *plunging* more like it. She was already soaked . . . She needed a flashlight. Why hadn't she thought of it before? Now she remembered there was one in her car which was in the garage . . . she had left the garage door open. She ran to the Mini, felt the flashlight in the center cup holder where she always kept her stuff . . . *there it was . . . oh my God, oh my God, what was that noise? Was he coming after her?* No, it was just the wind . . .

How could she even go back in the house? But where *could* she go? Could she even drive in this storm? Fool that she was, now she remembered her own car keys were in the silver swan tray on the kitchen sideboard. *Fool*, she told herself, *you stupid idiot fuckin' fool . . .*

The thin beam of her flashlight illuminated only a couple of feet ahead as she trudged up the driveway to the road, fighting the wind, slipping and sliding through puddles and gravel.

It was there. His black Range Rover. With its front end attached to the cypress tree she had planted when she'd moved in. "To bring luck," she said, or anyhow, that's what farmers in France, where she had lived for some years, believed. So much for that!

She remembered drivers always kept their registration in the glove compartment. Now she could find out who he was. She couldn't get the driver's side door open. Skidding in the mud, holding on to the car, she edged to the other side. The passenger door opened easily, she squeezed in, dripping water, trailing mud and gravel, lowered herself into the passenger seat, opened the glove compartment. Empty! How could it be? Everyone must keep their registration handy in case they were stopped by a cop, or were in an accident. Like this one.

Wet Hector stuck his face in at the open door. He gave her his best mournful what-are-we-doing-out-here-when-we-could-be-by-the-fire look. Hector was right but how could she go back? She remembered the man saying he'd had to cut himself out. And there it was, the severed belt, caught in the beam from her flashlight.

She sat for a minute, thinking. Could she trust this stranger? So far, everything he'd told her had turned out to be true. The man had obviously been in an accident and now the bastard was bleeding all over her good chair. He was hurt and probably in pain.

She got out of his Range Rover, put her head down and trudged back through the deluge, the wind pushing at her back.

He was sitting exactly where she had left him. She shut the kitchen door and stood there, dripping water, just the way he had.

She was right, the bastard was bleeding all over her nice chair! She got a kitchen cloth from the drawer, ran it under the cold tap, squeezed out the water, walked over to him and pressed it against his forehead. He groaned, looking up at her.

"It's all right," he said. "I'm not an axe-murderer."

He had read her mind. Fen said, "Then you had better give me that knife."

He looked down, surprised to see it still clutched in his hand, then turned it so Fen could take it by the handle. He said, "I'm sorry I scared you."

"I'm not scared," Fen said. Then, "Well maybe I was."

"Right."

He wiped the blood from his head with his fingers. She saw he really needed help. "Brandy," Fen suggested. Then, doubtfully, "Maybe brandy's not good when you're in shock."

"It's the classic." He lifted his head to look at her, and she saw him properly for the first time.

Hard to guess his age with the blood crusting on his forehead and hair so wet it might be any color. He was tall, over six feet and narrow, in a black leather biker jacket and jeans. He looked . . . well . . . good. Weren't killers supposed to look like monsters?

Fen poured the brandy, deciding she'd better have one herself. He wasn't the only person suffering from shock; she'd thought her end had come.

He threw back the brandy in one long gulp, which Fen thought was a pity since it was the good stuff. One of the girls had bought it for her a couple of Christmases ago. At least now it had come in handy.

She was soaked and shivering with cold, "Wait," she told him, becoming almost her old self. "I'll get my first-aid kit, clean you up. Meanwhile I have to get into something dry. And get you out of that jacket, you're ruining my chair."

"*Bossy*," Fen thought she heard the hopefully not "axe-murderer" say as she went upstairs and changed quickly into old gray chenille sweatpants and a lavender sweater. She looked down at her boots. Brown suede knee-high, pointy toes, new. And also covered in mud. Ruined. She could chalk that up to the stranger. Maybe she should put it on his bill, as well as the cost of medical attention.

She hurried to fetch sterile gauze pads and hydrogen peroxide and Band-Aids. *Band-Aids!* Was she *crazy*? The man had been injured in a car accident and she was bringing him Band-Aids! He might have a concussion, broken bones, need a hospital; *a doctor* . . . or— Oh my God, a doctor. Whatever had happened to Vivi?

3

D r. Vivian Dexter was on duty in one of the country's busiest emergency departments and it was not a quiet night. The San Francisco hospital's ED dealt with everything from drug overdoses to traffic accidents, from work-related injuries to crime injuries. It took care of over fifty thousand patients a year and usually had gurneys piled up in the hallways, waiting. In addition, the psychiatric emergency service department dealt with more than seven thousand patients a year. It was always noisy and crowded with the injured and distraught waiting to be helped.

Vivi had tried to call her aunt earlier to tell her there was no way she could make the journey in the storm, but without any luck. Now she was worried because she knew Fen would be worried about *her.* Not only that, she would have made a special dinner and would be looking forward to her company, and also be longing to know what it was that Vivi needed so urgently to tell her. Vivi heaved a tired sigh;

the phone connection was useless, all flights had been canceled, the roads were a disaster and she was exhausted.

She was wearing the same burgundy scrubs and white doctor coat she'd had on all day with a plastic cap pulled over her long brown hair, which by now definitely needed a wash. Her feet hurt in her sensible white clogs and she felt cold and sticky and in need of a shower. She had been on duty for ten hours. She had drunk a dozen cups of wishy-washy coffee, devoured two Snickers bars, was up for a third, and had snacked in between on potato chips and the salad somebody had brought in and which tasted like old garden weeds. All in all, she was ready for a martini and a good lie-down when the ambulance men came in at the run with a young woman strapped to the stretcher.

They had called fifteen minutes ago and the emergency team was expecting them, as were the cops who lurked in the background, conferring urgently with serious faces. This was no ordinary accident victim. This was a possible murder.

Vivi flung on a vinyl apron as she hurried to take a look. A *probable* murder attempt she thought as they slid the girl, her head stabilized with foam buffers, off the stretcher and onto the gurney. She had been lying in the woods for possibly seven or eight hours. Her face had the greenish hue of death. This one might be meant for the morgue, not the emergency room. There was no identification. She was simply a Jane Doe.

Vivi felt for a pulse. It fluttered feebly under her fingers. A miracle since it was obvious the attack had taken place several hours ago.

A severe neck wound, the ambulance guys were telling her, wrists cut too . . . The cops were hanging over her, getting in her team's way. Vivi snarled at them to get out. She took a look and stepped back, shocked. The girl's throat had been cut.

She waved the hovering cops away again; this was her scene; a life in danger, a life almost gone even as she and her team worked on her: epinephrine to give her heart a jolt, lines inserted for blood and drugs. Vivi noted that the incision was clean, obviously made with a very sharp knife, meant no doubt, for the purpose, but somehow the killer had missed the carotid artery. The girl's mouth appeared to have been stuck shut; duct tape, she guessed, but the cops must have taken that. It would be "evidence." The girl had also been savagely raped.

Sickened, Vivi knew, as everyone there did, that this was the fourth young woman to be attacked in this fashion in the past year. The difference was this one was not dead yet and would not be if she had anything to do with it. She and God. And the surgeons, who, anyway, thought they were gods.

She got one of the best on the phone just as he was about to brave the weather and leave for the night. The girl on the gurney was wheeled, with all her lines and drains and bottles and plastic bags of blood and plasma and drugs and paraphernalia into the elevator on her way to surgery. Watching the doors close behind her Vivi knew it was the girl's last chance.

Vivi had wanted to become a surgeon, she had studied for it for a couple of years before dropping out. Then, she had not known exactly why, but now, looking at that young woman, she understood. She did not have the nerves for it. Her role was here, as an emergency room doctor. This was what she was good at.

She took off the bloody apron. Leaning wearily against the wall, arms folded, she caught her reflection in the glass door. Thirty years old, five-three and a little too plump from too many snacks on the run; skin sallow from fatigue and too many cups of coffee; drab in her now bloodstained scrubs. With her long brown hair hidden under the plastic cap she looked like a turn-of-the-century scullery maid. And she felt like one. She might as well have been scrubbing floors on her hands and knees all day, except she supposed, giving herself some credit, she had helped a few people out. Customers. Patients. Victims. Call them what you liked, they were hers for a short while and she gave them her all.

"Excuse me, Nurse?"

Vivi swiveled her eyes to see who it was that wanted her. The cop was tall and solid-looking with big feet in big boots and a serious expression on his face. He had blue eyes and was in bad need of a shave.

"Excuse me, Nurse," he said again.

"*Doctor.*"

He nodded, still serious. "Of course, I meant Doctor."

"Of course you did."

"There's nothing wrong with nurses," he said.

"You don't have to tell me that." She was snappy and knew it and she definitely did not want to talk to him. She was too tired.

"I'm Detective Bradley Merlin."

He looked expectantly at her for a response.

"Forget it," she said wearily. "My shift was over five hours ago. I'm tired and I'm on my way home. Talk to one of the others, why don't you."

"Because I need to talk to you."

His face was still serious, not a hint of a smile. He was all business. As she should be too, Vivi reminded herself.

"I doubt she'll make it," she said. She felt it in her gut.

Detective Brad Merlin lowered his head. It wasn't from shock. He'd been there before, heard those words before.

"I know," he said. "I was first on the scene."

30

"This was a madman," Vivi said. "He cut her wrists, raped her and then cut her throat. Fortunately, he didn't get the carotid. It was a clean cut, though," she added, "with a very sharp knife. You'd need a surgical knife to make a cut like that, all in one go, not hacked at, if you see what I mean. I don't know how he missed the carotid."

"I see."

Assessing him, Vivi thought maybe he did. Hey, he was just a detective, he was trying to do his job, after all. Like her.

"Talk to Doc Lobavitch, the surgeon. He'll tell you all you need to know."

"Not everything," Detective Merlin said.

Vivi unraveled herself from her leaning position against the wall. Her knees trembled from fatigue. So did her hands. "What else do you need?" she asked, impatiently.

"Your phone number."

Vivi stared at him, stunned. "Jesus, Detective!" She pulled off the plastic cap and shook her hair free; it was sticky with sweat as she'd known it would be. "Why don't you just go and solve a few crimes!"

"I have to walk my dog first," he called after her as she strode away, wobbling a bit on the clogs. "We could walk our dogs together. Have a drink?"

"I don't have a dog," Vivi said, as she pushed open the door. "I have a life."

"I'll bet you do," Brad Merlin said. He'd just seen her in action and he thought she was pretty good at her life.

4

At Fen's house, the stranger had taken off his biker jacket and was still sitting at her kitchen table, closely inspecting her parrot plates, when she came back downstairs, warm and dry again in her gray chenille sweatpants and lavender sweater, carrying gauze, Band-Aids and the bottle of hydrogen peroxide.

"Nice plates," the stranger said, glancing up at her.

His eyes were brown. His hair was drying now and in the light from the hurricane lamp and the candles she could tell it was also dark brown. The front of his pink T-shirt was as wet as the jacket.

"Get that off," she ordered. "I'll get you a towel, you can dry yourself. I like parrots," she added, talking about the plates. "Very chatty birds. A relative of mine had one once, many years ago. His name was Luchay. He lived for more than a century, I believe."

"I didn't know that. About them living so long."

He stripped off the T-shirt and sat there, half naked, looking as though he didn't quite know what to do next. He seemed, Fen

33

decided, completely helpless. But then he *had* suffered a blow to the head in the car accident. At least that's what he'd said happened. Was it true? Or was she being a fool? Again! She took the sodden T-shirt, holding it in two fingers away from her, which made him laugh.

"Why pink?" she asked, dropping it into the sink, then turning on the tap and filling a small Pyrex bowl.

"Why not? Like you and the parrots, I liked it."

"Men don't wear pink. At least they didn't in my day."

He folded his arms, modestly covering his naked chest. "Your day wasn't that long ago."

Fen gave him a look, one eyebrow raised. What was he doing with the compliments? He was supposed to be half dead! Water spilled from the bowl as she walked over to him. Hector lumbered after her, licking up the spillage, then sat, eyes fixed on the stranger. Low rumbles came from his throat.

"Now why, I wonder, is Hector doing that?" Fen asked out loud. "He's usually such a friendly dog. I hope you are not an axe-murderer after all. Because if you are, it would mean that I have been a very foolish woman, and I rather hoped I'd outgrown that tendency."

She dipped the cloth in the water and began sponging off his forehead. She could see the gash now and it was nasty: two or three inches running from the scalp to above the left eyebrow, and certainly deep enough to need stitches.

He closed his eyes as she worked on him. She noted he had made no move to befriend the dog. In fact he'd ignored Hector, acting as though the dog was simply not there. Perhaps that was why Hector was making those growly sounds, to prove his presence, to impress, the way men sometimes did with women. Fen knew all about that. Three marriages later, that is. She was a slow learner.

"You married?" she asked.

His eyes were still closed. "Do I look like a married man?"

She shrugged and the wet gauze slipped, making him wince. "Ooops, sorry. You might. In the candlelight. You never know . . . a guy out alone, heading to an urgent rendezvous . . . probably with a married woman."

He laughed again, opening his eyes to look at her. "Why a married woman?"

"Because they're the easiest. Bored, lonely, a part of the furniture you might say. A little flattery goes a long way . . . a little of the how attractive they look, how attracted you are . . ." Fen shrugged. "And there you are."

His brows raised in mock horror. "You're a cynic."

The cut began to bleed again. "Don't wiggle your eyebrows like that," she said, soaking the gauze with the hydrogen peroxide again and pressing it firmly against the wound. "Not a cynic. A realist. And I know because I've been there. I was one of those 'married women.' You know that old cliché—hook, line and sinker. That was me, the catch of the day."

"Jesus!"

"There." She stood back. Frowning, she inspected her work. "Doesn't look too good. You need a doctor."

"Pity you don't have one handy."

"I almost did." Fen waved a hand at the set dinner table. "My niece, the doctor, was supposed to be coming for the night. I thought it was her, at the door."

"Instead it was me."

She said, "Of course it was you. And I don't even know your name."

"I'm Alex," he said.

"Fen," she said.

They looked into each other's eyes. A shimmer of connection passed between them.

"No last names." Fen smoothed her lavender sweater over her baggy sweats. "Let's keep it that way? A secret between us."

"Like a rendezvous."

She laughed. "It's been a long time since I had one of those." She took the bowl to the sink and emptied out the bloody water. "I used to like them though, those rendezvous."

"Sounds as though you've had more than I have."

Fen leaned back against the sink, arms folded, one long gray chenilled leg crossed over the other at the ankle. "And maybe I have. I'm older than you."

Hector came and fussed at Fen's feet. Outside the wind raised another decibel. Hail hit the windows. The hurricane lamp and the candles on the dining room table flickered.

She said briskly, "Good thing there's candlelight so you can't see the truth. I'd better put a couple of butterfly strips on that wound before you bleed all over my nice chair."

He closed his eyes again as she applied three Band-Aids to his forehead. "There." She stepped back to inspect him. "Now you look like the walking wounded."

He pushed back the chair and stretched his arms over his head. Suddenly nervous again, Fen thought he looked very naked, shirt-less, there in her small kitchen. His ribs stuck out the way they were supposed to and a fine thatch of dark hair crossed his chest. He was very attractive, this man she had rescued from the dark and stormy night. Skinny-hipped, jeans slung low . . .

She said, "I'd better get you a sweater."

He reached for his leather jacket, hooked over the back of the chair. "Don't worry, I'll just put on my jacket. Then I'll be on my way."

"No you will not! Not in your state, and in this storm. Wait here." Fen took a candle from the table, and walked to the guest room where she kept a collection of sweatshirts for friends who, imagining they were in for long hours of California sunshine, almost froze to death in the wicked ocean wind.

When she came back he was sitting on the floor next to Hector, who was allowing him to scratch that special place behind his ear. This man was a seducer.

She gave him the sweatshirt. Gray. With STANFORD in red letters on the back.

"Good school." He slipped it appreciatively over his head.

"Not mine, I'm afraid."

He walked over to her, took the candle and put it back on the table. "What was yours then?"

Fen had to laugh, he was so suddenly in charge. "The traditional school of hard knocks, that was mine."

"I want to hear all about it."

She quickly changed the subject. "How about a drink?"

He thought about it. "Okay. Drink *first*. Then the story of your life."

Fen ran a distracted hand through her hair. "And what would you like to drink?"

"I see you have some red wine open."

"A good Pinot Noir. I opened it for Vivi."

"Since Vivi's not here, how about we share it?" He picked up the bottle and poured wine into the two good glasses she had set on the table, then turned and handed her one.

"To two strangers together—like Bergman and Bogart in *Casablanca* riding out the storm together." He raised his glass to her.

"Two strangers," Fen said. She couldn't quite remember but she sure hoped Bogart had been a good guy.

Outside the wind raged and the ocean roiled. She smiled and took a sip. Whatever, she was suddenly enjoying it.

5

Vivi, freed at last, was walking fast to the hospital parking garage, as though if she lingered they might catch up to her and she would be back at work again, putting broken people back together. It didn't matter that *she* herself was broken. Life went on, didn't it? Somehow?

The big, echoing lot was almost empty, just a few scattered cars. She pressed the elevator button, glancing nervously round, shifting from one aching foot to the other, still in the scuffed white clogs she'd had on all day. She couldn't wait to get them off, get into the bathtub, sink in, chin deep, and let her tears mingle with the hot water. At least she hoped the water would be hot. Her apartment was on the basement level of an old San Francisco Victorian and it was a gamble whether or not the water, or the heating would work, or even whether the ancient gas stove might blow up. There were moments, like this, when Vivi wished she had taken the all mod-cons efficiency studio closer to the hospital, but as always, she had been influenced by charm, the peaked gables and fretwork, and of course, the beauty.

And there were also times, as on a night like this when still in the scrubs she'd put on ten hours ago, still with the image of the almost-dead girl with her throat slashed fresh in her mind, still with her own recent emotional despair to deal with, that Vivi wished she had opted for a nine-to-five job that left her with accountable free time. She wished the storm wasn't still raging outside and that the fuckin' elevator would come. She pressed the button again, heard it ping somewhere above, stamped her chilled feet.

She took out her mobile and tried Fen one more time. There was still no reception. And her aunt was the one person she'd so desperately wanted to see, to talk to tonight.

She worried about her, alone in that little cottage on the Pacific bluff where she knew the ocean must be raging and the wind howling strong enough to blow it and her right over the edge. She wished Fen had never moved there, twelve years ago now. She wished Fen had taken that apartment right here in the Bay Area, even Marin County would have been okay, but Fen had fallen in love with Big Sur, with the house, the view and importantly, the solitude. In essence, Vivi was very like Fen.

The elevator had pinged a couple of minutes ago and still no sound of it creaking down to her. Vivi pushed the button again but heard no answering ping this time. She would have to take the stairs.

The parking garage was silent, empty; no other workers in a hurry to brave the storm and get home to their families, or like her, to a hot bath.

She hesitated. The stairwell looked very lonely but the elevator was definitely not moving . . . *and someone was climbing the stairs . . . slow . . . heavy-footed . . .* The hair at the back of Vivi's neck prickled, her arms were suddenly all gooseflesh. She tried urgently to remember what you were supposed to do in lonely places like this . . . *rape spaces* some called these multi-story garages; she remembered the can of wasp spray in her bag, the modern woman's version of mace . . . it could take out a man's eyes at thirty feet . . .

"Hey, Vivi, why are you still here?"

Vivi's knees unlocked. She was shaking. It was only Dr. Sandowski.

"Oh, hi—or rather, goodnight," she said, giving him a relieved little wave. "I'm on my way home."

Ralph Sandowski was a kind of colleague, an internationally known psychiatrist who traveled the world, lecturing on post-traumatic stress, of which there seemed to be more about than people knew. At least that's what Sandowski had told Vivi, remarkably cheerfully, she had thought, over cups of the thin liquid they called coffee in the hospital. He'd also said that sometimes it seemed to him *most* people suffered from post-traumatic stress of some sort.

Vivi had mulled over that information until she realized she wasn't so surprised. She kind of suffered from it herself. Especially now. *Tonight.* When she was in emotional despair. For a second, standing in the parking lot, looking at Ralph Sandowski, she wondered whether he could help her with her problems.

He was a tall slight man, hunched, collar up against the cold in his black quilted all-weather jacket, dark hair, glasses—horn-rims of course, what else would a good shrink wear? In fact Ralph Sandowski was attractive. Vivi guessed there were women who would stand in line to get a date with him, or at least an appointment to spill out their troubles and have him tell them, oh so soothingly, how to cope, while handing them the Kleenex.

"Finally get off your shift?" Sandowski called, giving her a wave as he headed for the next flight of stairs.

"Finally," she agreed. "I had the new 'murdered' girl to take care of. She was attacked seven or eight hours ago and still made it through. Just. And no thanks to the would-be killer."

"Sorry to hear that," he said. "Hey." He popped back up again. "Feel like a drink?"

"You're the second one to ask me that tonight," she said, remembering Detective Brad Merlin.

"Popular girl," he said.

Vivi was laughing, even as she got her nerves together. Her fears seemed foolish now. "Once, I was 'a girl,'" she said regretfully. "Y'know, like yesterday . . . or some time before that."

Ralph Sandowski had stopped at the top of the steps and was looking at her. He shoved his slipping horn-rims farther up his nose. "Still are, if you ask my opinion," he said thoughtfully.

"You're a nice man, Dr. Ralph." Vivi walked down the stairs with him, grateful for his company. There was her Jeep, at last. "And thanks for the offer."

"Some other time, huh?"

She felt him watching as she let in the clutch, grating into gear, scowling at the racket she'd made. She smiled at him as she drove off, glad though, he had been there.

6

Detective Brad Merlin left the precinct house at about the same time Vivi left the hospital. Like her, he walked to his car, though his was parked on the street and was a Ford 250 twin-cab pickup, black of course, with a steel hitch bar at the back for when he trailered his little boat to the lake. He liked to camp, to fish, to sit round a makeshift fire and chat with the guys over, if they were lucky, a grilled fish they had caught; if not, then steaks; whatever. But a man needed time off for those pursuits and, also like Vivi Dexter, Brad did not get much of that.

His dog was sitting in the front seat, nose pressed against the window. A poodle. Not miniature, but certainly small. And a kind of rusty-pink color at that! It was his ex-wife's dog, named by her, *Bitsy.* When his wife had packed her bags and left, a couple of years ago, despairing Bitsy had stood at the window watching, then hurled herself thirty feet after her. Devastated, Brad had felt like following the dog. Instead he went down to the street and rescued it.

43

His wife told him she did not want Bitsy or him, and, defeated by the hurt look in the dog's eyes Brad kept it. Of course he'd had to change the name. He couldn't go round the park calling for a poodle named *Bitsy*. He'd remembered a story about the writer Dorothy Parker's dog, a spaniel who, impatient to join the guests on the terrace below, had made a similar thirty-foot leap. Parker had named her dog the Flyin' Fool. So Bitsy had become Brad's own Flyin' Fool.

He discovered that poodles were intelligent, trainable, likeable and they did not shed. It would have been better if the dog were not that rusty-pink, but Brad kept her unclipped and shaggy and put up with the smirks as he walked her, the big burly detective with his prissy-looking little dog. "Fuck them, Flyin,'" he'd say cheerfully. "You're your own dog and I'm my own man, and we know it."

Now, he let Flyin' out of the car. The dog trotted around, sniffing here, squatting there, then came back and sat beside him with a what-next expression.

"Guess," Brad said.

They set off in the direction of Veronica's Bar & Grill, a down-home old-fashioned saloon with a narrow curved zinc bar and a wall of glass shelves stocked with any booze you might dream up and which no one ever drank. They also had the Maker's Mark bourbon Brad preferred and his favorite Kirin on tap. The booths were covered in cracked red vinyl that probably dated from the sixties, as did the globe light fixtures that swung overhead in the draft from the AC or the heat, depending on the season, and which shed a comforting orange glow overall, sort of like a nice sunset.

The stools were new, however, and Brad hitched himself onto one where the bar curved and from where he could see both ends of the room, in particular the door. Once a cop, always a cop; he wanted to know who came in, who went out, and who was trouble. "Trouble" didn't happen a lot at Veronica's however, since it was a known hangout for the local squad, and besides, Veronica, a big woman with a big chest and a big voice, ruled her empire with a big strong hand. You didn't fuck with Veronica and get away with it.

Tonight, she was in black velvet, spangled here and there with a sequin—she was partial to a bit of sparkle. It fell in a deep V over a bosom that was lifted hydraulically to heaven in what Veronica believed to be a sexy and charming manner. Brad knew this because she had told him so.

Her hair was platinum and curly and everyone knew it was a wig but nobody cared. Veronica was every man's buddy and no man's wife. She was seventy if she was a day and as she said, speaking out of the side of that red-outlined mouth, didn't look a day over fifty.

She had owned Veronica's for forty years and nothing surprised her anymore. She lived "over the shop" and ran a tight ship, serving buffalo wings and burgers (no choice of cheese, you got American and liked it). The place smelled welcomingly on this cold rainy night of the "special," her hot chicken soup with dumplings. Veronica's mother had been Jewish.

Veronica liked the way Brad Merlin looked. But then women did. He was forty years old, a solid six-two in his socks, stocky with a bit of a gut, and despite a diet of mostly junk food and alcohol, he was still fit. His thick dark hair stood spikily up and had a life of its own. His bushy dark eyebrows grew at an alarming rate until they curled into his eyes and Veronica was forced to cut them back for him. His eyes were a darkish blue, a genetic throwback to some Norwegian ancestor, he'd told Veronica, and his chin, when unshaven, also had a bluish hue to it, a genetic throwback to some Irish ancestor, he'd also said. He also had a cop's big feet.

You couldn't call Brad good-looking but he was definitely on the attractive-to-women side. Veronica knew there had only been one woman for him though: his wife. She had left him for another man who, brokenhearted Brad told Veronica when he was still in the throes of the split-up, kept more sociable hours, had a more expensive car and could afford European vacations. He and Flyin' (then still Bitsy) had gotten the chop and Veronica knew it still hurt.

Brad lived alone in a small mews house in what had once been a stable, later a garage that had become almost derelict until he'd committed his free time and what was left of his money to putting it back together and making it his home. It was small, but he had his music, his books, his coffeemaker and his dog. "What more," he'd asked Veronica, "can any man want?" She could have told him, but she didn't.

"How're you doing, Whiz?" she asked now, reaching under the counter for a dog biscuit, kept specially for her dog-owner customers, and tossing it to Flyin'. Veronica always called Brad "Whiz" because of his name. In mythology, Merlin was the wizard at the Court of King Arthur and his Knights of the Round Table. "What'll ya have?"

She was asking what Brad would have to eat, not what he drank. The shot of Maker's Mark was already on the counter and Flyin' was already crunching her biscuit, making crumbs on the floor.

"I'll have the soup, please, Veronica," Brad said. "And how're you doin' on this rotten night when neither man nor beast should be abroad?"

"I'm doin' okay, but I'm not the one who's 'abroad.' You are."

"Had to walk my dog."

Veronica surveyed the peachy-pink dog, sitting, paws neatly arranged, looking up at her, hoping for a second biscuit. "Can't you get the poor little thing dyed black?" she asked, pulling a Kirin, making sure there was a good head on it, the way he liked.

Brad shrugged. "That's the way she came, that's the way she'll stay." He heard the door, and swung round as his colleague, Jerusalem Guiterrez, walked in.

Guiterrez was Mexican-Sicilian, a family man with four kids to put through college someday, a wife who adored him, and a mother-in-law from hell. He was short and skinny with skin the color of dried wheat and the whitest teeth known only to a color-blind dentist. Brad claimed Guiterrez could never do undercover work because the perps would see the gleam of his teeth and just take off. Like Brad, he had his Sig Sauer holstered under his jacket.

Veronica had the double shot of Patrón Silver on the bar before Guiterrez even reached it.

"So who's drivin' tonight anyway?" she asked.

Brad nodded in Guiterrez's direction; Guiterrez jerked a thumb at him. They both grinned.

Brad said, "Flyin' and I are walking. We always do after an evening here."

"I'll walk back with you." Guiterrez propped himself on a bar stool next to Brad. He took off his jacket, which was soaked, and slung it over the nearby chair.

"You're ruining my chairs," Veronica complained.

"Just think yourself lucky you have customers on a night like this."

"You shouldn't be *abroad*," Veronica said, winking at Brad.

Guiterrez looked mystified and Brad grinned. "A literary allusion, my friend," he said. He lifted his glass and drained it, then pulled a face. "Why do I like this stuff anyway? My father used to give me a slug of whisky when I was a kid and had a cold on my chest. Said it would cure it."

"And did it?" Jerusalem Guiterrez, known to all as Jerry, slammed back the tequila with gusto and no nonsense about salt and lime.

47

"I don't believe so, but he must have thought he did. Vicks would probably have been better."

Veronica polished glasses with an immaculately clean white cloth. "So, what're you up for tonight?" she asked Jerry.

"I'm guessing same as him. The chicken soup."

"Nothin' better on a night like this."

Veronica waved over the girl serving at the other end of the bar. She was a rosy-cheeked, fresh-faced, bustling young woman. Her long brown hair was pulled back in a ponytail, and she was plump and brimming with energy. They had not seen her before and gave her a smile.

"Hi." She smiled back.

"Kim's new," Veronica said. "These guys are regulars," she told Kim. "Treat 'em like royalty."

Kim giggled and made a mock-curtsy. "So what does royalty want, sirs?"

"Two chicken soups with dumplings," Brad said. "Please, Kim."

"Good choice." She beamed at them again and departed somewhere behind the bar where they assumed the kitchen was, though no one they knew had actually ever seen Veronica's kitchen. It might be some grime-mired hellhole for all they knew. What mattered was that the food came out hot and tasted good. Nobody wanted to know anything more, and anyhow, judging from the freshly laundered state of the cloth Veronica was cleaning the glasses with, there was no danger of grime in the back premises.

The door swung open again and a couple blew in on a gust of wind. Kim went over to them with the one-sheet menu. They chatted for a minute or two, placed an order, then she went back to the bar, returned again with a beer.

"More chicken soup," she told Veronica as she went through the door into the kitchen.

"Might as well cancel everything else," Veronica said. "This is a chicken soup night if ever there was one."

Brad laughed and turned his attention back to Jerry Guiterrez.

Jerry had been first to arrive at the scene of the murder. When Brad arrived he was standing in the storm, taking in the horror that no matter how experienced they were, never failed to sicken them. The fire truck with the paramedics had arrived almost as fast, found she was still alive. Barely. Gotten her to the hospital emergency room. Everybody had done their best, including, Brad was certain, Dr. Vivian Dexter. His team was still out there in the rain, searching the woods, futilely he'd bet, for any evidence. The killer knew what he was doing. He'd done it before. This time though, he'd missed his mark.

Jerry had gone to the precinct house to file the report while Brad went on to the hospital to follow up on the young woman's condition.

"You get the latest report on victim number four then?" Jerry asked now.

Brad hated that the girl was labeled simply "victim." She was somebody's daughter; somebody's girlfriend; somebody cared about her. "I did more than that," he said. "I saw her again. She's still alive. Barely."

Jerry stopped eating and turned his eyes to him. "Jesus Christ," he said.

Brad shrugged. "Don't get all optimistic, she wasn't alive enough to tell us who tried to kill her."

Jerry said, "The fucker used duct tape this time to make sure it stuck in the rain and all. The same message as before."

Brad said, "I'm just wondering *who* it is he doesn't want to know? Who it is that is so important to him, he doesn't want his victims to 'tell.'"

Jerry said, "Any shrink would guess it's his mother. It always is with these crazies. Anyhow, I've heard they've got one of the best shrinks at the hospital. Why not ask him?"

"Sandowski, you mean?"

"Yeah."

Their soup came and, hungry, they spooned it up, tearing chunks off the baguette that came with it.

Brad said, "I spoke with the emergency doctor, name of Vivian Dexter."

"Dr. Vivian." Jerry had met her several times at the emergency department.

"I did something bad," Brad added, looking at Jerry. "I don't know what came over me, I asked for her phone number."

"Jesus Christ! At a time like that . . ."

"I could see she was upset, tired, exhausted in fact and probably as shocked as I was. I thought we needed to share our feelings, over a drink." Brad thought for a moment, then added, "It was her name that did it . . . I mean she looked like hell but she's good at what she does, concerned, worried. And anyway her name and mine, y'know, they kind of coincided."

"What the fuck are you talkin' about?" Jerry tossed a piece of chicken to Flyin', who caught it daintily in her teeth, placed it on the floor, then wolfed it down.

"Vivian was the wizard Merlin's girlfriend," Brad told him. "In mythology, that is," he added as Jerry stared blankly at him. "Y'know, it was kind of an odd link."

"You bet it's odd. What are you? Goin' nuts? You oughta order that dog some food, it's starvin.' And leave the young doctors alone, we need 'em for better things than mythological flat-footed detectives."

"Speak for yourself," Brad said with a grin.

He was still thinking about Dr. Vivian Dexter when he walked home with his dog through the rain-washed streets an hour later. Brad was a loner, a man who lived for his work. He wasn't looking for emotional involvements. He told himself he just admired Dr. Vivian, that's all.

In Big Sur, Fen was still keeping an eye on the stranger named Alex who she'd thought earlier might be an axe-murderer. Maybe he still was and was just acting nice. She wondered, out loud, if she was being a fool.

By now, the two of them were standing in front of the fire with their glasses of wine. He was wearing the gray Stanford sweatshirt and the still-wet jeans. She had put on an old pair of black high-heeled leather boots that were definitely pinching her toes but which made the baggy gray chenille sweatpants look better. She might be in her fifties but Fen would never lose the habit of trying to look her best for a man.

He caught her anxious expression. He said, "Look, I'm really sorry I frightened you. You saw my car attached to your tree. It was an accident, I promise I'm a good guy." He grinned. "Or at least reasonably good."

She smiled back at him. His hair had dried and she saw it grew strongly back from a forehead that already had a few horizontal lines so she guessed maybe he was around forty. His eyes had lines around them too. Brown, as she'd noted earlier, and not twinkly, thank God. She couldn't abide men who twinkled at you. A lean jaw; she had always liked a lean face, it leant a man character. Lips a bit narrow but nice teeth. Obviously his mother had sent him to a good orthodontist when he was a youngster.

He was a bit on the skinny side too, but all in all, a good-looking guy. She thought he might have done very well for Vivi had she not been involved with that unfortunate French guy who Fen had always known was a shit, though she had never said that to Vivi who, as far as she knew, was still all aglow with love. Foolish girl. Love was two a penny these days. In fact it always had been.

"What are you thinking?" the stranger whose name was Alex asked her.

She sank back onto the sofa, cradling her wineglass, and he came and sat opposite.

"I'm thinking about my niece. I adopted her when she was small."

"The doctor? The one who was coming here tonight?"

"That one, and her sister. Vivi's thirty, the other is twenty-eight and still attempting to become a rock singer—pop, whatever you call it—and not making it. In my view she never will."

He settled back against the cushions, looking interested. "What about the real parents?"

Fen sighed. "They were killed in a plane crash. I was only twenty-eight myself. It was me or foster homes so of course I took them in, raised them, made sure they had a good education. Sometimes I think I was too tough, tougher than their own mother, but I had a responsibility."

"And what about their adopted father?"

54

"Do you mean *my* husband?"

"There must have been a *husband*?"

Fen decided to change the subject. "You must be starving." She glanced at the kitchen clock, a chrome disk with a shiny black Felix the cat draped over the top. She had picked it up in some junk sale and adored it. Vivi should have been here hours ago.

"That's not fair, you changed the subject," the stranger was saying. "You promised me you'd tell me your life story after we got our drinks."

"A woman can change her mind."

She went to the stove and turned up the light under the daube, dipping a spoon in to taste. Quite suddenly, she felt him beside her. She backed away, startled.

He held up a hand. "All I seem to be doing is scaring the hell out of you, when all I wanted was to see what you were cooking."

"You *are* scaring the hell out of me. Why can't you just stay where I put you."

"I knew you were bossy," he said.

Fen began to laugh. "*Now* you sound like a husband, and you're right, I am bossy. Always have been. That's because I always know best. Pass me the plates will you, from the table."

He went and got the parrot plates, handed them to her. She ladled out the beef stew and he carried them back to the table.

Fen took her usual seat, facing the door. He sat opposite. The candles flickered between them and the wind rattled at the window. Fen hacked at the crusty loaf, pushed the board over to him. He took a piece.

"Good for mopping up the juices," she said. "Tuck in, and don't dare tell me you don't like it, it's my specialty, and Vivi's favorite."

She was still worried about Vivi. She checked the time again.

"Oh God, what can have happened to her?" she asked out loud.

"She probably couldn't get you on the phone and decided, quite sensibly, not to attempt the journey. She's most likely at home, still trying to call you, having a bite to eat and a glass of wine, like we are."

"Vivi's more of a martini girl." Fen sighed, she missed seeing her nieces. "And I'm willing to bet she's still at work, helping those in need."

"A regular Florence Nightingale." He gave her a teasing grin.

Fen said, "I mentioned that name to someone the other day, a young person, fifteen or so years old. You know what his answer was? 'Who's Florence Nightingale?'" She rolled her eyes. "Florence was before *my* time but I know my history. Now *that's* when you know you're getting old."

"No it's not," he said, tucking into his beef daube with every evidence of enjoyment. "It's not *you* getting older," he said. "It's *their* ignorance."

He got up and poured more wine. Making himself right at home, Fen thought, feeling kind of pleased about it. Damn it, if she admitted it, she was having a good time. Dinner with this stranger wasn't all bad!

"So?" He settled back into his chair, the one with his biker jacket still draped around it.

His smile was charming, it kind of lit up his face. Fen cut off another piece of bread, pushed aside her empty plate, sliced a sliver of the Manchego . . . oh Lord she had forgotten all about the salad and the Parmesan . . . too late to bother now.

She took a bite of the cheese, a sip of the red wine and looked her guest in the eye.

"Okay. So I was a dancer," she said. "In Paris."

Their eyes met and lingered. He lifted his glass to her. "I'll bet you were always a beauty," he said. And to Fen the light seemed to shimmer and the wind stopped its sighing and there was only the beat of her heart.

Vivi's apartment in the old Victorian was too far from the hospital for convenience. It didn't even have a view of the Golden Gate Bridge and she couldn't even hear the friggin' famous sea lions barking their silly heads off at night. It was in the basement and she had taken it for two reasons: the first was she'd fallen in love with it; the second was it was on a quiet street and had a small garden where, in a burst of enthusiasm, she'd planned on growing parsley, basil and rosemary, thinking she might even cook. The fact that she neither had the time to cook nor a green thumb meant her garden was now a mess of weeds and mud. Plus there was no parking and she was forever searching for a spot on the street, like now, on what must be the stormiest night of the century.

She finally found a place. As she walked down the short flight of stone steps leading to the small basement area that had now turned into a pool and unlocked her front door, she felt sorry for herself. Fen had told her she was crazy to take this place, but she had been following her dream. She'd been in love and planning on sharing her little *pied-à-terre* with the Frenchman, François. Her lover. Her fiancé.

No more, though. Yesterday, the fiancé had canceled being a fiancé. Needed his freedom a while longer, he'd told her. In a *text*, for God's sake. François did not speak English, so instead of phone calls he usually texted Vivi in French, which Vivi's iPhone app translated into English. She would text him back in English, which his app then translated to French. Fen said it was the most modern courtship she had ever heard of.

They had met by chance—*"par hasard"* as François put it— bumping into each other on the Fisherman's Wharf. It was a soft, sunny day just six months ago, when Vivi had had a whole weekend off. She was thirty years old and had worked hard all through med school, then as an intern; now she was a resident emergency room doctor and still working hard. There had been other men in her life; a fellow medical student for four years; a couple of short-term "friendships," but "love" was currently playing no part in her too busy dedicated life. Except she loved *what* she did.

She had a small social life when she had the time: she attended parties when invited, putting on heels and her one and only little black dress and the small diamond brooch her aunt had given her when she'd graduated Johns Hopkins. She had thought about falling in love, tried a couple of times and failed, but she'd been desperately lonely. Until François.

The day they'd met Vivi had taken the opportunity to get herself together; she'd had her hair cut and styled that morning and it trailed smoothly over her shoulders, a few highlights glimmering through it. She was wearing lip gloss, and an actual summer dress instead of her hospital "uniform." She was also eating tiny bay shrimp from a paper cone, dipping them in tartar sauce, which was the reason she did not see the man walking fast toward her. And he did not see her, because he was in the midst of what sounded like a violent foreign argument on his cell phone, striding fast and gesticulating wildly. They collided; her shrimp went flying; his shirt was covered in tartar sauce.

"*Merde*," he hissed, glaring at her. He took a second look, stepped back, took another look. Then he smiled. "*Pardon, mademoiselle. Je m'excuse, c'était ma faute, évidemment c'était moi.*"

And that's how it had begun.

"A *coup de foudre*," he'd whispered in her ear an hour later.

Vivi immediately called Fen, who of course spoke French.

"A quick question," she said when Fen picked up. "What does *coup de foudre* mean?"

"Love at first sight. And *who* exactly, might I ask, is saying that to you? And under what circumstances?" Fen was a lioness when it came to her girls.

"Some Frenchman I've just met. He's here, sitting next to me, we're in Starbucks having coffee . . ."

"Hmm, you're having coffee in Starbucks, you've just met and he's telling you it's love at first sight? *Sex* is more like what's on that Frenchman's mind, you can be sure of that."

"Thanks, Fen," Vivi had said, cutting off the call. She'd turned and beamed at her new acquaintance. The "romance" took off from there.

Texts flew back and forth between them. François was a couple of years younger, doing graduate economics at Berkeley. He wanted to marry her, gave her a small sapphire ring. She took him to meet Fen, who acted cold and spoke only English to him. She so obviously did not approve that, terrified, François and Vivi had slept on their backs in separate beds in the guest room, hands folded over their chests, chaste as a knight and his lady on a tomb, afraid of making a move let alone voicing a complaint.

"Don't like him," was Fen's only comment as they were leaving the next morning. Vivi asked why, but all she said was, "Trust me, you'll find out."

Vivi had taken the new apartment so her fiancé could stay with her when he was free. Then he'd texted in French of course, just a couple of nights ago, "I need my freedom longer." Reading the translation, Vivi's heart plunged into her stomach. "Please, no, François . . ." she texted him back, she'd *pleaded* with him, humiliating herself. He had not even replied, and Vivi FedExed the sapphire ring back to him. It was over.

. . .

The shattering breakup was what Vivi had been going to talk to her aunt about. Her heart was broken. She needed her advice, her shoulder to lean on. Fen was always there when you needed her, always had been.

At work, Vivi was the strong, knowledgeable young doctor who knew what she was doing and did it well. At home, she was a lonely young woman.

Now, in her little basement apartment, Vivi lit the lamps and closed the cream linen curtains. Casting off her scrubs, she walked to the bathroom. It was small, of course, with a too-bright light over a sink so tiny there was nowhere to put her stuff, and an old claw-foot tub complete with rust stains. Still, it was wonderful to lounge in, once you got it filled that is, because the water pressure was definitely sluggish.

She turned on the taps, threw in some Kiehl's bath gel that

smelled prettily of lavender, wrapped herself in a warm blue bath-robe, a Christmas present from her aunt a couple of years ago.

She went to the cupboard that did duty as a kitchen and put on the kettle. A cup of tea, Twining Brit decaf was what a girl (a *woman*, attractive, older Dr. Ralph had called her tonight), anyway, it was what *this girl* needed now. Besides, she'd had enough caffeine in the past twenty-four to get her through the next twenty-four. What she really needed was sleep.

She took her phone and went and watched the bathtub slowly filling. Holding her face up to the steam, she called Fen one more time. The line was still out.

She fixed the tea, propped the mug and her phone on a stool next to the tub, slipped off the robe and climbed in. Leaning back in the bubbles, she let her long brown hair float around her shoulders. The heat slid soothingly over her skin. She wondered if she should have had a martini instead of the tea, but she didn't like to drink alone. Perhaps she should have shared a martini with Dr. Ralph after all? Or even the big burly detective who had a dog he walked? Jeesul That's how small her life had become, thinking about detective dog-walkers with big feet and older shrinks. She wished she was at Cliff Cottage instead of alone, here in this dungeon.

Then her phone rang.

9

Vivi scowled in its direction, not wanting to answer in case it was the hospital asking if she could do the early shift. They were perennially short-staffed. After a few rings the call went to message and she heard her sister, JC's voice.

"Vivi, I'm here in San Francisco. I *drove* in this fuckin' storm, can you believe me? All the way from the Napa Valley. All right, all right don't ask! It's a long story and not one I'm fond of . . . at least not anymore I'm not. Ooh, Vivi, I thought he would be the one, fool that I am. He was *perfect*! Had his own vineyard and everything, I could have grown grapes and had harvest dinners . . . you know, Vivi, kinda like that. Why am I such a fool? I'll bet you are on the verge of marrying the French guy. I'd like to meet him even though Fen told me, she thinks he's a shit. Please, please, Vivi, tell me it's not true. Let one of us be happy with a man. I mean, what's wrong with us anyway?"

The message ran out. Vivi sat up in the tub and stared at the phone. It rang again a minute later, as she had known it would. This time she picked up.

She said, "All right, JC, since you've driven this far, you can get yourself to my place. I'll put the coffee on, you can have the sofa, and anyway, are you hungry?"

"Jeez, Vivi, you didn't even give me time to say hello."

"You already said hello. Besides, I'm in the bathtub. And the Frenchman no longer exists, so we're in this together. Come to think of it, I'll have martinis waiting."

"Ten minutes," JC said.

Vivi heard her sister laugh before she clicked off. JC was as buoyant as a boat's lifesaver, she seemed to meet disaster on every corner but always came back smiling. Which was more than Vivi had. Shit, she wasn't going there again. She'd better find a pillow and a blanket for JC and clean the tub and run her a hot bath. Driving from Napa in this weather she must be half frozen, as well as tired and ready for a good cry. Okay, so they would cry on each other's shoulders and then get some sleep. She still had to go to work tomorrow.

· · ·

Jane Cecilia Dixon, known to her family as JC, would rather have been heading anywhere this stormy night than her sister's San Francisco apartment.

The first truth was, she had nowhere else to go. She did not even have enough money for a motel—even a cheap one, which she would not have stayed in anyway. Even hard up, she was used to better things.

The second truth was she'd had sort of an "epiphany" the previous night. She wondered if "epiphany" was the correct word. More like a "reality check." And she had not liked it. Not one bit.

Twenty-eight years old was a long hard way from the sunny eighteen-year-old who'd started out as the pretty blonde with the wide sparkling blue eyes and the small breathy sexy voice, copied, if she had to admit it, from the sixties icon Jane Birkin whose recording of *"Moi, je t'aime"* was top of JC's permanent hit list. Singing as though you were at the same time making love was easy, and JC was so young, so "ingénue," so vulnerable-looking on the stages of those little clubs, that older men in suits with money had wanted to take care of her, and the younger guys in black jeans with powerful positions had waved recording contracts at her. None of it worked.

"Rethink your life, JC," Fen had told her five years ago, knowing she was fighting a losing battle because JC was still so full of herself and showbiz, nothing anyone said could make an impression.

JC's third truth was her aunt had been right.

You could include in JC's CV all the men who'd chased her, and who had sometimes caught her. Hey, she was a sexy young chick, she did what she wanted when she wanted. In the end though, a few nights ago, she'd looked at herself in the mirror and seen a slightly-worn twenty-eight-year-old who had not worked in a year, who was involved in a relationship with an older man who owned a small vineyard in Napa Valley with a double divorce behind him plus custody of three teenagers and six dogs. Nevertheless, JC had been prepared to marry him, become a stepmom and settle down, though life in the country depressed her. And then she'd found there was "another woman."

She'd had the so-called "epiphany," sitting on the bed in the small two-room apartment she occupied, because what with his teenage kids and all, the vintner had said he could not have her living at his vineyard, she had come to the conclusion that life sucked, that too soon she would be thirty, that life as a wanna-be singer was not working. She suddenly regretted opting out of college, regretted the con men who'd told her she would be a star one day, regretted her own selfish beliefs. She had missed out on life and would have to start all over again. How, she did not know, but somebody would help her. Somebody always did.

And that's why she was here, credit cards maxed out and just enough money left in her pocket for a Big Mac and possibly a manicure, showing up on her sister's doorstep on the rainiest fuckin' night in years.

There were no parking spots and JC was forced to park two blocks from Vivi's, just managing to squeeze, though a bit sideways-on, between a Chevy Blazer and a motorcycle, which in JC's view had no right anyway to be taking up an entire parking place meant for cars, like her BMW 300i. Certainly, her car was old, and of course it was black: an artist, such as herself, would never dream of being seen in a white car, and forget about a color, though she might give red a go, if it was a Ferrari that is. Meanwhile, she had to drag her suitcase and an armload of slippery plastic garment bags all the way to Vivi's place in this deluge. She had not been happy before and she was even less happy now. Disgruntled, she pulled up the hood of her supposedly rainproof jacket, stuffed her long blond hair inside, and sloshed off in her red platform stilettos through the puddles.

The street was deserted. Of course it was; nobody but a fool would be out on a night like this. The wheels of her suitcase got stuck and she gave it a savage kick. Then the wind gave a sudden manic shriek whipping off her hood. In seconds her hair was soaked. Fuck!

JC stopped to get her bearings, checking the house numbers. She was almost there . . . she'd better be before she got washed away. How the hell had she driven all the way from Napa? She'd been crying so hard she'd thought it was tears, not the rain that had made visibility so bad . . . fool, fool, fool that she was . . .

She checked the numbers again; she had been to Vivi's once or twice before but these old houses all looked the same and she did not recognize it . . . that must be it, just a couple of more to go . . .

10

Vivi opened the door a crack. "Jesus, JC, stop pressing the bell, will you," she said crossly. "I heard you."

"Then let me in, why don't you?" The sisters glared at each other for a moment, JC still outside in the rain, Vivi standing in the doorway.

Vivi tugged the door open, took JC's case and dragged it in.

"Coffee or martini?" she asked.

JC squeezed past her and flung her armload of plastic garment bags onto the floor, slid off her platform heels and removed her coat all in one movement, before sinking onto the black leather sofa.

"Martini please," she said, her eyes roaming the room, taking everything in. "Why black leather?" she asked her sister, patting the sofa. "It's cold."

Vivi threw her a blanket. "Because it looks good," she said firmly. "And I don't get to spend much time on it. Anyhow, it's what you are sleeping on tonight."

"I'll bet nobody comes to sit on it anymore, now the Frenchman's gone," JC said nastily.

Vivi threw her a look back. "It's good to see you too, JC. It sounds like you're in trouble."

"*Again.*" JC's mouth twisted into a wry line. "I *know* that's what you were going to say."

Vivi hesitated, she didn't know whether to be encouraging or just say, "face it, baby, it's the truth." She decided on the latter course. "But it's not too late to change," she added.

She'd mixed vodka martinis a minute ago. Now she shook them vigorously, took a jar of olives from the refrigerator.

"Two please," JC said.

"You're not in a damned bar," Vivi said, irritated by her sister, as she always was, but nevertheless adding a second olive.

"To us." JC waved her glass. "May we both come out of this alive," she added, making Vivi laugh despite herself.

"I intend to change my life." JC's lovely, fine-boned face took on a determined look and her blue eyes narrowed. "I'm too old now to be a model, and nobody's interested in my music. Let's face it, I'm not that good anyway and I've always coasted on my looks and my youth." Her mouth pulled down, thinking about how old she was. "*Twenty-eight!*" she moaned. "I'll have to make a complete change, do something serious, like look after children."

Vivi snorted with laughter at the idea. "No woman in her right mind is going to let a girl who looks like you into her home and near her husband, so you might as well forget about that. Anyhow, you don't know the first thing about kids."

"True." JC's sigh was heartfelt. "I'll think about it," she promised. "I can always clean houses or wash dishes. I'll do anything."

"Of course you won't." Vivi knew her sister too well; as always,

JC would take the easy way out, which meant whatever fell into her lap. "You'll go see Fen," she decided. "You'll tell her everything and then she'll know what to do."

"You think so?" JC looked doubtful.

"Doesn't she always," Vivi said. "I was going there tonight, to tell her my troubles, but couldn't, because of the storm."

"*I* drove all the way from Napa," JC reminded her.

"Oh, shut up." Vivi was too tired for this conversation. "I'm like the walking dead, I have to get some sleep, and you should too."

JC had the endearing ability to express understanding and sympathy with her eyes, and she did so now, looking soulfully at her sister. She patted the leather cushions next to her. "Vivi, I don't want to be alone, I'd rather bunk in with you," she said.

Vivi sighed. It was impossible to be angry with JC for long. "Okay. But no more crying, right?"

"I won't if you don't," JC promised. "And you have to tell me *all*!"

The sisters had their arms round each other as they turned out the lights and finally headed for a bath and bed and another martini, and a long heart-to-heart instead of sleep.

11

It was very late. The wind was still gusting around Cliff Cottage, though the rain had let up a little. Now, though, the sound of it pattering on the windows made Fen's sitting room, with its dove-gray walls and silvery curtains and the pale linen sofas, the logs glowing red in the grate and the scent of the early hyacinths she had grown herself, feel even cozier.

It was also even more cozy because of the man sitting opposite. The low mirrored-glass coffee table was between them, with a newly opened bottle of the good Napa Pinot and their half-filled glasses, as well as the cheeses and rosemary crackers on a saffron-colored platter. Hector was sprawled, head between his paws, as close to the fire as he could get, and he had stopped making those suspicious little growls in the back of his throat. Fen guessed that, like her, Hector had accepted the stranger as being okay. As far as she or Hector knew, that is.

Alex was smiling at her. He said, "If I had to pick a place to be stranded in a storm, it would be this. You surely know how to run a good hotel."

She smiled back at him, the small pussycat smile that crinkled her eyes and which had endeared her to many men, a long time ago. "And who said you were staying?" she asked.

Alex laughed, threw up his hands, made as if to go. "Sorry, sorry . . . I did offer to leave earlier."

Fen didn't really want him to go, she was suddenly lonely and besides, she was attracted to him and wanted very much to know who he was, what he was, and why he had been outside her house anyway on a night like this, when even her own niece couldn't get there.

"Oh do be quiet and sit down," she said. "I was just about to tell you my life story. And then, of course, I expect to hear yours, though obviously yours will be shorter."

"And I'm sure, not as interesting. What about you being a dancer in Paris, then?"

He sat back down and began to spread goat cheese on rosemary crackers. He put two on a plate then handed it to Fen, looking expectantly at her.

She bit into a cracker and said, "I'd been dancing since I was six. Y'know the usual little girl longing to be a ballerina thing, though of course I was too tall. But I *was* a good dancer; I could do anything. Then, when I was eighteen my mother died. She was all I had. Dad had gone long before; it had always been just the two of us." Fen shrugged. "And there I was, suddenly all alone, with no one to tell me what to do. Actually, to tell me what I *could* or *couldn't* do is what I mean."

She gave him a meaningful look as she bit into another cracker.

"Anyhow let me tell you that when you're very young, 'freedom' is not all it's made out to be. And of course I did all the wrong things, like fall in love with a married man. I didn't find out until it was too late and then he said what married men always say—that there was no more sex between him and his wife, they virtually lived apart, he would get a divorce . . . Hah! I was smarter than he thought. I got myself a private detective and got the truth. No need to elaborate," she added, looking at Alex. "I'm sure you know what I mean. A married man like you."

Alex looked her straight in the eye. "I never said I was married."

"You never said you weren't."

He grinned. "This is your story, not mine, remember?"

Fen sighed again. "Oh, I remember too much. Some things I would like to forget. But there you go, you make mistakes and then you have to live with the consequences. You have wonderful times, wonderful lovers, and 'meaningful,' as they say nowadays, 'relationships,' which is what *I* would simply call 'being in love,' living for 'love.'"

"And is that what you did? You stayed with the married man?"

"Of course I did not! What sort of a girl do you think I was!" Fen kicked off her boots and slid her bare feet up under her, sinking back against the cushions, wineglass clasped in both hands, a host of memories hidden behind her eyes. "I simply got on with living," she said. "I was in New York because that's where *he* lived. They were auditioning for a show in Paris." She shrugged. "What more could a brokenhearted cheated-on girl want? I was nineteen years old then and had everything they needed. Would I take my clothes off, they asked, after assessing me this way and that, making notes, picking me out of the lineup of eager young dancers. Why not? I thought, I've taken them off for worse reasons."

Alex laughed again and so did she. "You must have been pretty darn gorgeous," he said, his eyes admiring her.

Fen fell silent. She wondered if he was sincere. Was she making a fool of herself? A woman in her fifties recalling her memories for a younger man, like a character on a soap opera.

"You're laughing at me," she said, nervous again.

"Oh my God, I am not!" Alex got to his feet, came round to her side of the coffee table, sat next to her, took her hand. "Listen to me," he said, "my savior from the storm, I would never laugh at you. I think you're pretty darn wonderful, as well as beautiful. Not to say courageous, taking your life into your own hands at nineteen, living and failing and picking up again and living some more. Why on earth would I be laughing at you. I want to *meet* a woman like you!"

"So you're not married then," Fen said, making him laugh again.

"Of course you know you're impossible," he said.

"And of course, I have just the woman for you," Fen retorted.

He rolled his eyes, pushing his hands through his thick dark hair, shaking his head, outwitted. "A 'niece,'" he guessed.

"I told you I have two. One needs to get a life and the second is dedicated to her work. Which would you prefer?"

"Jesus!" Alex patted her hand, then got up and walked over to the window. "I think I'd rather choose you," he said over his shoulder, looking out at the rain.

Fen was silent; she might almost have thought he meant it, but of course knew he could not; they had only just met and besides he was too young and she was too old.

"Not when you hear the rest of my story, you won't," she said lightly. "Now come back over here, why don't you, and pour me some more wine." She held up her hand, dismissing what she had just said. "I know, I know, there's no excuse for getting drunk, but I lived in France a long time, a woman gets used to imbibing a decent glass of wine, or even better, Champagne. I have a bottle of Perrier-Jouët chilling in the refrigerator. Shall we switch?"

Alex went to the refrigerator, took out the Champagne. "Tell me where the glasses are," he said.

"Top cupboard, third on your left. Get the ones that say Moët & Chandon on them. They're a souvenir of a visit I made to that vineyard with my first husband. We had lunch there, with the Moët people, the Compte de Vogué, white-glove service and a different Champagne with every course. So civilized!"

He came back, two glasses in one hand, the Champagne in the other. "You said the *first* husband?"

She watched him take off the foil and the wire cage and expertly ease out the cork. He was obviously used to the better things in life. Who the hell was he anyway? He poured and gave her a glass. Their hands touched again, and again attraction flickered between them. Fen felt a familiar lurch in the stomach. If she knew two things in life, one was that a broken heart felt like a lump of lead in your chest; the other was that sexual attraction felt like a jolt through what Shakespeare would have called your loins.

Alex took his seat opposite again.

"To this night," Fen toasted, "which came out of the blue, or I suppose the black. A grand surprise."

"To *our* night." Alex looked at her, his face absolutely serious. A silence fell between them. "Nothing like this has ever happened to me before," he finally said quietly.

Fen was not sure what he meant, not sure if he was feeling what she felt, but she knew she would not have missed this night for all the storms in the world. This was special, a sweet moment in time to add to that bank of memories.

But that was it. She must get back to reality. "Yes, I did say my first husband," she said, quickly changing the subject again. "The Frenchman, I mean."

12

It was after midnight and Brad lay in bed, staring at the ceiling. From behind the shades a suffused glow from the streetlamps silhouetted the branches of the pepper tree outside his window. Some early philanthropist, attuned to nature and after the 1906 earthquake and the great fire, had planted trees in the small alley in Chinatown where horses used to be stabled, so they would never suffer from the summer's heat. "Summer" and "heat" were not words that exactly fit together in San Francisco; more like summer and fog, as the boom of the foghorns now told. Though of course this was fall when anything might happen and usually did. Like, for instance, tonight's storm.

Sleepless, Brad got up. He paced the small living room in his blue boxers, cup of coffee in hand, Flyin' safely asleep on the sofa. She never used the padded velveteen bed he'd inherited with the dog, courtesy of his ex. The dog seemed to despise it and always slept on the sofa, a habit Brad had done nothing to discourage on the theory that it was better than the dog sleeping on *his* bed. Anyhow, there he was, pacing his low-beamed living room in what was originally a stable, later a garage and now his home, listening to the rain on his windows and the wind sighing through his pepper tree. "Nature's music," Brad called it. He thought it sure as hell beat rap.

He could not get the final image of the young woman out of his mind; her on the gurney being wheeled, ashen-faced as if in death; blood, plasma, drugs that might save her in plastic packets and tubes attached to her; a tired team in the emergency and an exhausted doctor whose name aligned in mythology with his own.

He put some music on the stereo: call him old-fashioned but he had a thing for Neil Diamond, always had since he was a kid, well, a youth anyway. He loved those lyrics: you just knew a guy like Diamond had lived through it, knew from where he was coming. Brad had been eighteen then and chasing girls in college. That certainly hadn't gotten him anywhere; he'd scraped through finals, contemplated life as a bum working his way round the world, surfing, drinking beer, sitting around fires on remote beaches, making love like the world was about to end.

His father had been a cop. He'd caught a bullet out there in the "wilds" of L.A.'s San Fernando Valley, lived long enough to be bitter about his disability, to regret the loss of a way of life that *was* his life. That's one of the reasons Brad had become a cop, not simply because he was following in his dad's footsteps, but because he was *like* his dad, with the urge to solve the jigsaw puzzles of crimes, aligned with the urge to fight those crimes. That's what he did. That's who he was.

And now he lived alone in the ex-stables ex-garage in Chinatown, close enough to the dim sum joints to always have a good breakfast—it beat the donuts the other guys ate—close enough to hear the calls from the street markets, close enough to keep an eye on the fake-Rolex business and any drug dealers crashing his turf. Everyone knew him. For God's sake even their kids knew him; he was almost an honorary Chinese by now, showing up for the New Year's and Lunar Festivals, applauding the Golden Dragon dance and smiling at the children's spellbound faces. He was one of them. A neighbor. A cop.

He'd done his time in the black-and-whites, patrolling the streets in the Mission District; gotten married and divorced with custody of a poodle. He'd scraped together enough to buy the dilapidated stable/garage with a Chinese temple at the end of the street because no one else wanted it, and with the help of his buddies had done it over in his spare time. The small living room was painted white—he wasn't creative with color, considered that a woman's department. He'd found the old green-tiled Victorian fireplace with the wooden mantel in a junk store, and installed it with a faux gas log fire for convenience. He had no time for logs. There was a brownish microfiber sofa, a couple of club chairs that went with it (matchy-matchy his ex had mocked when she came over and saw them), a coffee table made from a sawn-off hunk of redwood that had taken four guys to lift; a wall of bookshelves containing his stereo equipment; a TV next to the fire; two windows with rattan shades, one either side of the Chinese-red lacquered front door which had been donated by his Chinese new neighbors who were glad to have a cop right there on their patch; a black rug that showed every footfall, he should have gone for the white but hey, he was feeling hip that day.

The bedroom was the same décor only with a bed. There was a small tiled bathroom, a small white kitchen with a regular stove, a large refrigerator, a micro and—his favorite—the coffeemaker. Most everything else was unused.

Pacing his living room, circling the sofa, Neil Diamond singing "Sweet Caroline" softly in the background, coffee cup in his hand, Brad still could not get the image of the young woman out of his mind.

He slumped onto the un-plumped-up sofa cushions next to Flyin', who shifted grudgingly to allow him room, snuffling her irritation, making him smile. Women were all the same, give 'em an inch and they'd take a yard.

The coffee tasted old. It was yesterday's. He put the mug on the table, put his feet up next to it, arms behind his head, contemplating those low ceiling beams but still seeing the scene of the crime. How innocuous those words sounded, "the scene of the crime." It was the scene of an outrage, of an attempted murder so savage, so foul, he and Jerusalem Guiterrez, who'd seen a few "crime scenes" in their time, had found it hard to face. She was so young. She was so violated. Fear was still on her face, like the scream that had been cut off, sealed with a green Post-it and a strip of duct tape, while her blood seeped onto the dank woodland floor.

And then there was the message *Please Don't Tell*. How the fuck could she tell? She was dead. Or that's what her would-be killer had thought. Had he been caught in the act? In the *finality* of the act?

A squad had been sent immediately to comb the woods but the search had been called off because of the storm. Now though, the rain had slackened to a fine drizzle and the wind to buffeting gusts. If they were to find anything it would have to be immediately.

Brad swung his legs off the coffee table, picked up his iPhone and speed-dialed Guiterrez. His wife answered after three rings. "He's not here," she said, snappily.

"Chiquitita, I'm in love with you but I need your man."

Chiquitita was Brad's affectionate name for Maria Carmen because the first time he'd met her she had been dancing to the Abba song with that title, a wild Mexican dance of her own that made Brad understand why his friend had fallen for her.

Now she sighed loudly in his ear. "It's okay, I was up with the baby anyway."

How could he have forgotten the Guiterrezes were new parents? Their kid was two months old. He was godfather, for fuck's sake! "So, how is little Samson, anyway?" He did not ask how they had come up with the name Samson; for sure their boy was gonna give them hell over that when he was old enough, unless he grew up to be six-four and muscled that is, but knowing his parents Brad thought that unlikely.

"Samson would be better for knowing his father better, if his father spent better time at home. And maybe his godfather also. I'll go wake him."

She did not say goodbye-nice-talking-to-you and Brad heaved a sigh. He hated doing this but he and Jerry needed to get out there. Now.

"I'm already getting dressed." His partner came on the phone knowing what Brad wanted before he said it. "Better put on your wellies though, it'll be muddy out there."

"What the fuck are wellies?"

"Rubber boots, man. For walking in the country at night after a storm. Keep your feet clean and dry."

"They don't make 'em in my size," Brad said. "Pick you up at your place in fifteen."

He buckled his normal leather boots, holstered the Sig Sauer, threw on an old ski jacket—he hadn't been skiing since the bust-up and it smelled musty but it might keep out the rain, plus it had a hood. Him—in a hoodie!

Anyway. He slammed a baseball cap over his uncombed hair, gave Flyin' an affectionate pat, told her he'd be right back, and grabbed the keys to his Ford truck. He was glad he'd sprung for the top-grade tires—he'd need 'em on a night like this.

Then he called the hospital. Elaine was still alive.

13

"Frenchmen," Fen was saying to Alex, who'd gone to look out of the window again and was staring out at the storm, "are not to be trusted with women. Not under any circumstances."

He turned to look at her.

"It's in their blood," she said. "Simple as that. And the sooner women realize it the better. Though of course there are certain experiences that should not be missed. Depending on the man of course."

"The *French* man."

"My first husband. He was charming, attentive to my every need and handsome with it. We fell for each other at first glance." Fen paused, remembering Vivi calling to ask what a *coup de foudre* meant. Like her, she was certain Vivi would find out. She only hoped that unlike her, she did not marry him first.

"I'll bet it was across the footlights when you were a dancer," the stranger said, coming to sit opposite her again.

Fen laughed, remembering. "I must have looked about nine feet tall in those heels. But anyway." She pulled herself back from the memories, back to the man who had come to sit opposite again. "So that's my story," she said. "Now it's your turn."

"But I need to hear the rest, you can't leave me dangling in the front row."

"He was in the third row," she said. "And that's beside the point. You are here, sitting on my sofa, drinking my wine and I don't even know who you are." Seriousness lay behind her smile, as well as curiosity. "It's not often you get young men marooned at your front door in a storm," she added. "Nor does that man get free medical attention, a good beef daube and a clean sweatshirt, without telling all."

A lock of his dark brown hair slid over Alex's eyes and he ran his hand through it, pushing it back. "All right, I didn't want to tell you, but I will."

Her expression changed from interest to apprehension. "Start with how old you are."

"Thirty-nine. Forty next birthday."

Which is?"

"January."

"Hmm, Aries. And . . . ?"

"Born in Boston. Now I live in L.A. I'm in the security business, kind of a private investigator."

Fen sat up straighter, looking at him with interest.

"Not good husband material for a niece," he added, and they both laughed.

"So why are you here, in Big Sur, Mr. Detective? I never met a detective before," she added.

He shrugged. "Not for any good reason. In fact, it's a sad reason. My clients in L.A. have a daughter. *Had* a daughter." He clasped his

hands together, elbows on his knees, eyes cast down. "She lived in San Francisco, worked as a flight attendant. She was killed four months ago."

"You mean in an accident?" Fen was shocked.

"I mean she was raped and murdered," he answered. "'By person or persons unknown,' to quote the police report. There were no clues at the crime scene, the cops have yet to come up with any suspect; she was young, popular, a nice girl."

"And somebody's daughter." Fen's voice was hollow. "I wonder if murderers ever think of that." Fen shivered, she wished she'd never asked. She was aware of a sudden silence. The wind had stopped. The rain was a mere patter on the windows; a log tumbled in the grate. The house was suddenly very still.

"The police will find him." Fen put her faith in law and order; they had always come through for her. Small matters though, compared with this horror; a break-in; a car theft was about the sum of it. "Cops care," she added. "I know from personal experience. Maybe it's because I'm a woman but they took good care of me when my car was stolen, though they never did find the culprits," she added thoughtfully.

"Cops are on the streets, in the thick of it," Alex said. "Gangs, shootouts, violence, random murders, kids killing each other. I don't know which is more senseless but I do know they put their lives on the line every day. They drive those black-and-whites through the gang areas, knowing the risk they are taking, always having to have sharper eyes, knowing where the crack dealers are; the kids pimping; the crack houses with young people from nice suburbs getting ripped and raped. Every cop deserves an award and too many end up dead."

"And too many of those kids end up on gurneys in the emergency

department," Fen said. She knew that because Vivi told her how harrowing it was, and that the wounded and the dying from those shootouts were always young. "They're too young to die," she added.

"We're all too young to die."

"At my age I've been forced to consider it," Fen admitted, "though I prefer the option."

She made him laugh again, brought him back from a world she knew nothing about, and hoped she never would. "I hope you catch your killer, though, Mr. Detective," she said. He had not told her how the young woman whose case he was investigating had died, and she did not want to know.

He walked over to the window, stood silently looking out. Hector lumbered to his feet, watching him warily.

"Alex," Fen called and he turned his head.

"Now what?"

She smiled her pussycat smile at him, patted her silvery hair. She'd had curtains made to match that hair color. Call her vain, but there it was. He walked over and she shifted along the couch a bit so he could come and sit next to her. "What's your other name?" she said.

"Why do you want to know?"

"You were a wounded stranger who might have proved to be an axe-murderer. Now I need to know who you really are."

"Why wouldn't you have wanted to know my name then?"

"My God, if you were going to kill me do you think *that* would be first thing on my mind?"

He looked at her. He was suddenly very serious. He said quietly, "I've wondered exactly what would be on a woman's mind in that situation, facing a rapist, a killer, knowing as she must, what is to happen to her, what is to come . . . that she is totally helpless and that he has no mercy."

Fen shivered. She closed her eyes, picturing the sheer trembling horror of it. She said, "Perhaps, under those terrible circumstances, when all the fight is gone and they are helpless, perhaps they simply accept, put themselves in God's hands. Their only safety."

Alex got up, walked to the table, unhooked his biker jacket from the back of the chair, put it on.

He was leaving. Alarmed, she untucked herself from the couch. "What are you doing?"

"The wind's down, the rain's abated, no more biblical deluge. And thanks to you, my wounded head is fine. I must be on my way."

"But you could stay." She so badly wanted him to stay . . . she hurried over to him. She said, "Anyway, your car is wrecked. You can't go."

"The front bumper got the worst of it. My guess is it'll start okay, just be a bit of a rough ride."

"You're leaving me." Fen didn't know where those words came from. She felt abandoned.

Alex took her hands in his, held them to his lips. "Maybe I don't do that exactly like a Frenchman," he said, "but you made me feel like a Frenchman tonight." He ran a finger over her cheek, warm from sitting by the fire. "I had a wonderful time," he said softly. "You are a very special woman."

"Isn't this how it ended in the Bogart movie?" she said.

"But then I'm not Bogart."

Fen didn't say it, but she knew she certainly wasn't Bergman.

"I'll walk with you to the car, make sure you're okay." She went in search of her boots but Alex told her there was no need.

He opened the kitchen door and Hector shot past him into the night. Alex was right, the rain was no longer slamming against the house, and the wind had dropped; you could even hear the ocean again, foaming and roiling over the rocks at the bottom of the cliff. The night sky seemed weighted with black, not a color, just a mass of nothing. No stars out tonight.

Alex's hands were thrust in the pockets of his jacket as he gazed at the sky, breathing the clean cold air. He turned his eyes to her. "You're shivering," he said. "You must go in. But first I want to thank you. For everything."

Fen leaned against the doorjamb, arms folded over her chest. "Thank you for entertaining me so well," she said. "I haven't had such a good time in years."

"I don't believe that! A woman like you!"

He stepped off the porch and started down the puddled drive. She watched him from the doorway.

He turned, halfway, hands still thrust deep into his biker jacket pockets. He said, "I didn't tell you everything. My name is Alex Patcevich and I knew the young woman, the flight attendant who was murdered. I was engaged to her. We were to have been married in June. She was a beautiful girl. She didn't deserve to end like this. Now, I need to find who did it."

Fen clutched a hand to her heart. To say she was sorry seemed trivial. There were no words. He turned away and walked back up her gravel drive, back into the darkness, out of her life.

"Thank you," she called softly after him. "Thank you, Alex Patcevich."

Then Hector came bounding back and Fen went inside and shut the door, locking it this time. The night was over. She had met a man with a mission, a man bent on revenge. A man who had stirred her heart. She wished him luck.

"Ask me," Jerry Guiterrez said to Brad as they drove a narrow country road still awash in mud, "and I'd tell you I'd rather be anywhere but here."

"You mean with me." Brad, who was driving, smiled, but kept his eyes on the road. "I seem to remember I've heard that before."

"Must've been somebody else." Guiterrez flipped his mobile open, checked his messages. There was a text from his wife; she couldn't get the baby to stop crying. Screaming. Should she take little Samson to the emergency room? Didn't he know a doctor there? Maybe the baby had something really wrong?

"New-mother blues," Jerry said to Brad. "You'd think this was her first, not the fourth. The kid's a crier, is all. Some are, some are not." He shrugged. "That's the way it goes with kids."

He texted back though, reassuring her. "Love that boy," he said to Brad, smiling. "Y'know he was kind of an afterthought, meaning I should have 'thought' before I 'acted.' But I'll tell you what, I wouldn't be without him."

"He's only two months old," Brad objected.

"Glad you remembered. You should also remember godfathers are supposed to come up with gifts. Y'know, a small present, like five grand or so, to start a college education fund."

"My understanding was, as godfather I was supposed to take him under my wing, guide him through life, share my knowledge with him, take him out to lunch on his birthday."

"You got it wrong, you need more of the Marlon Brando style of godfathering . . . y'know with the money and the style . . ."

"And look what happened to him." The car went into a skid on the flooded corner and Brad steered confidently into it.

"One thing you are is a good driver," Jerry admitted. He spotted the squad car ahead, parked at the side of the road by the trees where the young woman had been found. Yellow police tape cordoned the area and as they approached a uniformed cop got out and waved them down.

Brad and Jerry rolled down their widows and flashed their badges. A second cop stood behind the first, a hand on his gun. "Sir," he said respectfully. "All's quiet here. What can we do for you?"

"Just gonna take another look around."

The two got out of the truck. The roadside had turned into a mud bath from all the rain, plus all the squad cars and foot traffic. Jerry had been right about the wellies. Another car was parked farther down the road, a red Camaro with an antenna sticking from its roof.

"We got TV news here?" Jerry asked.

"Last ones, still hanging in, hoping."

"Hah! Newshounds." Jerry snorted, irritated.

A young woman wearing a dark tracksuit and very white sneakers got out of the Camaro and came toward them, microphone in hand. "Detectives, sirs, could I speak to you for a minute, ask you what's going on, why you're back here? Is there any further news for our viewers?"

"Pardon my French," Jerry said coldly, "but I don't give a fuck about your viewers, and nor does the woman who is the reason we are here, doing what cops do."

"Just asking . . ." she said.

They turned away and she hurried after them, skidded and ended up butt down, in the mud. "Shit," she said angrily, trying to get to her feet. The pristine white sneakers were no longer white.

Brad went back to help her. He offered her his hand, gave her a tug up and said in his most fatherly way—he was not yet forty and not a father but it worked at times—"Ma'am, please get back in your car and go home. This is no place for you or your viewers. A young woman, not so very different from you, was savagely attacked here, she lies now between life and death. I do not think your mother would want you to be anywhere near this scene, at one in the morning on a stormy night. So tell your cameraman who very sensibly is waiting in your car, there is no news and get yourself back home where you belong."

"Shit," he heard her snort angrily again as he turned away.

"We're going in there," Jerry told the guys in the squad car who were on guard. He could see from their look they thought he was on a losing streak with that. Nevertheless, toting his flashlight, he walked with Brad into the wooded area.

The short path to the crime scene was worn down by the booted feet of emergency personnel and police and Jerry had no trouble finding it. He shone his lamp on the place under the tree where she had lain.

The imprint of the girl's body was still there under a plastic cover, on the soaked mass of dead leaves. You could see clearly where her outflung arms had rested, the convex dent where her head had been; the spread-eagled legs; the rust-dark stains of blood. Forensics had been here, taken their samples; photographs and videos had been taken, everything necessary had been done. After that, the search had to be called off, until morning they'd said. Brad and Jerry were taking matters into their own hands.

"He was interrupted," Brad said. "And frightened. A frightened man makes mistakes, forgets things."

He crouched over the compressed bed of leaves, scanning the ground. Her clothes had been found and taken away by forensics. There was no identification; so far nobody had called in saying their daughter, their girlfriend, their roommate was missing. Soon, though, somebody would wonder why she hadn't shown up for work, or for an appointment, or a date. Somebody would come looking for her and Brad badly needed to put the jigsaw pieces together so they could find her family, get them to the hospital before it was too late.

Earlier, he'd interviewed the two young men who'd found her, eight hours after the attack. Shattered, they'd sat on hard plastic chairs at the precinct, heads in their hands repeating over and over, *oh man, oh man, let this not have happened, let me not have seen it . . .*

Brad felt sorry for them, being questioned by the police about a murder when he was sure they were simply unfortunate to have stumbled on something that did not involve them.

They hadn't seen anyone, they'd come into the woods just to take a piss for God's sakes. They were both under the alcohol limit, both stone-cold sober, both wanted to get home to their wives and kids, never wanted to think about this again . . .

"We didn't think," the other said . . . "I mean why would ya? Until we saw her." He began to cry then and Brad sent for coffee all-round, and said the officers were just doing their duty, questioning.

His flashlight caught a low branch, twigs broken off, a slippery trail of flattened leaves.

"He ran out through here," he said to Jerry and the two moved toward the tree and swung their lights over and around it. Jerry spotted it first, a gleam of white at the base of the trunk. He crouched low. "It's a name tag," he said.

Brad crouched next to him. The name was Elaine.

"I'll bet she was a waitress," he said. "From the black skirt and white shirt she was wearing, I'd guess a coffee shop. Your more up-market waitresses wear all black, kinda Versace-looking."

Jerry was photographing the name tag from every angle. Brad walked on, feeling like an explorer tracking an animal's path through the jungle. It was almost child's play, it was so obvious from the broken twigs where the panicked killer had fought his way out to the road and his car, where the storm had successfully removed all tire tracks. A piece of wire stuck out from the pad of leaves, though. In the beam from his flashlight Brad saw it was a small tripod, made to hold a video camera.

"Jesus Christ," he yelled to Jerry. "The bastard was filming her. *Filming* what he did! *Jesus Christ, man!*"

Sickened, he realized the tripod might well lead him to the killer. "Elaine" might not be dead—yet—but three other young women were. This time the killer had left his mark.

V ivi was woken by a phone call at eight the next morning; not JC, though; *she* snored on, oblivious. Not only that, JC had taken up three-quarters of the bed, leaving Vivi to lie all night, straight as a pole, unable even to bend her knees while her sister snuggled a pillow to her chest in the comfy fetal position.

There were traces of tears on JC's rounded pink cheeks. Looking at her, Vivi thought all her sister needed was the thumb in the mouth and JC would have reverted completely to childhood. But Vivi was *not* JC's mom, and now she had a mind to send her right back home to their aunt. Let *her* straighten her out. Somebody had to.

The phone was still ringing. What the hell had happened to her answering machine? And who was calling so early, anyway? She checked the time. It wasn't *that* early, it was just that she'd had a late night.

She swung her legs over the side of the bed and inspected the caller ID. It was her aunt.

"Fen," she said, snatching up the phone. "Are you all right?"

"Of course I'm all right, I was worried about you, though. I thought you might have gotten stuck on the road in the storm."

"I didn't even set off, it was impossible because of the weather, and your phones didn't work."

"Never do, even when there's only so much as a bit of a breeze."

Vivi knew her aunt's "a bit of a breeze" was what most people would call a gale. She asked if the house was okay, how was Hector, how was she; she was sorry she had missed her favorite meal but asked Fen to please save the beef daube because she would be coming down to see her in the next few days, and this time she would bring someone with her.

"I hope not the Frenchman again," Fen said.

The disapproval in her voice made Vivi laugh. "Not him. Your favorite girl."

"Well, now, that would mean *you*, wouldn't it?"

Vivi could hear the amusement in her aunt's voice. "*Of course* it's JC," she said. "She showed up last night, the proverbial drowned rat, jobless, man-less, and, if I'm not mistaken, penniless."

"That sounds like my favorite girl," Fen acknowledged.

"She needs straightening out." Vivi turned as she heard the sheets rustling. JC was sitting up in bed, in the same white T-shirt she had been wearing when she showed up on the doorstep, blond hair streaming over her shoulders, blue eyes as bright, Vivi thought enviously, as a summer sky. JC looked like an angel when she was sleeping and now she looked even more angelic waking. It was not normal.

JC reached over to grab the phone but Vivi yanked it away from her.

"Hi, Fen," JC yelled, "I'm coming to see you."

"Tell her I'll be here," Fen told Vivi, "whenever she can make it. Meanwhile, I had quite an exciting time last night. An Intruder." She gave the word a significant capital.

"What!" Vivi leapt to her feet, shocked.

"Don't worry, he turned out to be charming, in fact I thought for a while there he might be ideal for you, until I encountered a little problem he has."

"He's gay," Vivi guessed.

"No, he is not. An 'orphan of the storm,' I guess you might call him."

Vivi could hear the reminiscent tone in Fen's voice and knew she had better get down there soon. She would sort out her Intruder, unload JC on her, then get back to her own life. Dr. Vivian, emergency life-support system. Work beat out loneliness every time.

"We'll try to be there tomorrow afternoon." She said goodbye and put down the phone and looked at JC, sitting expectantly, staring at her. "You might at least have put on the coffee."

"Oh, let's go out for coffee, it'll be so much better than anything I make. Besides, you never know who you might meet. Dibs on first shower."

JC flitted across the room, all brown legs and blondness. How did she stay so brown anyway? Guessing, Vivi bet her sister spent a good deal of whatever money she had in spray-tan salons. Looking at her own pale legs she thought it might not be a bad idea but knew she would never keep up with it. And anyhow, nobody was looking at her legs.

"Brains," she called out to JC who was singing in the shower (that girl's spirits never sank for more than half an hour at a time, regardless of the state of her heart or her finances, or her future.) "*Brains* are what get you somewhere in this life, little sister. Brains and hard work."

JC pulled back the shower curtain and reached out a hand for Vivi to deposit a towel in it. "I know, and I'm so proud of you," she said humbly. Or at least Vivi thought it might have been humble.

JC stepped out of the shower wrapped in Vivi's new cream towel, bought the previous week at Costco and laundered by Vivi, as per instructions, prior to use. Except *she* had not gotten to use it yet.

She met JC's eyes.

"Truce, Vivi," her sister said with a new real humility. Vivi was almost sure about it.

Standing there in her tiny bathroom which in any case was not big enough for two, Vivi felt herself droop; tears of weariness brimmed and trickled down her cheeks. "Oh, JC, I'm sorry I'm being mean to you; I'm just so tired and yesterday was so horrible, a girl with her throat slashed . . ."

"Shh, shh, don't talk about murders."

JC's arms were round her: they were suddenly as close as when they were little girls. "You need a break, that's all, you need to meet some nice man . . ."

"Oh, God, now you sound like Fen."

"I'll bet she'll tell you to forget the ex-fiancé, to just get on with things." JC laughed. "Fen's like that, always 'briskly moving on.'"

"She was married three times, no role model there."

"Oh yes there is! Our aunt is a role model for how to live your life, how I should live mine. She brought us up properly."

The phone was ringing again and Vivi ran to answer. It was Dr. Ralph Sandowski.

"Hey," she said, surprised, thinking immediately about work and who needed her at the hospital. "Is everything okay?"

"Everything's almost okay. It will be perfectly okay though if you will do me a great favor."

"Of course. Name it." It must be important for him to call this early.

"Remember last night when I met you on the stairs, I asked if you'd like to have a drink?"

"I remember." Of course she did, he was the second man to offer to take her for a drink that night. The burly blue-eyed cop with the big feet was the other, though she seemed to remember that also included dog-walking.

"You turned me down then, so I'm calling to ask you again, if you would care to have a drink with me this evening? Perhaps a bite to eat after?"

JC had her ear to the phone alongside her.

"Get away," Vivi hissed under her breath, but JC was jumping up and down, clapping her hands.

"Go," she was mouthing, "*go, go, go . . .*"

Vivi looked at her blue flannel pj's, at her pale feet stuck in furry slippers, remembering the Vivi who was the Frenchman's girlfriend in strappy sandals and a skirt short enough to at least show she had legs. "I'd love to, Dr. Ralph," she said.

"It's *Ralph*, Vivi." He reminded her of their new status, friends—with maybe a vibe—and not merely colleagues.

"I'll remember that," Vivi said smiling as they arranged to meet at the bar at Top of the Mark on Nob Hill, famous not only for its stupendous views, but as Ralph said, also for its "100 Martinis" menu.

"I heard you were a martini girl," he added.

"Oh? Who from?" Vivi wasn't aware they had friends in common who knew her habits and likes and dislikes.

"I made it my business to find out," he replied lightly. "I aim to please."

"Thank the Lord for that," Vivi heard JC exclaim from behind, making her laugh.

It was arranged they would meet at eight. She would be coming straight from the hospital and would change there.

Of course, JC took over and got her outfit together, top to toe.

16

Brad had been up all night, combing the woods by flashlight with the extra detail summoned to help, then back at the precinct house. Following his instinct that the girl worked as a waitress in a coffee shop, he'd searched the Internet for diners and coffee shops within a twenty-mile radius. There were a lot. It would be a long haul to contact each one and inquire if they had a waitress named Elaine, who had possibly not shown up for work. Finally, he left others to it, hauled his weary body out of the chair and went home. In the car he called the hospital again. Elaine was still in a coma, the loss of blood had been severe, as was the shock . . . but she was holding her own. At the moment.

Back home, Flyin' was waiting behind the door on her hind legs, doing her best to look neglected and forlorn. Brad swung her up into his arms, gave her a hug, grabbed her lead and said, "Come on, poodle, we're walking."

To tell the truth, he was just glad to have something alive, something warm and breathing to hold after the night he'd had.

They walked a long way, pushing down crowded streets filled with the sounds and smells of China, past small temples with pointed red-and-gold roofs and storefront cafés where old men clattered mah-jongg tiles; past the fortune cookie factories where they stamped out your future on slips of paper; past schoolchildren in single file following the teacher, all wearing red knee socks and giggling and shoving each other; past souvenir shops selling trashy bobble-head dolls and embroidered scarlet jackets, and cafés where slick golden ducks hung in the window, destined to be Peking duck on your table that night, and whose wonderful aroma drifted onto the street.

Owners of shops, out hosing down their sidewalks, waved a greeting. The schoolteacher called hello, the children giggled some more and the pretty young girl at the vegetable stand gave Brad an encouraging smile, showing cute dimples. He'd known her since she was a child in the red knee socks. He was one of the community, he served on committees for the maintenance of Chinese history in California. He liked where he lived.

Remembering he had not fed the dog he stopped at one of the storefront dim sum houses. He was a regular there and they smiled a welcome. He ordered two pork and two shrimp *sui mai*, steamed not fried. The food came quickly and he fed the pork to Flyin' and ate the shrimp himself. No sauce. He liked his *sui mai* straight. In his view you couldn't get a better breakfast. Of course he shouldn't be feeding it to the dog, but needs must; Flyin' was hungry and so was he. It was well past breakfast but when a guy was up all night he kinda lost track of time.

He saw his "friend," Chang Liu, aka Charlie Lew, elbowing his way through the crowd of eaters toward him. Charlie was in his late twenties, smooth-haired, smooth-spoken, a man for the girls who loved him for his flashy ways, his street smarts that got him a customized red Mustang convertible with white leather seats, chrome spokes and a V-8 engine that roared like a Harley in heat.

"Detective . . . how're ya doin'." Charlie beamed and smoothed back his already smooth dark hair. A diamond sparkled on his pinkie, two more in his ears. He was small, thin, groomed to the hilt, smelling of Chinese pomade and French scent. His English-country-style tweed jacket and his red-striped shirt looked like Armani though Brad guessed he'd had them copied in Hong Kong, where Charlie spent a lot of time. The rest of his time, Charlie filled in as the owner of a couple of shops and bars, here in Chinatown.

Of course Brad knew Charlie was always up to something and that it was usually not good, but though Charlie skirted the law he also kept Brad informed when really bad things were going to happen, right there on his turf; like gangs bringing in cheap drugs, heroin cut to the bone with wash powder, or else so pure it killed as soon as it hit the vein; or who was using punk little kids to deliver rock crack for the urban hipsters, and cocaine for the suburbanites. Charlie knew who had guns, where they got 'em and where they kept 'em. Charlie knew who was losing at *pai gow*, who was cheating on his wife; who was about to sell up and go back to China with illegal proceeds and start a new life in the homeland.

And Brad knew Charlie was a big gambler—illegal games in back rooms tucked away in forgotten alleys, serious men, all of them Asian and all ready to stake everything they owned. Sometimes they won, sometimes they lost. Charlie told Brad this, in confidence over cups of green tea that had little round balls of sago floating in them, and live crickets for sale in little wire cages to feed to the birds the Chinese kept as pets.

"How're you doing, Charlie?" Brad gave him a comradely pat on the shoulder, which meant, Charlie knew, that there was no trouble between them, at the moment that is. Brad kept to the letter of the law and Charlie broke it; both of them knew that, and each respected the other for what they could offer. Right now, Charlie was offering information.

"I saw about the murdered girl on TV. Elaine," he said.

Brad rolled his eyes. Elaine's name had not yet been mentioned on TV and would not be until they were able to contact the family. "How'd you hear that name?"

Charlie shrugged. "Doesn't matter how. I also heard the killer videoed her."

Brad's brows rose even higher; he tightened his grip on Flyin's lead and sensing his tension the dog sat very still at his feet.

"We sell cameras here." Charlie indicated Grant Avenue, round the corner. "You need a pretty expensive camera to shoot that, at night in the woods. Maybe some guy came into our shop, you get a good price there, nobody asks questions what you buy, what you want it for. You want night vision? A tripod? You can buy anything you want."

Brad gripped Charlie's shoulder. "You're saying you know this for sure? That a man came to your shop recently and bought that kind of equipment?"

"Detective, Detective . . ." Charlie wiggled free of Brad's hand. "All I'm saying is somebody sold such a thing a week or two ago. And my bet is, a man like that would also have bought night-vision binoculars somewhere."

Brad put his hands back in his pockets, looking intently at Charlie, who said, "I don't want a man like that on my turf, in my space. I'm not saying it was him, I don't know who he was, all I know is what he bought. I don't want him here." He waved his arms round indicting Chinatown. "We do not kill young girls."

Brad understood. Charlie had given him a lead, maybe to nowhere but it was all he'd gotten so far.

He thanked Charlie and walked quickly to the camera store on Grant. The window display was impressive and the man who came forward to speak to him had obviously been warned by Charlie that a cop was on his way. He said he couldn't remember the purchase exactly, so many customers came through his doors, but he did remember the camera. The sale was printed right here, on the sales sheet. He remembered him mostly because the man had paid in cash, but then, in this area, with tourists and fly-by-nighters, that wasn't unusual. Cash left no trace, he reminded Brad, who had been hoping for a credit card.

He showed him the camera, an Olympus Stylus Tough Camera with a Monocam Night Vision Camera Adapter, and the tripod, the same one Brad had found in the woods.

Another piece in the jigsaw.

Brad pushed his way back through the crowded fish market where live amphibians slid slowly back and forth in glass tanks, gazing their last on this world. Looking at them Brad thought again about the girl. Elaine. He texted Jerry, left a message. Called the precinct, did the same. Someone would visit the camera shop and get the info down. He needed to get to the hospital, see what was going on. Picking up a coffee at the local shop, he hurried back home.

Half an hour later he was showered, shaved, dark hair combed obediently into place, clean jeans, plaid shirt, a new pair of shoes he'd bought just the other day—brown suede loafers they were and mighty comfortable. He was ready to go.

He drained the now-cold coffee—story of his life—threw on a wool jacket, zipped it up—it was cloudy out and still with that bitter wind. Calling Flyin', who was also ready to go, he locked his exotic Chinese red-lacquered door behind him, opened the passenger door of the Ford 250 for the dog, who leapt into her place in the shotgun seat; opened his own door, climbed in and took off for the hospital.

Brad had sent Jerry home early the previous night, told him to get some sleep, well, it *had* been three in the morning. He himself had had no sleep but the coffee and the shower had done miracles. He contemplated phoning Jerry, advising him where he was headed but decided against waking him. The man needed to see his baby, and his wife who by now was probably not speaking to Brad anyhow.

At the hospital he parked where he shouldn't because he could and also because it was convenient, slapped the police light on top and opened the window a crack for Flyin'.

Inside, the woman at the desk directed him to the ICU. He took the elevator and walked down a long, brightly lit corridor. He knew where to go because two uniforms were standing outside the door, looking in need of a cigarette and caffeine. They were both young, early twenties, clean-shaven, crisp, eager. Brad remembered when he'd felt like that before the anger at the senselessness of the gangs and the killings. Now he told himself the world had always been that way, all he could do was try to stem the tide. You're just world-weary, he told himself, from too much work; too long a night; too many bad guys.

"Afternoon, sir." The young ones were always polite, anxious to be doing the right thing.

"How're y'doin', guys? More important, how is she doing?"

"A nurse is in there with her, sir. 'Holding her own' is what she said."

Brad looked at the door. Her name was slotted into the metal holder. ELAINE.

He knocked and a nurse came to the door. She was young, around the same age as the girl in the narrow hospital bed with her life supported by machines. The girl's head was immobilized, pads of gauze over her neck, wrists bound where they had been stitched together. Tubes fed vital fluids into her body. Zigzags of luminous green traced the beat of her heart on a small screen, monitored her pulse, her blood pressure. Her eyes were shut so tight the lashes seemed imprinted on her cheeks and her small feet came to a point under the white sheet.

The nurse had summoned the doctor in charge and now he entered the room, white-coated, older. "Careworn," was how Brad would have described him: gray-haired, thin-faced, furrowed brow. He introduced himself as Dr. Harvey.

"We're lucky," he said to Brad. "The would-be killer severely damaged the throat, but he could have hit the thorax or the jugular, or the carotid. Thankfully, he didn't, he only nicked the artery. If we can call that 'lucky.'" He grimaced, looking at his patient, then at the notes he held in his hand. "Otherwise she would have died almost immediately from blood loss and shock. They were clean cuts though, using a professional knife."

"Dr. Vivian in Emergency told me that," Brad said. It was the first time he'd thought about Dr. Vivian since the previous night when she had practically told him to get lost. And rightly so. It was inappropriate to ask an emergency room doctor on duty and half-dead herself after dealing with what she had just dealt with, for her phone number.

Dr. Harvey said, "It's all up to her now. Elaine, I mean. About how

111

strong she is. Whether she'll speak or not?" He shrugged. "It may be impossible with this kind of damage." He glanced at Brad, and asked, "Do we know who she is yet? I'm thinking of her family, of course."

"So far, sir, it's only 'Elaine.' We're working on it though. I know Elaine can't thank you right now but I'm sure she would if she could. And Dr. Vivian too."

"Dr. Vivian is the hero in this drama. She saved this young woman's life before I even got to the scene."

"She's quite a girl," Brad agreed.

The doctor didn't know whether he meant the girl in the bed, or the doctor in Emergency, but he nodded anyway. "We'll keep you posted, Detective," he said, as he left.

Brad lingered a moment longer. He was thinking of the scene in the woods, the imprint of her body on the fallen wet leaves, the tripod where a video camera had filmed what looked likely to be the last moments of her life and her brutal rape. He was thinking of the jigsaw puzzle of the crime, the small pieces that might lead him to the killer. Of the coffee shop badge which might give a clue as to where the killer had met her. Of the tripod, small enough to hold a powerful night-vision camera. He was thinking of the type of car the man had driven away in, how he had gotten Elaine into that car in the first place.

He got on the phone and called forensics. The woman in charge told him Elaine had been knocked out first with a blow to the neck, then a needle jab in the arm, probably Rohypnol she said, answering one of his questions. They would know for sure later. The man had used a condom, no semen—no DNA. And an eight-inch knife. Clothing still being inspected for anything else they could find. It all took time.

Brad clicked off and his phone bleeped again. It was Jerry.

"Her name is Elaine Mary McCarthy. Age twenty-two. Native of Portland, Oregon. Parents saw it on the news, just called in. They were supposed to be driving down to see her today, but she never called them to confirm . . . they were worried . . ."

"Jesus!" Brad's anger simmered but he kept a lid on it.

"She had a boyfriend; he worked as a waiter also, only at one of our swankier cafés."

Brad thought only Jerry would have used a word like "swankier."

"He call in or what?" he asked.

"The parents called him first, worried y'know. They were all to have had dinner tonight. Now they're on the next flight from Portland. We'll have them met at the airport, bring them to the hospital." Jerry paused. "Just tell me they're not too late," he said.

"Maybe."

Jerry sighed. He gave Brad the address of Elaine's apartment and told him he would meet him there.

Brad nodded goodbye to the two cops still on guard, thanked the nurse, and took the elevator back down. The bell pinged when it stopped at the ground floor. The doors slid open and there, looking at him, all wide brown eyes, pretty rose-lipsticked mouth in an oh of surprise, her brown hair pulled back into a neat bun, white coat immaculate, white clogs scuffed on newly-tanned-looking legs, was Dr. Vivian.

"Hey." Brad felt the smile coming from somewhere good; she had that effect on him.

"Hey yourself," she said, demurely.

He could swear she was blushing. "How about that drink tonight?" he asked, stepping out and holding the door for her.

"Sorry, too late, I've already got a date," she said.

"You could always break it."

"I'm not that kind of girl."

"Too bad, I know a good Chinese place, best Peking duck in town, a sight to behold, and the jasmine rice . . ."

She was laughing. "Oh, go walk your dog, Detective," she said as the elevator doors clanged shut.

He turned away but the doors slid back open again. It seemed Dr. Vivian had had a change of heart. She was smiling at him.

"Listen, Detective," she said, holding the door open, "you caught me in a good mood. Something about you makes me smile."

He was smiling back. "Wait till you see my dog. Flyin's gonna make you laugh."

"*Flyin'?*" She cocked her head to one side.

"It's a long story."

"Then I'd like to hear it." She gazed brightly at him, sheaf of notes clutched to her white-coated chest. "I'm free tomorrow night, if you are?"

"You mean we have a date?" Silly, but he felt like jumping up and down with delight, nothing this good, this positive had happened in he didn't know how long. He contented himself with a grin.

She said, "You could pick me up here, eightish? Is that okay?"

It seemed Vivi knew how to use a smile when she wanted. "More than okay." He'd leave Jerry in charge, this was important.

Vivi said, "I'll bring my sister along too. She's visiting, I can't just leave her all alone."

Brad stared blankly at her for a speechless second. Then, "Right. You got it. And I'll bring Flyin', make it a foursome. Peking duck all round."

"Perfect."

She was still smiling at him as the elevator doors clanged shut again, leaving Brad wondering if he was being taken for a ride. He thought being set up for the sister was more like it. Fuck!

His phone beeped. It was Jerry again. "We got the place she worked," he said. "Bobo's; about twenty miles from where she was found. I closed it down, cordoned off the parking lot, I have guys searching there, and we're questioning the staff."

Brad got the address and said they would go there later. First though they would check out Elaine's apartment.

V ivi still had the smile on her face thinking abut Brad Merlin
as she stepped out of the elevator and walked briskly back to
Emergency. He was just so cute . . . well, no, you couldn't exactly
call such a big man, all blue-chinned maleness, *cute*! Sexy, maybe,
with that light-up-his-eyes grin, his broad-shouldered loping walk,
his big feet. She'd noticed the loafers as he'd stood there, chatting
her up in the elevator: brown suede and so obviously new. She
thought they looked a whole lot better than the buckled whoppers
he'd had on the previous night. God, was that only a night away?
Time seemed to have lost its sequence, what with the long day at the
emergency room, the murder victim being wheeled in, the trauma
team taking over, the girl now holding her own in the ICU, where
Vivi guessed Brad Merlin had just been visiting.

"Elaine" was still all Vivi knew her as, though she'd heard it said
they now had positive identification and that the parents were flying
in. She also knew Elaine was halfway here, halfway there, and that

kind of middle ground did not bode well. She hoped the parents would arrive soon. She also didn't want to say "before it was too late"; negative thinking, at least medically, was not her style. She was all-out until the last moment when time and life ran out. That was her job.

She walked into Emergency and almost bumped into a man walking toward her. He was holding a hand to his head. Blood seeped through his fingers.

She stopped, pulled his hand away and took a look at the deep two-inch gash, amateurishly held together with butterfly strips.

"You need stitches right now," she said. "Follow me please."

She was taking care of him before the others already waiting on plastic chairs, talking loudly, sipping coffee from cardboard cups or Coke from the machine that never ran out. Infants fretted and wailed; a kid with a jelly bean stuck up his nose was whisked into the next cubicle; a pregnant woman complained her belly hurt.

"Of course it does," Vivi said, giving her a smile as she passed. "You're having a baby. I'll send someone with a wheelchair to take you to Obstetrics."

The young man followed her into the cubicle and she drew the curtains. "Please take a seat." She indicated the gurney with its clean white paper covering. "Now, let's see what's up with you."

So far, he had not said a word. She looked properly at him for the first time. Alex Patcevich looked back at her.

"I'm Dr. Vivian," she said, calmly she thought, considering she was looking at a very attractive man whose really nice brown eyes were looking back into hers.

He said, "I know who you are."

Surprised, Vivi raised her brows. He pointed to the name embroidered on the pocket of her doctor coat. Of course. "So? What happened?"

"A car accident. In the storm, last night."

Vivi slipped on her surgical gloves, then pulled off the butterfly strips, making him wince. "Sorry," she said. "It's better a quick tug than trying to ease them off. Anyhow, what did you hit?"

She was cleaning the gash now, examining the torn edges of skin. She summoned a nurse to bring the equipment necessary to stitch the wound.

"The cypress tree at the top of your aunt, Fen Dexter's, drive."

Vivi sat back, needle in hand. Realizing who he was she said, "You must be *the Intruder*!"

Alex laughed, crinkling his brow, causing the wound to ooze blood again. "Is *that* what she called me? I thought she was going to kill me, and she thought I was going to kill her."

Vivi held up a hand. She said, "Wait just a minute," and speed-dialed Fen.

Fen didn't even bother with the hellos. "Don't tell me JC's gone and married somebody unsuitable this morning."

"It would be like her to do that," Vivi admitted, "but Fen, I have your 'Intruder' here."

"You mean right there, in your emergency room? I told him that wound needed stitches. How sensible of him to follow my advice."

"He came in because he was bleeding, and you were right, it does need stitches, I'm about to do that now. Meanwhile, I want to know if you are okay, I mean . . . what exactly *happened* last night?" Vivi threw a wary glance at the Intruder, who smiled charmingly back at her.

"Oh, we had a wonderful time, I told him my life story and he . . .

well, he almost told me his." Fen was obviously aware that Alex was able to hear her gusty sigh over the phone. "I'm afraid my friend Alex—he did tell you his name was Alex Patcevich, didn't he? Yes, well, my friend—I think I can call him 'my friend' even though we knew each other such a short time . . . well, Vivi dear, I think I should advise you that he may have . . . well perhaps he doesn't but you never know . . . I mean . . ."

"FEN! For God's sake *tell* me what you mean!"

"Well, sweetie, he has a Past."

Vivi rolled her eyes, sometimes Fen could drive her crazy. "We all have a past. Get to the point," she said firmly. "Tell me *exactly* what you mean."

"What I mean is he showed up on my doorstep with a knife and a bloody head, frightened me half to death, until we both got our stories straight. Then . . ." Vivi could hear the smile in Fen's voice. "After that it was all plain sailing, as they say."

Vivi threw the Intruder a wary glance; he'd better not have any knives concealed about his person here.

"Anyhow," Fen suddenly came right to the point. "He's in the security business, a private investigator, and he's investigating the death of a young woman who lived right where you are, in San Francisco. She was what I would call an airline stewardess but I believe is now known as a flight attendant. She was young, she was beautiful, and he was engaged to be married to her. She was raped and murdered four months ago. My new friend, Alex Patcevich, is on a mission to find that killer. You may remember it, it was in all the papers, on TV endlessly."

Vivi stared at her patient.

"He was driving from L.A. to San Francisco, ended up in Big Sur, crashed outside my door in the storm. You might say," Fen added thoughtfully, "that we 'found each other.'"

Vivi's heart seemed to have sunk into her stomach, not medically but certainly emotionally. She said, "Thanks, I'll get back to you." She clicked off her phone, and looked at Alex Patcevich.

He looked calmly back at her. "Sorry," he said. "I would have told you eventually, but I only came in here to get stitched up."

"I'll do that right now." Vivi dragged up the little wheeled stool and sat next to him, busying herself with the lidocaine shot to numb his head; then the needle; the fine thread. She was an expert, had done this a thousand or more times, making tiny, very even stitches. "I don't want to leave a scar," she explained, leaning in to him, concentrating.

"I recognize your perfume," he said suddenly. She sat back, startled, and he apologized. "Sorry, it's just that you were so close I recognized it."

Vivi gave him a skeptical glance; he wouldn't be the first to come on to her in the ED. He looked pretty good, sitting there, at her mercy, in his blue shirt, lean and narrow in his jeans. She liked the set of his jaw, his high cheekbones under golden-retriever brown eyes. His dark hair even grew in a peak. Shaggy, rock-star hair. Unlike Detective Brad Merlin, this guy could certainly be called "cute."

"The perfume's my sister's," Vivi said crisply, leaning close to him again, getting back to her work.

"Versace Bright Crystal," he said, flinching under the needle.

"I'm usually more of a Chanel No. 5 woman, myself." Vivi put in the final stitch. "Middle of the road. You just know Chanel's always good because it's been there forever and everybody says so. And anyhow those women in the ads must be telling the truth otherwise they wouldn't look so great."

Alex Patcevich stared at her, bemused. "That's female logic, I guess," he said doubtfully. "But anyway, the Versace's good on you, and my sister also wears it."

Vivi breathed a sigh of relief. She'd been afraid he was going to say his murdered fiancée had worn it.

"I had a wonderful time with your aunt last night," Alex said, bringing a smile to her face.

"Nobody else has an aunt like Fen," Vivi admitted proudly.

"You know what?" Alex said. "I think you take after her. You're open, the way she is, she kind of took me to her heart even though at first she was afraid of me."

"I'm not *exactly* like her," Vivi said cautiously. "I'm only stitching your head, not taking you to my heart. And I'm certainly not afraid of you."

She patted the stitches, made sure everything was correct, wrote out a prescription for painkillers. "You could always just take Tylenol, but you might get a cracking headache, after leaving the cut like that for so long."

Alex slid off the gurney and stood opposite her. "Thank you, Dr. Vivian. You've worked magic. I feel much better."

"No more blood," she said briskly.

"I'm wondering . . . I mean would you please have a cup of coffee with me? I have something I need to talk about."

So! It wasn't just her clean hair and sexy perfume; the poor man wanted to talk about his dear departed fiancée. Vivi told herself she was being a bitch, of course she would help him.

"You really need to meet Detective Merlin," she told him. "He knows all the details on the latest case and I'm sure he'll help you.

To find out who did it, I mean," she ended lamely, blushing because she knew she had said too much, interfered even.

"Please?" he begged, exactly the way he had the previous night when he'd asked Fen to help him.

Vivi melted. She told him she was due for a break anyhow, that she would get someone to take over and would meet him in the parking lot outside the ER. They would go to the local Starbucks and she would do her best to help him.

Just like Fen, she thought, slipping off the white doctor coat and combing her hair. It must be in the genes.

18

Jerry was waiting for Brad outside Elaine Mary McCarthy's studio apartment on the third floor back of a small inexpensive complex whose cheap rents brought in young people. Like Elaine, they worked small jobs earning just enough to cover expenses and allow a night or two at a bar, so they could consider themselves "living the life" that had lured them to San Francisco in the first place.

A couple of black-and-whites were already parked outside and uniformed cops had several residents lined up, questioning them. Brad guessed all were under the age of twenty-three, and he'd bet most of 'em had dropped out of college. You could almost get the whiff of weed as you passed. You certainly got the full blast when you walked inside.

The door to Elaine's room stood open. A uniform lounged next to it, springing to attention when the two detectives strode in. He told them it was just as she had left it, nobody had set foot in there. Forensics and the photographer were waiting in the hall, smoking indoors, illegal in California. When they saw the detectives they stuck their heads out the windows.

"Fuck, guys, what are you? Addicts or something?" Jerry complained. "Couldn't you just wait?"

"You took your time," the woman from forensics, who they knew well, followed them into the small room that had been Elaine's home for seven months, when she had come to San Francisco from Portland, Oregon, looking for the good life, a good time, a good man, a young girl's dream. She'd ended up waitressing in a tired coffee shop frequented by local retirees. Still, she had always paid her rent promptly on the first of the month. Jerry had all the information. The owner of the building had sent a representative to keep an eye on things and make sure his property was not damaged in any way.

The two detectives walked the small L-shaped space. There was a low black futon draped with a crocheted blue shawl; a nineteen-inch TV on a shelf next to the single window, a wire-mesh café table with two matching chairs in front of a small kitchen counter that held a microwave, a single electric hotplate and a drip-style coffeepot. Under the counter was a shelf containing two saucepans, a small frying pan and a bottle of Palmolive dish detergent. On the shelf above was a flat Pyrex dish, two earthenware plates and two mugs, one of which was bright orange with I-POTT printed on it in white; the other was from Disney World with Mickey ears and ELAINE in scrolled writing.

A white fluffy rug covered the worn green carpet, and the single-size bed was hidden round the corner of the L. It had obviously been slept in and Elaine had neglected to make it. A clutter of underwear and shoes on the floor; a metal rack with her clothing. On the small bedside table was a photo of a nice-looking couple, sitting on lawn chairs, a dog at their feet. A souvenir of home.

"Probably in a hurry to get to work," Jerry said, as the two stood there, looking at the sadness and the intimacy of a young single woman's life, both of them thinking about the loss of her hopes and dreams.

They checked the tiny bathroom. The same sort of thing: old pink tiles dating from another era; the usual girl stuff stacked in a basket under the sink. There was no window; no daylight ever reached here.

They went back into the main part of the room, sifted through the magazines stacked on the small coffee table, examined the pile of papers in one corner. CVs; applications to smaller colleges and for better jobs.

There was no telephone; Elaine had not paid for a landline. "Cheaper just to use her mobile," Brad guessed. "How I wish we could find that, but there was no handbag, nothing."

"Which means the killer must have kept it."

"She probably dropped it when he grabbed her. He would have put it in his car." Brad turned to look at Jerry. "You get the feeling he was here? *In here*, I mean. Looking at her things, touching her stuff? He's a sicko, crazy enough to do that too."

Jerry stroked the stubble on his unshaven chin, thoughtfully. "There's nothing random about this killing. He knew who she was and what he wanted. The other three women were the same physical type. I'll bet he *was* here."

They turned the apartment over to forensics hoping for fingerprints, hairs, any dropped clue that might help, and went and stood outside, where photographers and TV cameras had suddenly shown up.

"Tell us what's going on, please, Detective," someone yelled as flashbulbs flashed in their eyes.

"Later guys, nothing to say yet. Please." Brad shaded his eyes. His phone rang. He answered, listened, hung up and turned to Jerry.

"They've got tire tracks in the coffee shop parking lot, under the shaded part where the rain didn't hit so hard. It's the staff lot, and they're checking all the cars, though the manager said the staff never parked there, they always parked in the light. Nervous, y'know."

"I'll bet they were," Jerry agreed.

It was one more piece in the jigsaw.

19

Vivi saw Alex waiting, two cups of coffee already on the table, when she walked in.

He got to his feet, held out his hand to her and said, "Good to see you again."

"We just met fifteen minutes ago, it can't be all *that* terrific." Vivi slid in the seat opposite him, inspected her coffee and added approvingly, "Black, no sugar. You got it right."

"Just what the doctor ordered."

"Oh God." Vivi put her head in her hands. "If only you knew how many times I've heard that."

He grinned at her. "Sorry, sorry. How about something to eat? A muffin? Sandwich?"

Vivi contemplated a muffin but the gray pencil skirt was already so tight she could hardly breathe. It was JC's of course. Her sister had talked her into wearing it for her date tonight with Dr. Ralph . . . shit, she couldn't go on a date calling him "Doctor." He was *Ralph*.

And right now this was Alex Patcevich, the Intruder/friend of her aunt's, and with a dead fiancée. She stole a glance at him over the rim of the coffee cup. He certainly was cute, obviously unavailable though, due to grief.

"Dr. Vivian?"

She glanced up, startled. "Sorry, I got lost in my thoughts. How can I help you?"

"I'll begin at the beginning," Alex told her, and she sat back, looking expectantly at him. "Her name is . . . *was*—Julia Mastro. She was about your height. Five four? Petite, long brown hair she mostly wore in a bun. Like you also," he said.

Vivi always pulled her hair back for work.

He said, "We met four years ago on a flight from L.A. to New York. I'm not a guy who chats up flight attendants, but I spotted her on the concourse, dragging her little flight attendant bag. One of the wheels got stuck so of course, I stopped to help her."

"And I guess that was that." Vivi finished his story for him.

He said, "I had a house in L.A. She had a house near Nob Hill. My job kept me in L.A., or I was traveling. I'm not really a detective, I have a security business, keeping important clients safe, whether it's in Dubai, or Paris. Turns out," he added bitterly, "I couldn't even keep my girl safe."

Their eyes met across the table, Vivi's were full of sympathy. "You had no reason to think she might not be safe," she reminded him.

"Anyway . . ." Alex pulled himself together, and asked, "More coffee?"

"I have to get back soon."

"Okay, well, what I wanted to ask you was, about this new victim, I mean, I heard she was still alive."

"She's stable," Vivi said. "That's hospital-speak for it could go either way. Let's hope for your sake, as well as hers, she lives to tell the tale. Meanwhile there are uniformed cops outside her room, nobody can get to her. She is absolutely safe, I can guarantee that." She thought for a moment about his sorrow, then leaned across and gave him her hand. He gripped it in both of his, looking intently at her.

She said, "It's not me you need to talk to, it's Detective Merlin. If anyone can help you, he can." Remembering good, solid Brad Merlin, a man who loved his dog, somehow, she felt sure of that.

"Thank you. Again." Alex hesitated. "Look, Dr. Vivian . . ."

"It's Vivi." She smiled. "After all, you know my aunt, that makes you almost family."

Alex smiled. "Okay, so Vivi . . . I'd like to see you again."

Startled, she gave him a long level look. He was attractive, nice, troubled, everything she liked in a man. Then why wasn't she falling over herself to get a date? He was too troubled, she guessed. Maybe she should help put him back together. Wasn't that what she always did, in her job? And in her personal life? Wasn't it what she'd done with her Frenchman, and most of the other men who came before him? And now with her sister? She wasn't exactly Mother Teresa but all she seemed to do was offer a helping hand. A wistful little thought slipped into Vivi's mind of how nice it might be for someone to look out for her for a change.

She suddenly remembered her dinner date that evening with Dr. Ralph—oh for God's sake, she must remember to call him *Ralph*—and her double date with Brad Merlin and his dog and her sister the following night. For a woman who'd had nothing but time on her hands for weeks the dates were suddenly stacking up. Plus she had to get JC to Big Sur, let Fen sort her out.

"Look, Alex." She smiled at him as she said his name. His eyes never left hers. "The fact is I'm busy for the next couple of days, work and . . . well, you know . . ."

"Of course you are, I shouldn't have expected you to be free on such short notice."

He didn't say "a woman like you" but Vivi thought that's what he meant and was flattered. Impetuously, she said, "But why not let's meet for a drink tomorrow evening? I have a sort of dinner date later, well, not really a *date* date, kind of just a friend thing, with my sister, and actually with Detective Merlin. Maybe you could come along, get to meet him, see what he can do to help you?"

Now Alex smiled. "Wonderful, I was going to contact him anyway, but this will be much better, on a more personal level rather than just a cop thing, not just another relative seeking help. When what I want to do is to help him. Any way I can."

Vivi recalled the young almost-dead Elaine on the gurney and thought about Alex's fiancée who had not been lucky enough to survive. "We all want to help," she said simply.

She wrote her phone number on the back of a napkin and got up quickly to leave. "I get off work earlier tomorrow, so let's say around six? Yes? Call me first. If I'm not home, JC will be there, she'll look after you." With a hint of misgiving, Vivi bet JC would.

The man was in the narrow garden, at the back of his house, clearing up the mess left by the storm. The clematis vine had been ripped from the wall where it had been safely espaliered for twenty years; now there would be no spring blooms. Plus his treasured non-fruiting olive was stripped of its silvery leaves and several branches had broken off, exposing gray-white wounds. It was not easy growing olive trees in San Francisco's intemperate climate; in winter he wrapped the trunk, to protect it from the cold. The small greenhouse where he grew his beautiful orchids was missing a few panes and several of his most spectacular specimens were damaged.

He stroked their splintered stems with tender fingers, their drooping rose-and-white heads. He would have to get rid of them. He was not a sentimental man. They could be replaced. Sweat prickled his neck. The temperature in the greenhouse was shooting up, because of the wind blowing through the broken panes.

He looked up "glazier" in the yellow pages then called, stressing the importance of the task. The glazier said he would have someone there that afternoon.

"*This* afternoon," the man told him. "It is already *afternoon*." He couldn't wait; he had a busy evening planned.

He swept up the broken glass, cleaned the spilled dirt off the planked shelves, checked the pots for moisture. They were doing as well as could be expected.

Not unlike, he thought with a bitter sigh, the young woman in the hospital, who by all his calculations should have been dead by now. The fact that she was not disturbed him greatly; he had the nagging fear that she would wake up and talk. Would she be able to describe her attacker? Tell the story of how he had come into the coffee shop, how he'd called her over to his car? Was he going to have to do something to prevent that? It might be for the best. Still, he'd wait, let matters cool down, keep himself appraised of her progress, or her decline. Then, if necessary, he would act.

He put the broom back in its designated spot in the corner, arranged the pots so they were perfectly aligned, stood back to make sure everything was as it should be, then went and washed his hands under the spigot.

The tripod was also on his mind. When he'd realized it was missing he had felt that tightness in his chest, like a cord binding his ribs together; his jaw had clenched, sweat poured off him.

It was the middle of the night and he'd shot up in bed in a frenzy. Staggering to the desk where he'd left his messenger bag, searching it frantically. He went to the garage, searched the car. Nothing— except Elaine's handbag. She'd had it clutched in her hand when he'd saved her. He always called what he did "saving." It meant he was the strong one and he was "saving" them from a life they should not be living. His studies told him that.

He had started "saving" girls after the death of his older sister with whom he had lived for more than ten years. He had two sisters and the older one was everything he was not: sloppy, loud, drunken, promiscuous. But she was family—there was nobody else, so he took her in when she hit rock bottom, put her in rehab, got her some therapy, barred alcohol and men from the house. It was a kind of living hell but it was his duty. Finally, five years ago, she had gotten herself run over by a truck, leaving a bar in Salinas. He had taken care of everything, had her cremated and spilled her ashes onto his roses. At least in death she might as well be useful.

As a boy he'd understood he was different. What he *was*, was not something that developed over the years, a result of abuse or an inferiority complex or bullying. He was born that way. A "psychopath" his own terrified mother had called him when he had given her one of those dead-eye looks that he knew inspired fear. He was only five years old at the time, but he knew. He learned the power of fear early; knew it was an emotion he could inspire simply with a look. Because behind that glance was a killer.

"Callous-unemotional behavior" experts called it nowadays, when they encountered it in children. And they were correct, all those do-good therapists who wanted so much to change what he was. He'd fooled them though, because he had been born not only with a sense lacking, but also with the talent of "charm."

He was a good-looking child, when he was behaving himself and not wrecking the family home in a garrison town in the Midwest, throwing fits and tantrums, screaming, hurling chairs, choking his sisters.

Nowadays, everyone knew about the ratings on the Childhood Psychopathy Scale and the Inventory of Callous-Unemotional Traits in children, which measured up to the same cold, predatory behavior found in adult psychopathy.

The phrase described him as a child perfectly, though he had been clever enough to disguise it when confronted with a test. He was intelligent and could turn on the charm in a second. "Just like a normal boy," the therapists told his mother.

The turning point for him had come on a train journey. Ironically, it was on a train heading for Florida's Disney World. He was eleven years old. It was one of those cute special trains with separate compartments and no connecting corridors. His mother and sisters were with him; they were on vacation. He sat, kicking his legs, eyeing the trio opposite: a man, a woman and their ten-year-old daughter, who avoided his insistent gaze. The parents were watching him though, the man wary, the woman nervous. He leapt suddenly to his feet, hands fisted in front of him, posed like a fighter ready to take on this stupid family; that look in his eyes; ready to kill. The girl's father knew it, but his own mother and his sisters just sat there with lowered heads, avoiding looking, avoiding the issue, unwilling to know what might be coming, though of course they feared they knew.

It was the first time he'd understood the real power he had over people. The power of fear. That father was on the edge of his seat, a tall man, ready to protect his family, ready to take him on. He'd wished he had his knife but his mother had taken that away . . . he could have dealt with the father then, and the rest of them. Easy. A pleasure in fact. One smooth slit across her throat and that daughter would be a dead daughter.

The train had jerked to a halt, sending him falling backwards. The man was instantly on his feet, collecting his small family. They were out of there. And he was laughing. "I just wanted to talk to them," he said sweetly to his mother. "You know I'm a nice boy really."

This scene at Disney World remained clear in the man's head even after all these years. It was the first time he'd really understood what he could do. What he was capable of. The first time he realized the thrill of intimidation, of fear, and of *their* fear of what he *might* do. As well as the sexual thrill he got from a woman's fear, the idea of a knife against her smooth throat, her blood spilling.

• • •

Looking now at Elaine's handbag, he hesitated, uncertain what to do with it. Of course he would have to get rid of it. But how? Where? What would be safest? The river was an obvious choice, but rivers could be swept to find evidence; sometimes things washed up on the banks. There was always the ocean, he could drive south, somewhere quiet, lonely, throw it over a cliff. Right now, though, there was no time. He put Elaine's bag in the trunk and continued his fruitless search for the tripod. It was no good, he would have to get a new one.

He went back indoors, looked up the sales receipt from the shop on Grant Street. It was tempting to go back, he'd gotten a good price there. He doubted they'd even remember him, he had paid in cash and the sales clerk had counted out the bills in front of him, taking forever. Patience was not an asset he possessed, unless he was on the hunt, watching, waiting.

Otherwise his life was as normal as anyone else's. He had work that involved international travel; the respect of his colleagues; a good social life. He had his home; his Mrs. Meade who was the best and most uninquisitive housekeeper, and who came in twice a week to keep the place tidy. Not that he was ever untidy; she complained he was the neatest man she had ever worked for.

He wasn't simply neat: he was obsessive-compulsive. Everything had to be in its place; every ritual respected; every woman perfectly chosen.

With Dr. Vivian he had come up with something different. This one would be difficult but she intrigued him, and he liked a challenge. No rush, though. He would clean up after Elaine, buy a new tripod, maybe even a new camera . . . he liked all the gadgetry involved. Only one thing remained the same, sure and true. His eight-inch chef's knife. Pure and supple and strong as his heart.

Which reminded him, he'd better make an appointment with a cardiologist; get himself checked out.

It was easy for Alex to find Fen Dexter's phone number; she was in the book. Sitting in his banged-up black Range Rover in the hospital parking garage, he punched it into his mobile. She answered promptly, sounding out of breath and rather annoyed.

"Whoever it is, I don't recognize your number and I'm out walking the dog, so I can't talk now."

Alex grinned; that was the woman he'd met last night all right. "I'll bet you'll talk to me," he said.

There was a small silence, then Fen said, "Who are you? And why should I talk to you?"

"I'm the man in your life? Have you forgotten me already?"

He was teasing and heard the answering smile in her voice as she said, "Well now, if it isn't my Intruder. I'm wondering if I should have called the police after all. I would have, if Hector hadn't given you the once-over and declared you safe with older women."

It was Alex's turn to laugh. "Then I owe my life to Hector and your Band-Aids. I wanted to thank you again, and tell you that I just met your girl."

"Which one? I'm praying you're going to say Vivi."

"Dr. Vivian Dexter. I met her in her professional capacity. She stitched me up pretty good."

"And did she kiss you better?"

"You should know better. Your girl is a complete professional."

"I'm glad to hear it but I wish she'd get more of a proper private life, like a dinner date, dancing, flowers, perfume."

"Sort of like you, in fact."

"Exactly. I'm the best example any woman could have."

"I think you're right there." Alex meant it. "In fact, she did invite me out to dinner, tomorrow night."

"What!" Fen was stunned. Vivi had never, in her entire life asked a man out on a date. "Did you accept?"

"I did, but it comes with conditions. She's having dinner with the detective in charge of the serial killings. She met him at the hospital where the latest young woman . . ." Alex paused remembering his fiancée . . . "where the latest young woman to be attacked is. Her name is Elaine and she is, in medical jargon, holding her own. Vivi thought it would be a good opportunity for me to meet Detective Merlin, and maybe talk about my own involvement, see if I could offer any insights. Or, more like it," he added, "I'm just chasing dreams, might-have-been's, wish-there-were's, and there's nothing I can do to help."

"After the fact, you mean," Fen said. "Still, worth a try," she added, gently. "You're a good guy, Alex Patcevich, and life must go on. I found that out the hard way years ago, so don't you go and let me down. Besides, it'll put your mind to rest. You'll know you have done everything you can, and the rest is up to the man in heaven and the police."

Alex guessed she was right. "I'll give it my best shot," he promised. "Though I'll probably be the one who gets shot down. Anyhow, I wanted to say hello again, to say thank you again, to tell you what a magical woman you are, Fen Dexter."

"I'm too old for you," she reminded him. Just in case he had forgotten.

He was laughing as he said, "You're like a girl to me. I'll drop in and see you again, on my way back to L.A., next week perhaps?"

"Call me first," Fen said smartly. "My social life is always in a whirl."

He heard laughing as she hung up. He touched a hand to the stitches on his still-smarting forehead. He thought the Dexter family was quite something. He couldn't wait to meet the other member, the naughty sister, JC.

Later, Fen was on her terrace cleaning up the mess left by the previous night's wind. Broken roof tiles, an old bird nest, a splintered terra-cotta urn that was her favorite geranium pot. In the twelve years she had lived there, she had never experienced such a wild storm. Her small home was tucked behind a little copse of trees which sheltered her, except when the wind blew in from the ocean.

The wind still had an edge but the sky was as cloudless and innocent as the face of a child who was done with the mischief and back to being an angel again.

She had put on her ancient English Barbour windproof jacket, a long red cashmere scarf wrapped twice around, a sheepskin hunter's cap, earflaps firmly tied under her chin, jeans tucked into raspberry-pink rubber boots, hands mittened in matching pink, dark glasses against the glare. With her long bristled broom she pushed the debris to the end of the terrace where Hector had parked his big rear end right in her way.

"Oh, get out of there you silly dog," Fen grumbled out loud, but Hector merely gave her his "blank" gaze which meant he wasn't moving for anyone. So of course, Fen swept around him.

When her mobile rang again, she dropped the broom and shuffled in her pocket with a mittened hand. When she finally found it, it was too late. She checked the message; it was Vivi again. Fen called her right back.

"I worry when you don't answer," was Vivi's immediate response.

Tired, Fen dropped onto the wooden bench that faced her own particular ocean view, today a turbulent bluish ocean fringed with white spray. It always gave her pleasure. This place was the next best thing to Paris. Paris of course always came out tops. Golden city; city of lights; city of love . . .

"*Fe . . . en?*"

"Oh, sorry," Fen said, "I was just thinking about Paris."

"I was in the middle of talking to you." Vivi sounded suspicious. "And anyway you're not thinking of taking off to Paris again, are you?"

"No. Of course not. Why would I do that?" Fen sounded deliberately innocent; she was always thinking of taking off for Paris. A little fun never hurt a woman did it? "Anyhow if I did, what would I do with Hector?"

"*Fen!* Stop it. You can't just go dashing off to Paris on your own anymore, and besides you have your other 'girl' to think about."

"Oh! That one." Fen contemplated JC silently for a moment. "I suppose you're going to bring her down here so I can give her a talking-to."

"A pep talk. She needs to straighten out." Vivi was genuinely worried.

"I suppose I could always take her to Paris with me," Fen said. The idea didn't sound so bad to her; her and JC having fun in Paris.

"Really, this conversation is going nowhere!"

Fen sighed; she got the feeling Vivi was too much like her for her own good. Fen had always taken care of her friends, her relatives, the broken ones. A "woman in any storm," she thought, smiling as she thought of Alex and their connection, of how much she had enjoyed him.

"So what about Alex Patcevich, anyway?" she asked, remembering Vivi had seen him that morning. "Cute, huh? And right up your street, a man who needs fixing."

"I'm not 'fixing' him. But I have invited him for a drink tomorrow evening."

"A *drink*?" Fen was shocked by Vivi's ignorance. "You don't ask men like that 'for a *drink*' . . . you get yourself all slinked up in your best frock and go *out* for drinks, and then dinner and then maybe some dancing—*my* kind of dancing I mean, close stuff, not your whirling about, separately. The whole point of dancing is it's an excuse to hold each other."

Vivi was laughing now. She said she'd invited him to dinner too, and that she also had a "date" tonight with another doctor, a psychiatrist. Fen wasn't impressed.

"I'll bet he's older and wears horn-rims and drives a Volvo station wagon," she warned. "Be careful, he's also likely to have a wife and three kids tucked away in the suburbs."

Vivi assured her Dr. Ralph did not, though Fen wasn't far wrong in her description. "He's nice," Vivi said defensively. "Good with women, you know, kind, caring . . ."

"Boring!" Fen didn't go along with the "kind and caring" bit. Where was the excitement? "Where's he taking you, anyway?"

"Top of the Mark for martinis, then for dinner somewhere."

"So you can mingle with the conventioneers having a night out! My dear, Vivi, I thought better of you."

Vivi supposed now it did seem a bit lame. "It was his suggestion."

"A woman can always change her mind. Find somewhere more exciting," Fen ordered. "If you think he can stand the pace, that is, him being so old and all."

"Fen, he is *not* old. He's maybe forty-eight . . ."

"Everyone's forty-eight. I've been that myself a few times." Fen heard Vivi giggle. "Cheer up, baby," she told her. "You can always pass him on to JC. A little free therapy might be just the thing."

Hector lumbered to his feet. He came over and leaned his bulk against Fen's legs. She patted him absently, listening while Vivi told about her other date with Brad Merlin, the detective investigating the latest "attempted" serial killing, and that she had also told Alex to get in touch with him.

"I also told Brad Merlin I was going to bring my sister along, I thought I might pass him on to her," she admitted. "He's the strong, tough type, the kind every woman can rely on."

"No woman can rely on any man." Fen had been there, she knew all about that. Remembering, she modified that a little. "*Most* men anyway."

"This one has a dog called Flyin.'"

"Hmm, a literate type, he reads Dorothy Parker."

Vivi obviously had no idea what Fen was talking about but then she told her what her detective had said about their own names, Vivian and Merlin at the Court of King Arthur.

"Definitely a literary man," Fen said. "You should cultivate him, broaden your mind. Or JC's," she added. "If it's not too late for that."

Vivi told her she intended to bring JC down to visit her in a couple of days, to get "straightened out." Fen said she would defrost more beef daube, she might as well get rid of it while she could or it would stay in her freezer forever. She would prepare the guest room and was there anything special they might want?

"Just you," Vivi said, and her voice was so sweet, so sincere, it brought unexpected tears to Fen's eyes.

"See you then," she said, wiping them away with a pink-mittened hand. Then she hung up, kissed Hector's nose and went back to her sweeping. Nothing like good hard work to take sentimentality away. Though never love.

23

To say that Dr. Ralph Sandowski was looking forward to his date with Dr. Vivian was, he thought, the understatement of the year. He had seen her around since he first started consultations at the hospital where he dealt with the mentally disturbed, who were sometimes brought in in cuffs, were often violent and cursing, and more often than not the worse for wear, via drink, drugs and the homeless route. The hospital would accommodate them, he and other staff would do their best to get them back on track and send them out in the world again. Ready or not, he thought with a grim smile. He could only do what he could do; society would have to pick up the slack.

Then, of course, there was the other type, the quietly despairing, often suicidal, brought down by a depression so deep, so intangible, there seemed no way out. He would try to find that way for them. He was good at what he did, internationally renowned, a sought-after lecturer at medical conferences around the world.

Dr. Ralph was, in fact, forty-eight years old just as Vivi's aunt had predicted; he wore the horn-rims she had also predicted; yet he was also attractive in that offbeat lean-faced, tweed-jacketed way academics sometimes have, and he genuinely cared about his work and his patients.

He'd first met Dr. Vivian when he'd been called to Emergency almost a year ago. The hospital was a big place and their paths would not normally have crossed but there was a child in trouble, a truculent father, a silent downtrodden mother. Dr. Vivian suspected child abuse, and so did Dr. Ralph. The child had been placed in care, the father arrested and the mother sent to him for therapy. It was not one of Dr. Ralph's better moments; he disliked having to deal with child abusers, the very idea was an anathema to him; to him that man was lower than an animal.

Still, Dr. Vivian had handled the case perfectly and they had become "Dr. Vivian" and "Dr. Ralph" to one another. In fact afterwards, he had found himself going out of his way to catch her in the cafeteria, to suggest a cup of coffee, but when she told him she'd just become engaged to the Frenchman he'd stepped abruptly back, though he had still kept his interest. In fact Dr. Vivian had a special allure for him: she was his ideal woman: strong, fearless, expert at her job, dedicated, and attractive. He liked her slightly plump body, her alert brown eyes, her ready smile even when she was tired at the end of a long day. But he'd never had the courage to risk inviting her out on a date until he'd heard on the hospital grapevine that her engagement was off.

His timing had proved correct; Dr. Vivian—Vivi he could now safely call her—had accepted and he was in his car, waiting for her outside Emergency. It was eight o'clock; "the witching hour," he thought with a smile because, though it wasn't midnight he'd bet that Vivi could be a special kind of witch, when she wanted that is. Quiet, caring women like her, with her looks, were exactly what he preferred.

He saw her swing through the glass doors and got out of the car to meet her. "Over here, Vivi," he called, raising his arm so she could spot him.

She arrived, pink-cheeked from rushing, surprisingly smart in a gray pencil skirt, lavender turtleneck and heels. "Sorry, Ralph, a last-minute case, a female basketball player, all of six feet and with a broken femur. Poor darling, I'm afraid she won't be playing again for a long while."

Ralph held open the car door, and Vivi got in, butt first, knees together in the proper ladylike fashion Fen had taught her (so you don't flash your underwear, Fen had said, making Vivi giggle, but she had never forgotten, and had never inadvertently flashed her underwear in her entire life because of that).

"A Range Rover," she said approvingly. "My aunt said you would drive a Volvo."

Ralph, who was in the driver's seat now, turned, astonished, to look at her. "Why on earth would she have thought that?"

"She said that's what shrinks drive. She also said you'd probably have a wife and three kids in the suburbs somewhere."

His usually stern face softened into a grin. "Sorry to disappoint her: no wives, no kids, no suburbia. I live alone, right here in San Francisco, when I'm not traveling on business that is. No responsibilities, not even a dog, I simply don't have the time."

Vivi heaved a sympathetic sigh. Leaning across she patted him on the knee and said, "Me either. I mean, I don't even have a dog, but I do have a sister who's suddenly descended on me with a multitude of problems *I'm* supposed to solve."

Ralph didn't ask what the problems were but he did ask what she meant to do about it.

"I'll send her off to my aunt. She'll sort her out."

"The fount of all wisdom."

Vivi laughed. "That's Fen exactly."

They'd cut through the clanging cable cars and trolleys and were plowing up California Street, heading for the Mark Hopkins. Vivi recognized the route but couldn't bring herself to ask to be taken some other place; he seemed to be looking forward to this so much, already asking which type of martini she preferred.

Ralph gave the car to the valet, placing a guiding hand lightly on Vivi's back as they walked through the sumptuous lobby and waited for the elevator, which whisked them, all in one smooth move, to the penthouse cocktail bar with its 360-degree view over the lights of San Francisco. They were shown a window table and given cocktail menus. There really was a huge choice but Vivi ordered what she always did: Grey Goose vodka on the rocks, a splash of tonic and two olives.

"I like a girl who knows her own mind," Dr. Ralph said approvingly.

Vivi still had to keep on reminding herself to call him *Ralph* and not *Dr. Ralph*. "You mean 'woman,'" she said and he laughed.

"Haven't we had this conversation before? On the parking garage stairs, at the hospital?"

"Of course you could always call me just plain 'Doctor.'" Vivi gave him a flirty little smile, though she wasn't sure she felt like flirting with him, he was so "grown-up," so serious, quite unlike anyone she had been out with before. This was her first experience with an "older" man.

"In case you're wondering, I'm forty-eight," he said, reading her mind, then stared perplexed at her when she burst out laughing.

"Sorry, it's just that Fen said you would be forty-eight. She said she'd been forty-eight herself a few times."

Ralph put a hand over his heart. "Honest to God, I swear, I'm forty-eight. And sometimes I feel every year of it."

"Because of what you do? Your work?"

"Probably that." He fell silent and Vivi was glad when a jazz combo began to play. The cocktail lounge was crowded now and there was a pleasant buzz about the place; it had turned out to be a good choice after all, not too small, not too intimate. She could keep a safe distance here, though why exactly she wanted to, she didn't know. Of course it was because she had never been out with an older man before; the gap between her thirty and his forty-eight loomed large.

He'd ordered Jack Daniel's on the rocks, and now he took a sip, looking at her over the rim of the glass.

She looked back at him, taking him in, in this new venue away from the hospital. He really looked quite good in those horn-rims, sort of *Mad Men*-ish . . . maybe this would be okay after all. Vivi's phone bleeped and she excused herself, embarrassed, explaining she didn't usually answer when out on a date, but this was her sister.

"The sister who keeps you permanently worried?" Ralph asked, and she nodded yes, it was her.

He turned to look out of the window, giving her some sort of privacy as she whispered, "JC, why are you calling me now?"

"I'm going stir-crazy, all by myself. Can't I come and join you, up there at Top of the Mark? God, Vivi, I haven't been there since I was a teenager."

"And you should *not* have *been* in a bar when you were a teenager." Vivi's frown expressed her annoyance. She added, "It's not fair to Dr. Ralph, we're having drinks."

153

"I'll join you, we can all have dinner. Actually, Vivi," JC admitted, "I lied to you. I'm down here in the lobby, all dressed up and no-where to go."

Vivi glanced at Ralph, who was gazing stoically at the sparkling view, sipping his whiskey. How did she explain this to him? There was only one way. To his credit he took it calmly; that's why he was a good shrink, Vivi supposed.

"The more the merrier, isn't that what they say?" Ralph raised his glass to her, but Vivi thought his smile had become rather tight. She didn't blame him, JC had no right to do this, but *that* was her sister.

She said, "I'm going to send JC to you, Ralph, she really needs your professional help," but he merely smiled.

He said, "It seems to me that what your sister needs is a little more self-control and a lot less selfish behavior. What she's doing now is giving no thought to you or what your evening might be, or even to myself, or what I expected from this evening."

Vivi hung her head. He was right. Anyway, what *had* he expected from this evening? Surely not a couple of drinks, then dinner and then a quick tumble into bed? She eyed him closely but his face was smooth, his lips sealed. She could not tell if he was angry, but she was suddenly glad JC had shown up.

And here she came, glamorous in a short silky red dress with a ruffle from shoulder to hem and a swirl to the skirt that showed off her perfect brown legs. Vivi felt suddenly drab in the plain gray pencil skirt and the lavender turtleneck sweater she'd felt so good in earlier.

JC's long blond hair fell forward as she leaned over to kiss Vivi, then swung her wide blue gaze upward at Ralph.

He was standing, holding out a chair for her, and now he smiled at her. Who wouldn't, Vivi thought? Her sister looked stunning, barely made up, a magenta lipstick that clashed perfectly with the red of her dress, a sweep of black mascara, and her golden skin, was all.

"Sorry," JC apologized again, shifting her upward gaze between her sister and Ralph. "I got so bored at home, nothing on TV except all that news about murdered girls, it got me quite scared, so anyway, I thought I might join you here. Only for a couple of minutes, though, I mean, I wouldn't dream of staying . . ."

Of course she would and Vivi knew it. Drinks, dinner, JC would be there. She decided it wasn't so bad her sister came after all, because she had kind of come to a blank with Dr. Ralph. He was definitely too old for her. This would be their final date.

JC realized her sister was irritated with her and therefore she directed all her charm as well as her beaming smile at Dr. Ralph. "I know all about you," she told him.

Ralph glanced coolly back; he thought she was lovely. Still, he wasn't exactly thrilled that she had upset his private evening with Vivi. He summoned the waiter and JC ordered a cosmo, not too sweet and very cold. Ralph thought that, despite the fluffy, girly surface JC was a woman who knew exactly what she liked.

He said, "And exactly *how* do you know all about me?"

"I Googled you, of course." JC beamed again, pleased with her forethought. "I like to know who I'm having dinner with."

Vivi threw her a glare: who the hell had invited her to dinner anyway?

"I know you are an eminent psychiatrist," JC went on, "one of the top in your field; I know where you graduated from, all your degrees, and I know you're in demand for lectures around the world. That must be so much fun, all that traveling. You know, I've only ever been to Paris once in my life when I was sixteen, with Fen."

"I'm sure you'll get to go again." Ralph's dry tone was not lost on Vivi, though it was on JC. Nothing and no one could put her down. If Fen was the "fount of all knowledge," then JC was the "fount of all enjoyment," and she kind of carried everyone along with her.

"So, Ralph," JC addressed him again, calling him by his name, of course, smiling from under her lashes. "What about this serial killer? It makes a girl afraid to go out alone."

"A *woman*," Vivi corrected her automatically. JC threw her a questioning look. "You are 'a woman' JC, not a 'girl,'" Vivi explained.

Dr. Ralph said, "Vivi and I discussed this point earlier. She is, of course, correct."

JC continued. "Anyway, I mean, any *woman* might be in danger, just walking the street, or in her car, even in here." She waved her martini glass around the crowded cocktail bar. "I mean, you just never know. At least *I* don't know, but Dr. Ralph *you* must be able to tell us what kind of man does this? What makes him a killer? And why does he hate women so?"

Ralph folded his arms across his chest. He sat silently back in his chair, eyes cast down, obviously thinking seriously about what she had said.

JC looked questioningly at Vivi. Had she brought up the wrong subject over dinner? The waiter arrived and they ordered. Dr. Ralph seemed to come back to life long enough to order a steak, then fell silent again, apparently still thinking about her question.

The sisters looked silently at each other: Murder wasn't exactly a subject for new acquaintances to discuss over cocktails and a nice dinner; they should be talking about the latest movie, or what was new at the theater, or a gallery opening.

Dr. Ralph said suddenly, "A man like this might be very much the same as any man you meet. On the surface, that is. He might be a married man, with children even. Whatever his circumstances, he is essentially a 'loner.' The compulsion to rape is foremost, because what he seeks is power over a woman."

"You mean he hates women that much?" JC asked, stunned.

"He does not 'hate women.' Or perhaps he hates one woman and these others are substitutes for that hate."

Vivi said, "But he kills them, cuts their throats . . ." The image of Elaine was indelibly fixed in her mind.

"Of course. I believe it's quite simply that he doesn't want them to be able to tell. The dead don't talk," Ralph added, with a wry smile. "Anyway, for what it's worth that's my analysis of the situation."

Vivi thought "situation," was a very clinical description of a murder, but she guessed what he had said was true. And anyhow, now JC was on to something else . . . like eating dinner. She said she was starving.

Neither Vivi nor the doctor had a second drink since both were driving. But JC had another cosmo and then ate a hearty filet steak with as many fries as she could manage. Conversation kept on the work side of things, JC's of course, and her lack of it and her intention to find a new career.

They were surprised when Dr. Ralph told them that, as a sideline and because of his love for antiques, he ran a high-end antique shop, in nearby Nob Hill. He said he needed an assistant and wondered if it would suit JC.

JC turned, delighted, to her sister. "Didn't I tell you something would turn up?"

And for you, JC, it always did, Vivi thought.

F en wasn't surprised when her phone rang around eleven that night. Nor was she surprised that it was JC calling.

"I'm sure you're in trouble," she said, dispensing as always with the formalities of hello how are you. "What do you want?"

"*Me?*" JC sounded astonished if a little tearful. "Why, nothing at all. I mean, like, what *would* I want?"

Fen said, "I'd appreciate it, JC, if, during this conversation, you could eliminate the word '*like*' from your vocabulary. It is quite irrelevant; it's valley-girl-speak and it has absolutely no meaning as far as what you need to say."

"Jesus! I mean, *like*, I was only calling to complain."

"*JC!*"

"Oh *God!*"

Fen could visualize the eye roll. She said, "Let's start again, shall we? I know you're at Vivi's, I know you're out of a job, I know you're out of men, and out of money. So? What's new?"

There was a long silence, then JC said, "Did anyone ever tell you, you were—like—*mean*?"

"If I think about it, there were probably one or two. Yes. You might be correct on that, JC." Relenting a little, Fen smiled. "Like, so, okay, what's up? Tell me your new troubles." *All over again*, she added silently, because with JC they were always pretty much the same three topics: men and money, or lack of it, and how hard life was for a singer.

"Fen, I just thought, I'll bet you were *sleeping*! Oh, gosh, I woke you, didn't I?"

"I am in bed, yes, and you did not wake me, but you did wake Hector, who resents his routine being disturbed. He is getting on a bit now, you know, feeling his age."

"Like you, I suppose," JC said.

Fen was silent for a moment, then she said tartly, "If I were not a lady, which you know I am and always will be, I might have said 'fuck you.' One day you will be fifty-eight, then you'll know how age feels."

"I know, I know, you're the eternal spring chicken."

JC was laughing and Fen felt better about her; she was truly worried about her niece, who always lived for the moment and never looked the future in the eye. "So tell Fen, sweetheart," she said, gently now, "what's going on with you?"

"It's all over with me. The singing, I mean. I know I'm not good enough, never really was except now they're all younger than I am. I'm too old to get away with just being cute and outrageous, wearing all that rock-girl stuff, tattoos . . ."

"You have *tattoos*?" Outrage colored Fen's voice.

"Only a couple, really, nothing much, though I do have his name . . ."

"*Where* do you have *whose* name?" Fen heard the hesitation in JC's answer.

"Just, you know, like . . ."

"*JC!*"

"Okay, so it's the guy I was with and it's on my lower back, well, actually, just above my butt-crack if you must know."

Fen thought she would faint; strutting the stage in feathers and sequins was nothing compared with butt tattoos. "What about the next man you make love with?" She asked because it had been her first thought. "What's he going to think?"

"I can have it redone, altered into a rose, something sweet like that."

Fen said, "JC, I'm going to ask you something right now, a favor for your aunt. *Please*, no more tattoos."

"Okay."

JC sounded too obliging. "A *promise* to your aunt means something. I want you to remember that."

This time JC sounded sincere when she said she would, of course she would and it would never happen again. "Anyway, I can't afford it," she added. "But, Fen, I have a new job. Maybe even a new career."

Fen listened while JC bubbled on about dinner with the renowned psychiatrist who also owned an antique store where she was now to become an assistant.

"How much is he paying you?" Fen got right to the point; work was something you got paid for, not a debutante thing where you whiled away the hours between shopping and husband-hunting.

JC said they hadn't quite gotten that far over dinner, but she was sure tomorrow they would, and he was a rich man, she was sure of that also.

"The rich do not always pay well," Fen warned her, but wished her luck anyway, glad that at least JC would be off Vivi's hands, though no doubt she would still be living with her sister.

JC did not tell Fen how she had barged in on Vivi's date because she was lonely, but she did tell her Vivi had asked her to go with her the following night. They were to have dinner with Detective Brad Merlin, who was in charge of the serial killer case; the one whose latest victim Vivi had taken care of in the ER. "And also," she added, in a moment of triumph, "with your *Intruder*. Alex."

Fen told her to have a good time, to keep an eye on her sister who never knew where she was with a man unless she could find one to look after, adding she was afraid the Intruder was a prime candidate in that department.

"I love you," JC said, as she rang off. "I'm coming to see you, day after tomorrow."

"I'll defrost something," Fen said, smiling. "And I love you too, you are my craziest girl and I need to sort you out."

"Oh, I do wish you would," JC said, seriously.

After JC's phone call Fen thought the house seemed suddenly very quiet. JC had that effect on people, on places; she was a life-bringer, even though she was hopeless at dealing with her own life. Fen loved her for it.

She pushed Hector, who was of course sleeping on the bed, out of the way, flung back the covers and padded barefoot, in her gray T-shirt and her pink cotton pajama bottoms, down to the kitchen where she put the kettle on for a cup of tea. Chamomile of course, at this time of night.

She went and sat at the table where the Intruder had sat, where she had bathed his badly cut head, that later her other niece had stitched up for him. Nothing like keeping it in the family. She knew

Alex was heartbroken about his fiancée, but still perhaps Vivi could take care of him.

Couldn't be a better match, Fen thought, then quickly asked God to excuse her for not putting the poor murdered girl first.

"You have to understand," she told Him out loud, "I'm their aunt by adoption."

But it wasn't her niece she was thinking about. It was Alex, and the special connection between them. She told herself she needed to see him again, get this ridiculous "feeling" for him out of her system. Still, she couldn't help wondering what, if anything, Alex felt about her. Perhaps she should call him, find out. Oh my God, she was crazy after all. Crazy for a guy more suitable for her girls than her. She had finished her tea and was still thinking about him when she went to bed and finally fell asleep again.

The man had not intended to pick up the woman, random killings were not what he was after. He needed to make his choice carefully, to match point-for-point, physically, the way the woman he had loved looked. Of course there were variations on the theme. He smiled, rather liking the way he had phrased that—similar to a Bach fugue, the "Variations on a Theme." Musically he was very literate. He attended San Francisco Opera's prestigious First Nights and enjoyed himself immensely. They were white-tie events for which he'd had the outfit custom-tailored. Actually, in Hong Kong, where it was so much cheaper and where the tailoring was first-class, if you went to the right man of course. He also bought his custom shirts there, from Ascot Chang: they had his measurements on file and FedExed his semiannual orders, unless he was on an official trip and could pick them up himself.

Tonight, though, driving through San Francisco's never-quiet North Beach, he was restless, as were the teeming crowds on the street. It was long past midnight and still hopping; still music blaring; still strip joints, still guys loitering on corners and women struttin' their stuff. Not his type at all. Except maybe one.

She caught his eye when he stopped at the light, she came sauntering toward his car, one shoulder lifted in a question. Petite, in tall patent heels, fake-leopard jacket flung open to reveal a black lacy bra and a skirt so minimal it probably wasn't even legal. Her skin was coffee-colored, her hair a flamboyant array of tiny red braids that stuck out like firecrackers, and her full mouth was painted a juicy orange. Quite suddenly, he wanted her. It wasn't the usual, this was not the way he behaved . . . this was different. He pulled a ski cap over his hair, put on his dark glasses, rolled down the window, said, "Get in."

She leaned against the car. "Don't ya wanna know how much?"

"You can tell me in the car."

She hesitated, throwing a glance over her shoulder at the lurking pimp on the corner, then climbed in, slamming the door after her. She turned to appraise her catch, giving him a full-on smile. He knew she couldn't tell what he looked like, with the cap and glasses, but she also knew from the car he was better class than her usual john.

"I like you, rich boy," she said. "Anythin' you want you can have."

He said, "How much for the night?" Heard her gasp.

"Y'mean, like the *whole entire* night? Baby, that's pricey, that is . . ." She wiggled in her seat, searching for the phone in her pocket.

He put a hand over hers to stop her. "No phone calls," he said. "I'll give you the money up front if you'll do as I say."

He was driving away from the street now, onto another, less well-lit, less busy.

"So how much y'thinkin', for a whole night, baby?" She snuggled against him. "You want two girls? I got my blond friend who's really into threesomes. Only I gotta warn ya, I don't do ass. You S&M, anyway?" She glanced suspiciously at him and he laughed.

"Sometimes," he said, putting his foot to the pedal, heading fast for the area near the park.

"Stop!" she yelled in his ear. "Where you think you goin'? I haven't seen the money yet, I ain't even heard how much."

"How much do you want?"

She went quiet for a moment, thinking, then said, "A thousand for the whole night. In cash." She knew she didn't have a hope of getting it and suddenly needed to be out of there, like a bat outta hell. Cost her a friggin' taxi back, he'd driven so far, but he was behaving weird.

He took a wad of cash from the inner breast pocket of his jacket and sitting at the light, counted out one hundred ten-dollar bills then handed them to her.

"Shit," she said. "I'm yours, honey." She was laughing now as he drove away.

"So, where we going anyway?" She settled comfortably back in the leather seat. "Nice car, hon, but then you a rich boy, ain't ya?"

"My place," he said, calmly. His heart was as icy as his voice. "Random" was not his style, but tonight it would come in useful; it would set the cops off on a different track, take the heat off him, and his thoughts off Elaine, though he had already planned how he would take care of that situation. Soon, that "situation" would no longer exist.

And nor would this delightful young hooker with the sparkle in her eyes when she'd seen the money, and the coffee-colored legs and spiraled hair. She was exactly what he felt like tonight.

When he was in this mood, he would risk anything. First though, he took some precautions. He stopped the car in a dark place alongside the park. She turned to look at him.

"*Here?*" she asked, puzzled. "You want a BJ, or what?" She'd thought he'd want more for his thousand which, even as she spoke, was burning a hole in her fake-leopard pocket.

He opened the center console, took out a black wool ski cap, like the one he was wearing, told her to put it on, pull it all the way down over her eyes. He saw from the look she gave him she was suspicious but she wanted that thousand. He thought about tying a cord around her neck to make sure she kept the woolen hat pulled down so she could not see where he took her, but that would frighten her too much. He didn't want her dead. He wanted her very much alive.

"I'm not going to hurt you," he said. "I'm taking you to a house, you'll love it there, but you will not know where it is. Understand?"

"Yes, sir." She suddenly sounded very young. At a stoplight he took another long look at her. What was she? Seventeen, maybe? Dangerous territory. He smiled, thinking about it. He enjoyed that edge of danger, the thrill of it, planning it, executing it. Still, this was different, this was new. What he wanted with the girl was sex and he wasn't about to have it in the back of his car, on the leather seats that reclined, on some side street with maybe a cop shining a light in his—albeit blackened—windows. He was taking this one home, and when he got there he would fix a proper mask over her eyes, he would have her take off her clothes—however minimal they were; he would have her perform certain acts on herself, not him, while he watched. Maybe he would take some photos on his cell, not with the expensive equipment he used for the other "variations."

They had arrived. He rolled up the garage door and drove in, closing it behind him, heard her sighing gasp of fear.

"It's okay," he reassured her, hurrying to help her out. He took her hand, it was very cold.

Scared, she suddenly jumped back from him. "I don't want your money," she yelled. "I just want to get outta here, let me go or I'll scream . . ."

She screamed. He hit her across the face with the flat of his hand and she staggered back, hands pressed behind her on the car's trunk. "Just let me go, please," she whispered.

Worried by the amount of noise she was making, her screaming at the top of her lungs, he realized this was a big mistake. Neighbors might hear, might call the police, might come looking to see what the trouble was. Quickly, he grabbed her round the waist, flung her back in the passenger seat, got in himself, pressed the ignition, clicked the garage door open again and reversed out onto the street. He looked at her. She was still wearing the improvised hood.

"Shut up or I'll kill you," he said, in a conversational tone, as though he were suggesting afternoon tea.

The girl shut up. She slumped against the car door, allowing her fake leopard coat to fall over her hand to hide it as she felt for the door handle. She would jump out when he stopped at a light but he was driving too fast . . . He suddenly braked and she shot forward, smacking her head on the windshield, yelping with pain.

"Get out," he said, clicking open her door.

She got out. Fast. Running on those big heels, ankles turning, she was on grass now . . . heard the car start up, roar away. Sobbing, she sank down, wrenched the hideous wool mask up over her head, blinked in the meager light shed by an old-fashioned streetlamp. She was in a park. She was alive. And he had gone.

She must hide, in case he came back again. She started off at a fast trot down the cement path that led to a street where there were lights, people . . . then she remembered. She felt for it in her pocket. She still had his thousand dollars! She shoved the woolen ski cap in her pocket over it to keep it safe.

She took a deep breath, smiled, thought about what to do. She would take a taxi; she would tell no one what had happened; she'd tell the pimp the guy had only paid her a hundred, hand the hundred over to him. She would keep the rest of the money. For fuck's sake she had earned it. In fact it was the hardest money she had ever earned.

26

Brad spent a sleepless night, worrying about Elaine, and about who might be next on the crazed killer's list. Because he was sure the man had a list: four identical attacks; the rape; the slit wrists; the throat cut, and of course the same Post-it with the same message, *Please Don't Tell*. All four were the same body type: rounded, slightly plump, fair-skinned, long brown hair. Only the age range was different. The first victim had been in her early forties, the other two in their late twenties, this one, Elaine, twenty-two. It followed that age was not a decider in the killer's needs: what he wanted was a woman who looked a particular way.

Why? Brad asked himself again, and came up with the same answer. Because it reminded the killer of a woman he knew. Perhaps it was a woman who had rejected him, demeaned him. Could even be a wife who'd belittled him, made him feel small, insignificant, and certainly sexually inadequate.

This killer was bent on revenge, on getting his own back and feeling good about it.

It was five A.M. Brad sighed. It was no good, he might as well get up, go get some coffee, walk Flyin' who, ever alert to his movements was already climbing off the sofa, lengthening herself into a lazy stretch, ready for anything.

He let the dog out for a few minutes; fed her, then brushed her curly coat. He showered, looked in the mirror, ran a hand across his stubble, decided to skip shaving, save it for that evening when he had his "date" with Dr. Vivian. No more calling her "Doctor." When she was off duty, she would be "Vivi." He said her name out loud, smiling at himself in the mirror. It felt good.

In minutes he was out on the streets of Chinatown where the markets were already setting up. He stopped to buy a couple of oranges then walked back to the little pagoda-like temple at the end of his street and placed them, with a candle, as an offering to the household gods who, he hoped, might keep an eye out for Elaine. The coffee place opened at six and he was their first customer. There was a five-minute wait for the dark roast to brew but he was impatient and took it "as was," which meant before it was ready. It was thick, dark, bitter, caffeine-loaded and wonderful. Exactly what he needed to set him up for the long day he knew was ahead.

He called the hospital. Elaine's condition had not changed. No one had been admitted to her room other than the nurses on duty, all of whom had been vetted, and the doctor in charge, along with those he might consult with. And of course, the girl's parents, who were now staying at a nearby Holiday Inn, exhausted, praying for their daughter, and hoping for the blessing of sleep when they would not remember this had happened.

Jerusalem had personally met the parents at the airport; he'd seen to their luggage, consoled them as much as he could, reassured them their daughter was still alive.

Brad had been at the hospital when they arrived, a nice, regular couple in their early fifties; he gray-haired, stocky; she blond, un-made-up; both exhausted.

It had not been easy, showing them what was left of the no doubt once vibrant daughter they remembered, her life supported by machines they did not understand.

He'd had a tray of coffee sent up, sandwiches, which they did not eat. They sat mutely, for hours, side by side, simply watching their daughter breathe, occasionally reaching out to touch her arm, above where the gauze pads covered the cuts in her wrists.

"Who would do such a thing to a young woman?" her father, Jim McCarthy, asked Brad, before they finally left for the hotel to get some rest. "A woman in her prime. Why my Elaine?"

That was the question Brad had been asking himself all that sleepless night. He did not understand either, but what he did know was that he must stop this from happening. They had to find the killer before he killed again.

He walked Flyin' until his watch said seven, then turned and walked back again, stopping for the pork and shrimp dim sum at the storefront place next to the Peking duck joint where he would probably take Dr. Vivian in their date tonight. *And* her sister! Fuck!

His phone beeped. It was Jerry.

"We've checked every tire print in the coffee shop parking lots, the front for customers, rear for the staff. Not much luck with the customers, too much exposure to rain and wind. But we checked all the staff cars' tires, those who were on duty and those off, got 'em pretty well matched up, except one, blurred but newish so the tread was readable. From the size and weight distribution it was a big

SUV, an Escalade perhaps, or a Range Rover, that type of vehicle anyway. None of the staff drives anything like that, yet it was parked in the staff lot, under the overhang where it was darkest."

"And that's where he got her, coming out from work, walking to her car in the rain."

"They also checked her car; an old clunker, she probably shouldn't even have been drivin' it but y'know how these girls are . . ."

"Women," Brad said automatically. "They're *women*, right?"

"You comin' over all feminist on me?"

Jerry sounded plaintive, making Brad laugh. "It's just that her father called her a young woman last night. 'A woman in her prime,' the poor bastard said. He didn't cry; neither of the parents cried, they just sat there next to their daughter, hoping, praying."

Jerry said what Brad was thinking. "She'll never be the same, if she comes out of this, I mean. How could she?"

"Let's just hope for a miracle." Brad was silent for a minute, thinking, then he said, "Jerusalem, we can't let this bastard do it again . . . now we have another clue. Range Rovers and Cadillacs don't come cheap, he's driving an expensive vehicle, buying expensive photographic equipment, paying in cash. This is no downtrodden blue-collar suburban psycho-husband. Our man has money and he's willing to spend it. Forget coffee shops, he only went there to stake Elaine out. We have to look more upmarket, my friend. This guy has money, he has a position in life and he has no trouble finding women."

"So now we're searching for a good-looking rich serial killer?"

"Something like that," Brad admitted. "I'm certainly betting he has a good job, and that he's brimming with confidence. Except for one thing."

"He's afraid Elaine will wake up and be able to identify him."

"You got it, Jerusalem," Brad said.

27

Brad had been summoned for an interview with the chief of police: the mayor was getting restless, the public was anxious, there was a serial killer in their midst and they wanted to know what the cops were doing about it.

He took the chief through his jigsaw theory, the small details that would eventually add up to the big picture; he said they were on the trail of a man with money, a confident man, a man who knew what he was doing and Brad suspected he knew why he was doing it.

He also gave the chief his "abuse" story, said he believed the man had been subjected to abuse, perhaps even as a boy, certainly as a young man.

Brad said, "Despite a confident exterior, sir, I'm betting he's not one of those 'born-to-it' killers, the ones who kill whatever they can at an early age, the kids who decapitate cats, string up dogs, strangle little babies. I think our killer came to his . . ." He hesitated, searching for the right word. "—*craft* is the only way I can describe it, sir . . . by a long slow process of abuse. Not purely physical, perhaps it was the mother who mentally 'played with his mind.'"

The chief sat behind his desk in his shirtsleeves, rolling a pen between his fingers. His gray hair grew the way Irishmen's hair did, thick, full, turning to silver, as were his brows. He was a good-looking older man who had started where Brad had, on the streets, though his streets were Philadelphia. His experience was unbounded. He said, "Did you ever consider the killer might be a woman? Someone with a grudge against women?"

Brad thought about his question, then said, "Sir, the only woman serial killer I can recall is Aileen Wuornos."

"I expect there have been more, but she's certainly one that sticks in the memory."

"I don't honestly think this has a woman's touch," Brad said. "Sexually, there was rape, though it could have been with an object, we don't yet know from forensics. There was no semen, no DNA. Still, we'll keep it in mind."

"You're working with Jerusalem Guiterrez, right?"

"Yes, sir."

"I'm going to suggest something to you, to *both* of you. We need to get a handle on this killer—man or woman. We know he plans carefully. Picks out his victims for a certain look, a style. Why?"

"I've asked myself exactly that," Brad admitted, "and so far haven't come up with any answers."

"Then I suggest we ask a professional."

The chief took his pencil and wrote something on the notepad in front of him. He tore off the page, handed it to Brad. "This is the name of the best psychotherapist in San Francisco," he said. "Call him, tell him who you are and that you want his opinion. His *advice*, I guess." The chief smiled as Brad got up to leave. "Men like this always enjoy being asked for their 'advice,'" he added. "So let's get this mess cleared up before we all lose our jobs. The mayor is definitely not happy, and you, my friend, are on the firing line."

Jerusalem was waiting, hovering over the coffee machine, nibbling on a jelly donut. Powdered sugar dusted the front of his blue shirt and his dark eyes looked inquiringly into Brad's. He didn't speak, merely raised an eyebrow.

Neither did Brad answer: he shrugged a shoulder, handed him the piece of paper with Dr. Ralph Sandowski's name written on it, and said, "We'd better get an appointment with the doctor pronto or we're both out of a job."

Jerry got online, Googled the doctor, raised his brows again, in admiration, this time, said, "He's got credentials coming out of his ass, this guy. World-renowned." He grinned looking up at Brad, who had taken the last donut and was eating it while pulling a face and asking *why*, when even Singapore noodles—his least favorite Chinese dish—tasted so much better and probably had fewer calories.

"Know how much sugar there is in one of these things?" he demanded, holding aloft the final bite, before putting it in his mouth.

"All I know is there's enough sugar to get me along till the next cup of coffee." Jerry printed out the information on Dr. Sandowski and handed it to Brad, who scanned it, got the number, dialed it and got a brusque know-it-all-sounding woman who said Dr. Sandowski's list was full, that he had a business trip to the Far East planned and would not accept any new patients for two months.

"He'll accept us," Brad told her gently, not wanting to be as rude as she was. "We're the cops. Detective Brad Merlin and Detective Jerry Guiterrez. The chief of police personally asked us to contact the doctor and see him as soon as possible. Which means, in fact, right now."

"Ooh." She sounded flustered and Brad smiled; he guessed she didn't get a lot of calls from the cops. Jerry later informed him he was wrong; Dr. Sandowski dealt with a lot of criminals, did good work apparently, trying to rehab them.

"In fact Dr. Sandowski is at the hospital this morning," she told him, eager to help now. "I don't usually do this but I'll give you his cell phone number; I'm sure you can reach him there."

Brad dialed. Sandowski picked up on the first ring and surprised Brad, since it was Sandowski's personal cell phone, by answering with his name. "*Sandowski?*" the doctor said, almost as a question.

Brad made himself known, apologized for bothering such a busy man, asked was there any way they could meet that day. The chief of police had personally asked him to call, said if anyone could help it would be the doctor.

Brad winked at Jerry, who was leaning against the desk, arms folded, listening to his colleague butter up the psychiatrist. He heard Brad agree they would meet at the doctor's office in the hospital after lunch.

"*After* lunch?" Jerry asked, brows raised again when Brad clicked off. "Like what's wrong with *now*?"

It was Brad's turn to shrug. "Famous psychotherapists have lunch," he told Jerry. "You and I have donuts." He remembered Flyin'. She was stretched out on her own special plaid wool rug where she liked to snooze when Brad was busy.

"Anybody asks, I'm walking the dog," he called over his shoulder as he pushed through the door.

"That's what I tell the chief, when he asks how you're doing catching the serial killer?" Jerry called back and got a finger in response.

28

Jerry accompanied Brad to their two-thirty after-lunch appointment. Dr. Sandowski's office was surprisingly modest for a man who, Jerry had established, had degrees from Harvard as well as Johns Hopkins, and who was esteemed as one of the experts on just about every personality disorder that had so far been found to exist.

"From schizoid to schizotypal; from borderline to avoidant, from dependent to dissociative," Jerry said as they exited Brad's truck and gave Flyin' a quick run.

"You've done your homework," Brad said. He gave the dog a push back into the car, where she sprawled elegantly. Head to one side, he admired her. "Look at *that;* class always tells, Jer, my boy."

Jerry reached in his pocket for the chew-bar, which he tossed to the dog. Flyin' snapped it up before it could even bounce, but Brad was there just as quickly.

"Do not give my dog those things," he said. "Flyin' only gets good food, food I choose for her."

"Yeah, like shrimp dim sum." Jerry had heard all about their morning walks.

"Pork *sui mai*," Brad said, slamming shut the door and striding to the elevator. They had been forced to park in the multistory, something he hated, but due to traffic, parking out front was impossible today, even for cops. From the number of wailing ambulances Brad guessed Dr. Vivian must have her hands full. Roll on eight o'clock.

"About Dr. Vivian," he said to Jerry as the two men strode (loped was more like it since Brad was long-legged and fast on his feet and Jerry had to half-run to keep up) toward the elevator.

"I remember, you got that date with her tonight." Jerry didn't say it but he did wonder how Brad could have thought he might have forgotten, since Brad had remarked on his "date" practically every time they had spoken that day. He checked his colleague out: he was in a gray-checked short-sleeved shirt, no tie, jeans and a worn woven belt with a silver Indian head buckle. The head had a turquoise eye. Brad had bought it in a Taos, New Mexico, tourist market many years ago, and it looked it.

"You goin' like that?" Jerry eyed him, as they waited for the elevator.

Brad rubbed a hand thoughtfully across his chin. "Thought I'd go home first. I saved my shave for later." He threw Jerry a grin. "Got to make a good impression on a first date, even if it is a double date. Shit, Jer," he complained, "why did Dr. Vivi do that to me?"

The elevator came. Jerry got in first and held the door for Brad. "Maybe she guessed you'd show up looking like that and didn't want to be humiliated all alone." He grinned at Brad, who stepped in and pressed the button. The elevator lurched up.

"Well, I told her I'd bring Flyin', double dates all round."

"Better hope she likes poodles," was all Jerry could say.

The elevator stopped and the doors swung back. They were on a typical pale green hospital corridor lined with doors, each with the number of the suite, its function and the names of the doctors involved. Sandowski's was to the left, at the very end.

"Hmm," Brad commented. "Must be all you said he was, Jerusalem, my friend. Our doctor has the corner office with the big windows."

He knocked and they went in. Three people sat on the row of uncomfortable-looking chairs arranged along the walls. They glanced up at the two cops, took note of their badges, and glanced quickly down again. Brad knew some of Sandowski's patients came via the ER, or straight from the streets, or straight from the holding cell.

Jerry nudged him and whispered, "Think any of these are violent?"

"I believe the doctor sees the criminally-minded some other place where they can deal with that sort of thing," Brad said.

The receptionist who had been so arrogant on the phone was all smiles; in her fifties, ashy blond hair with dark roots tied primly back; skirt well below her sturdy knees. She looked what she was: efficient, capable. And protective of her esteemed doctor.

"He's waiting for you," she said, picking up a blue folder containing a few sheets of paper. Ignoring the three people waiting, who glared angrily after them, she knocked on the door to the inner sanctum.

"Detective Bradley Merlin and Detective Jerusalem Guiterrez, Doctor," she said, waving them in and placing the blue file on the desk in front of the doctor.

Sandowski came from behind his desk, hand outstretched, to greet them.

"Detectives, I hope I can be of some help to you. Not in specifics, of course. You are the experts there. I am merely the expert on 'types.'"

He indicated the chairs opposite his desk. The two detectives sat. They looked at him across his impressive desk, a slab of black glass the size of three coffins and thick enough to cripple anyone who tried to lift it. The doctor had to have used a crane to get the thing in there. And there was almost nothing on it: a white phone; a thirteen-inch MacBook Air; a yellow legal pad with a Bic ballpoint lying on top of it. The chairs were of the Eames variety; black plastic with a thin black cushion that did little to protect the sitter's behind.

Brad saw none of the usual framed certificates, orders of merit, medical degrees. There were no family photos, no little-kid drawings, no grandpa stuff, and yet Sandowski must be what? Fifty years old? Graying dark hair, nice-looking behind the square horn-rims, no ring on the left hand, or on the other hand for that matter. There was only a very thin gold watch, an expensive Blancpain lunar model. He was not wearing a doctor's white coat over his very well-cut dark gray suit though Brad spied his initials embroidered on his blue shirt cuffs when the doctor reached out to shake hands. There was some vanity after all, some sense that Dr. Sandowski might have an ego and maybe even a personal life, one he was not eager to show to his patients. Brad didn't blame him; he must get a lot of sickos here.

He took all this in in the space of the minute it had taken to greet, be offered a seat, say thanks for seeing us, we know it's a big interruption in your day.

"So, now." Dr. Ralph leaned back in his own, much plusher, antique black leather Eames chair (Jerry told Brad later he recognized it was authentic, the real thing, must have cost him a bomb). "So, how can I help you?"

Without giving away the police investigation, Brad explained his theory, based on small details that added up to one conclusion.

"And might I ask what that conclusion is?"

Brad hesitated, his eyes met Jerry's. "Sir, we were kinda hoping you might offer some insight on that. Exactly what type of man would commit crimes like these, against young women we suspect he does not even know."

Dr. Sandowski leaned his elbows on his desk, hands steepled in front of him, and looked directly into Brad's eyes. "What you want to know is *why* he is doing what he does."

"Right on, Doc," Jerry said. He'd once lived in Haight-Ashbury and still occasionally threw out some of their lingering sixties-speak.

Sandowski opened the file, read the two pages of notes it contained, then looked up at them again. "I think I am correct that you have come to the conclusion that our killer is seeking out the same type of young woman. There is nothing random about this. It is who and what he wants. It's who he wants to harm. The difficulty in catching him is that there are thousands of young women, right here in San Francisco, who must approximately match that description. Our killer could have his choice, a field day in fact."

Brad was puzzled. "Then though you say this was not random, there is some sort of random choice he makes. I'm thinking he picks one out, stalks her, plans his attack . . ."

"In a way you are right. Our killer has a severe passive-aggressive personality, probably combined with a borderline personality disorder. I would guess he is a young man, a loner, of course, though he may have a job and he may carry out that job efficiently."

"A blue-collar worker, sir?" Jerry was taking notes.

"Or he could be a businessman of some sort, probably his own business where he has the freedom to come and go. An executive would have to take a more definitive part in the day-to-day office work. Of course the man may also be married. Difficulties there, especially sexual, can lead to violence. Uncontrolled violence, of the sort you find yourself dealing with."

Dr. Sandowski pushed back his chair and got to his feet. He walked to the corner of the room and stood, staring out of the window. "I dealt with a case like this years ago. A young man. He'd suffered family abuse, a loner, could never get a girlfriend, worked as a garage mechanic, hid the bodies in trunks of old cars. He got four before they finally caught him."

Brad glanced at Jerry, who raised his brows in an are-we-getting-anywhere look. They both looked back at the doctor, who had taken a small object from a side table and was pressing it between his palms. Brad saw it was a rounded glass paperweight, the kind they made in Murano, Venice. The light from the window flickered through its brilliant blues and greens, a pretty thing that he would not have expected the doctor to possess, let alone caress. Sort of like worry beads, he guessed. Maybe the doc had problems too.

"Tell me, Doc, *sir*," he added respectfully. "Do you think this guy, this *killer*, might be holding down a job with other people? Mingling with society in some way, going about his business until . . . well, until he cracks, I guess."

"You said it exactly, Detective. And he's cleverer than you think. Remember that." Sandowski was smiling as he said it. He walked over and put the paperweight on the big glass desk that was wide enough for three coffins. It looked very small there.

"I see you're admiring my Murano weight," he said affably. "In my other life, my *alter ego* you might say, I am a dealer in antiques. It's a

passion of mine, gets me away from the down and dirty of everyday. I feel like I'm taking care of things, objects, furniture, paintings, objects people treasured in their lifetimes. You might say I'm saving them."

"Good for you, Dr. Sandowski." Brad got to his feet. "And my partner and I thank you for taking the time to give us a clue on how our killer might be thinking, and why."

He and Guiterrez pushed back their uncomfortable plastic Eames chairs, which Brad was pretty sure nobody had ever treasured in their entire lives and could have done with not being saved, but he smiled his thanks at Sandowski, who walked them to the door.

Sandowski paused, his hand on the door handle. "I hear you know Dr. Vivian," he said, looking directly at Brad.

"Indeed I do, sir." Brad hid his surprise and smiled at the unsmiling doctor. "In fact I'll be seeing her tonight. A little Peking duck together, we thought. That's Dr. Vivian *and* her sister," he added, and was surprised again when the doctor laughed.

"I had dinner myself, with both of them, last night," Sandowski said, ruefully. "It was meant just to be Vivi but then JC butted in and took over and there was no getting rid of her. *And* she eats enough for two," he added, as though, Brad thought, he was remembering the size of the bill.

Brad and Jerry thanked him again. They waved goodbye to the receptionist, who gave them a brief harried smile. There were now half a dozen tense-looking people lining the walls in those hard plastic chairs.

"Oh by the way," Sandowski called after them.

They turned in unison to look.

"I took Vivi to the Top of the Mark," he said. "She told me she liked it there."

"Right," Brad said, and Sandowski closed the door.

Out in the corridor, Jerry said, "What the fuck was all that about?"

Brad said, "That, Detective, was a bit of doctoral jealousy. Our Sandowski has the hots for Dr. Vivian and he was pissed off because I'm the one who gets to take her out to dinner tonight."

"Albeit with the friggin' sister," Jerry said, making Brad laugh.

"That's okay," Brad said, "I've got Flyin' to balance things out."

"By the way, am I right that the Doc is right and we are wrong?" Jerry asked.

"You *are* right! And I guess *he* is right. Now, we may be looking for a businessman loner with sexual problems and a wife. Which leaves us," Brad ended gloomily, "absolutely nowhere."

"Or even," Jerry said, even more gloomily, "one more time, right back where we started."

Vivi finished her shift ten minutes late, which wasn't bad going. The rush hour usually kept them busy from five on, people on freeways driving home from work, doing dumb things like texting or phoning or drinking hot coffee and smoking at the same time, no hands on the wheel thank you very much. She thanked heaven she'd missed the later emergency shift when they got the drunks, the gangsters, the homeboys who wanted to rip each other up, gangs of them hanging outside under the eye of security while one of their members got a bullet pulled out of him and a rival gang was given the hook, escorted away from the premises by the police.

Nerves of steel were not part of a doctor's long and arduous and very tiring training but somehow you grew them, extra little nerve appendages that got you through, cut out everything happening around you except what concerned the patient, the victim, whose blood loss you were going to attempt to stave, or whose earache you were going to diagnose. Emergency room work was not all blood and guts; it was a lot of little kids with broken ankles and babies with high fevers and frazzled young moms with teenagers, grandmas worried about grandpa who'd taken a fall. It was quite simply a slice of real life every single day.

Now, Vivi changed quickly out of the scrubs and the clogs, and into a black long-sleeved boat-neck jersey top, a black cotton skirt which of course was too tight because it was JC's, but her sister had sworn Vivi looked good in it. "Good enough to eat," was exactly what JC had said with a wicked grin that had earned her a glare, then a laugh from Vivi. She put on her good black cashmere jacket, slipped on JC's red platform heels and took a wobbly step. She kind of liked them.

She removed the scrunchie holding back her long brown hair and brushed it smooth, letting it fall across her shoulders. Unfortunately the effect was somewhat marred by the imprint where the scrunchie had held the hair back, but what the heck, a girl could only do what a girl could do. She powdered, dotted a thin black line across her upper eyelids, a little mascara, then Chanel's Rouge Coco Shine lipstick in Deauville—bought impulsively in Macy's that morning on the way to work and now she was glad. She really liked it.

Stepping back, she took a look in the half-mirror which was all they supplied them with at the hospital. She thought it would have to do, but wait a minute. A spray of her new perfume, also bought that morning, Tom Ford's Jasmin Rouge.

JC was meeting her outside and so was Brad Merlin, except the detective was not there. Of course, JC was, though, looking lovely in white jeans and silver flat sandals adorned with what looked like large diamonds and which were totally unsuitable for the weather (her feet must be freezing, but for JC looks always came first) and a little orangy faux-rabbit jacket over a black turtleneck.

"You look as though you just shot that rabbit." Vivi looked round for any sign of her date. "Where is he anyway?"

JC lifted her shoulder. "Why not find out? Check your phone."

Vivi did. There was a text from Brad. It said, *sorry delayed, please meet me at the Virgin Duck.* He gave an address in Chinatown and said he would be there almost as soon as she was.

"Fuckin' nerve," JC said, when Vivi told her. "On a first date? I mean, who does this guy think he is?"

Vivi said nothing, she was wondering whether to cancel the whole evening anyway, but then remembered Alex was supposed to be coming. She checked her phone messages: there he was, *"Hi, it's Alex, I'm looking forward to seeing you tonight, just let me know where and what time."*

He left a number and Vivi called immediately back. "We're leaving the hospital now," she said. "Be there in half an hour. It's in China-town." She gave him the address. "It's the Virgin Duck," she told him and heard JC, next to her, dissolve into giggles.

"The *Virgin Duck!*" JC was still giggling as they walked to get Vivi's car, but then Vivi decided against driving since she would never be able to park, and they took a taxi instead. Somebody would take them back to pick up her car.

The taxi dropped them off at their destination twenty minutes later; of course there had been traffic. It was stacking up to be one of those nights, Vivi just knew it.

She got out, knees neatly together, sliding across the seat, no glimpse of underwear, while JC simply flung herself out without a care in the world as to who saw what, if anything at all anyway. Vivi smoothed her skirt, adjusted her jacket and the long sleeves of her black top, checked her heels worrying about the cobbled street, then looked up at the hole-in-the-wall that was the Virgin Duck.

Behind its steamed-up storefront windows hung a row of polished golden ducks.

"Virgins all," JC marveled, making Vivi laugh.

Outside, to the left of the door, sat an apricot poodle. Well, a *pinkish* poodle anyway. Vivi guessed it was a poodle though it had none of the accoutrements of "poodledom": the fluff-ball tail, the powderpuff topknot. This dog was untouched by human primpers. This dog owned her space on that sidewalk and a cool glance from her round brown eyes let you know it.

"Dare we walk past her?" JC hovered nervously behind Vivi. "You think she might bite?"

"I'll bet my boots that poodle's Flyin'," Vivi said. The dog, hearing its name, got up and wagged its tail. "That's the dog the detective always has to walk," Vivi added, giving the tail-wagger a quick pat as she strode into the restaurant, noting in passing how soft its thick fur was. Brad kept his dog in good shape; the man groomed as well as walked. However, though his dog was there, Detective Merlin himself was not.

A smooth, smiling young Chinese man came forward to greet them, hands pressed together in an eastern greeting.

"Good evening, good evening, misses." He bowed his head over his steepled hands. "Welcome to Virgin Duck. I am Charlie Lew, this is my place and I will make sure you are well looked after tonight."

Charlie beamed while at the same time giving them a sideways assessing glance: he thought Brad Merlin had done well for himself. He also thought it was about time too, after that bitch of a wife dumped him so publicly. Everyone in Chinatown knew about that and everyone had admired the way Brad had picked himself up, as well as her dog, and simply gone on, doing what he did and, as Charlie knew, doing it well. Almost too well from Charlie's point of view, but then he always managed to keep one step ahead. And he always helped when things turned bad. That was how Charlie gave back to the community for the good fortune that had befallen him, in off-beat ways certainly, but then he'd never been one to look a gift horse in the mouth. So to speak.

He said, "Detective Merlin is not here yet, but I have a table ready for you."

He led Vivi and JC to a round table, dead center. It had a white cloth, a mirrored lazy Susan, a plastic red rose in a glass jar and six chairs.

"Six?" Vivi questioned, surprised, as she took a seat. "I thought we were four. And a dog."

"The Merlin said six, Miss Doctor."

Vivi gave Charlie a sharp glance. This man knew more than she did. Hadn't this started out as a *date*? Just her and "the Merlin," as Charlie Lew called him, a name she thought oddly suited the detective; big, broad-shouldered, and always, it seemed, in need of a shave. He surely didn't look much like a mythological wizard though. *This* Merlin was definitely of this earth and not King Arthur's.

A red-jacketed very young waiter brought jasmine tea in steaming little white pots, with tiny handless cups. "Like egg cups," JC said. Charlie told them to please call him Charlie, added that he was a good friend of Merlin, and what would they like to drink.

"We have full bar," he said, waving a genial hand toward a shelf stocked with the usual. JC ordered a margarita, which they could tell by the sudden blankness of his eyes, threw Charlie off a bit. Mexican margaritas were not the usual drink of choice in a Chinese restaurant, but Charlie owned the bar next door and within minutes a huge frosted pale lemon glass—more of a bowl really—was placed in front of JC, who gaped admiringly at it.

"I guess one of these is enough to finish any girl off," she said, taking a sip through the straw and rolling her eyes in appreciation. She gave Charlie, who was watching anxiously, the thumbs-up and he smiled and went to stand by the door, dapper in his Hong Kong Armani suit, to await his guests of honor. However, it was Alex who was next through the door.

Charlie escorted him to the table, told him the Merlin was running late, asked what he would care to drink. When Alex said a glass of white wine would be good, he hurried off to command a minion to bring the wine list, then went back to hover near the door, while Alex decided on his choice.

"Sorry I'm late," Alex said, dropping a quick kiss on Vivi's cheek, then turning to smile at JC, whom he had not yet met. "I know you're Vivi's sister," he said, his eyes admiring her. "She told me you were staying with her."

"And you're my aunt's 'Intruder,'" JC replied. "When we heard about you, we thought you might be the serial killer, you know, with the knife in hand, all that business."

"Then I hope your aunt explained it was all an accident."

"She did," Vivi said. "In fact she said she hadn't enjoyed herself so much in years. Anyway, your scar looks good."

Alex threw back his head and laughed. He told JC her sister had done a good stitching job and ran a hand through his light brown wavy hair. Vivi thought he was quite something, this Alex, and with his sad story he especially tugged at her always vulnerable heart.

"Fen is impossible," Alex said. "She is without doubt the most entertaining woman I've ever met. She told me she had been a dancer in Paris."

"Oh, you got the whole feather-headdress, spangles and stilettos story, did you," Vivi said, laughing.

"Not the whole story. I only got the first episode."

JC took another sip of her blended margarita. She'd slipped off the faux-rabbit jacket and her golden-tan arms gleamed nicely in the cutaway white linen summer top she wore, even though it was fifty degrees out. In fact, Vivi thought, her sister looked as though she was ready for a Mexican beach, not a steamy little restaurant in November-damp San Francisco's Chinatown.

"Ah," JC addressed Alex, "then you got the *first* husband. The Frenchman."

Alex took in the pink-and-golden blondness of her, her round blue eyes, her long slender limbs and the up-tilt flirt in her voice. There was no doubt JC was easy on the eye; and somehow he knew she was also a challenge.

"I got the French husband," he agreed. "As well as a lecture of the danger all Frenchmen are to any woman."

"I can vouch for that." Vivi's voice held an edge that made Alex turn to look at her, surprised. "Sorry." Vivi shrugged. "Didn't mean to be bitchy, that's just the way it came out."

"Vivi had an unfortunate engagement to a Frenchman," JC told the attentive Alex. "Fen told her two in one family was quite enough." JC laughed, thanking God when Vivi laughed with her; maybe she was getting over François after all. Meanwhile, she scanned the door for any sign of Brad Merlin.

The dog was still there, sort of on guard. Vivi wondered if the pink poodle could really be the brawny detective's dog. She smiled at the thought, half listening while Alex told JC about how much he enjoyed his night with Fen. She wondered about him, he seemed so nice, and he'd charmed Fen, but . . . But? What? Vivi shrugged, she didn't know. He was here to get to know the detective who had worked on the "case" of his murdered fiancée. He was here to try to help find a serial killer, whose latest victim still lay in a darkened ICU unit, her life held together by machines. Vivi reminded herself this was not exactly a "date" night, wondering again, puzzled, hadn't it somewhere along the line, started out like that? She and Brad Merlin? On some sort of date?

And then there he was, striding in, his broad shoulders almost filling the doorway, running a hand through his thick windblown hair to try to calm it down, greeting Charlie who was beaming at him, snapping his fingers at the red-jacketed busboy to get the hot tea on the table, quick before the detective sat down. The poodle was at Merlin's side and behind him walked a Latino-looking man, short, skinny and with a smile that dazzled even at the range of forty feet.

"Here they come," Vivi told the others, though she did not know who the second man was, and certainly was not expecting him. Her "date" was growing by the minute. They were now five, which meant there was still a chair left for someone else. Unless it was for the dog, of course.

Alex got on his feet as Vivi introduced JC. She saw a flicker of surprise cross Brad's face, as well as that of his companion, who Brad introduced as Detective Jerusalem Guiterrez.

"My partner in crime you might say. By the way, he answers to Jerry, most of the time."

"Except to my wife. Maria Carmen always calls me Jerusalem, says it gives her a bit of extra class." Jerry showed his dazzling teeth in a smile and they smiled back.

Brad took the seat next to Vivi. The dog slipped under the table at his feet.

"Some intimate *date*, huh, Merlin?" Vivi murmured in Brad's ear. "Is the pink poodle really *yours*?"

"Every curly pink hair of her. And her name is Flyin'."

"You told me. You also said you would tell me how she got that name."

"Later."

He grinned at her. She noticed he had shaved recently, that his chin was bluish-smooth and he wore a crisp white shirt, jeans and a dark jacket. He looked good.

More hot tea appeared in the little white pots with fresh cups and, though no one had ordered it, small bowls of a fragrant broth, each with a single soft pork dumpling. Alex's choice of white wine was presented and poured; Flyin' was sneaked a dumpling under the table and Brad Merlin lifted his cup in a toast.

"Glad to meet you, Vivi's sister," he said, giving JC a smile that privately JC thought was to die for: my God, there were two men here who might just knock her socks off! She'd better find out how the land lay with Vivi, she didn't want to make any wrong moves. Still, Merlin was cute, and so was his poodle whose panting breath she could feel on her ankles. She debated whether she should shove it away with her foot then remembered she was wearing sandals. The dog might bite her too. She kept very still instead.

Brad was still toasting and smiling. "Very glad to see *you*, Dr. Vivian, though since this started out as kind of a date I'd prefer to call you Vivi."

Vivi felt herself turning red but she was smiling too. All this teeth-flashing at one table might be too much. "Go right ahead," she said primly, though she did like Brad's smile, now that she thought about it.

"So, who's the sixth chair for?" JC asked.

Vivi kind of hoped Brad would not say it was for his wife. She was not sure how matters stood there, though married men did not usually ask other women on dates. Did they? Hah! According to Fen they did and, she had told Vivi, more often than she might think.

"Since Brad told me Dr. Vivian was bringing along her sister, I kinda thought it would be nice if my wife Maria Carmen could join us," Jerry explained the vacant sixth chair. "If she can get her mom to babysit that is."

Knowing his mother-in-law from hell, Jerry wasn't at all certain Senora Angelita would pick up the slack and give her daughter a night off. She was about as far from an angel as Vivi's sister, JC was close. Now *that* was some fine-looking young woman. He glanced at Brad to estimate his reaction to JC, but his buddy was in close conversation with Dr. Vivian, loud enough for Jerry to catch what he was saying, and also for Alex, across the table, who was listening intently.

Jerry took a sip of the jasmine tea and lifted a hand to order a Heineken. He'd have preferred a Mexican Modelo but in a Chinese joint like this, knew it was a lost cause.

"Detective Merlin," Vivi was saying but Brad quickly told her she must call him Brad, or even Merlin if she preferred, since after all this was a date. "I'd better just call you Detective," Vivi said, "because this is more than a date. Alex was engaged to be married to the flight attendant who was your serial killer's third victim."

Brad's eyes darkened. He threw a glance at Alex, said, "Sorry, man," offered his hand across the table. "A tragedy. I can only promise we are doing everything to catch the . . ." He did not want to use the word "killer." Instead he said, "To catch the man responsible."

Alex leaned across and said eagerly, "And I want to help *you.*"

Jerry said, "I'm sure you've already done everything you can." He felt sorry for Alex, but he was barking up the wrong tree if he thought he could help the investigation. Jerry remembered Alex now: he was the boyfriend who'd been checked out at the time of the murder. He'd been in L.A. when it happened, the girl in San Francisco. There wasn't a speck of suspicion on this guy.

Alex said, "She'd told me she was being followed."

Brad remembered that from the case files.

"She said she felt like she was being watched, for weeks before this happened. She was scared, y'know, but yet she never saw anyone, never was approached, no one ever threatened her."

"But I felt like that too, the other night," Vivi remembered suddenly. "I was alone in the empty parking garage, waiting for the elevator. It was as though . . ." She shrugged, chilled. "As though eyes were crawling over me."

"Did you see anyone?"

"No one. But then I heard footsteps on the stairs." She smiled, remembering. "It was only a colleague, Dr. Sandowski. He walked me down to my car, just to make sure I was okay." She didn't tell them that he then asked her out to dinner but JC said, "He's okay, is Dr. Ralph. He took us for dinner and then he offered me a job in his antique store. Two birds with one stone," she added.

"For you, or for him?" Brad was thinking about Dr. Ralph's date with Vivi and how the doctor had said JC had butted in.

"For me, of course. I needed a job. I got lucky, that's all."

"I'm interested in antiques myself," Alex said, seemingly to emerge from his gloom over thoughts of his fiancée. "I'll have to come and check your store out."

The poodle's head poked up from under the tablecloth between them and Vivi stroked it absently, thinking how soft the dog's fur was. "What does she eat?" she asked Brad, who was giving Vivi that long intimate kind of look that meant he didn't really care what the dog ate right now: he was more interested in her.

Just then, the Peking duck arrived, two varnished golden ducks carried in with great ceremony on a silver platter: with a mound of puffy round buns; sliced spring onions and cucumber and bowls of plum sauce. And all of it smelling as though Buddha himself had reigned over this meal.

Ooohs and ahhs greeted Charlie, who took his bows with his usual prayer hands, then on a side table proceeded to expertly carve the ducks while his assistant made up plates of the steam-roasted meats with layers of cucumber and onion folded in the bun, adding long wafer-thin strips of crispy skin, with the dipping sauce on the side.

Vivi thought the skin was the best part of it. It crackled as she bit into it. The buns were ethereally light and the duck meat drizzled with a little plum sauce was melt-in-the-mouth.

She looked up at Brad. He had sticky sauce on his chin and in-stinctively she took her napkin and wiped it away. His eyes met hers, a long deep look that sliced right through to her "downstairs" as Fen called it. And Fen knew what she was talking about. Vivi's fingers trembled as she attempted to put together another bun.

"Allow me." As Brad fixed it for her, the conversation seemed to drift over Vivi's head; she felt alone with Merlin the Wizard, aware of the bigness of him, of his shoulder almost touching hers, of his blue eyes that were definitely touching hers.

"I think I'd like a glass of wine," she said, quickly pulling away.

Brad called for one. Charlie came and poured. JC had one too, and Alex had a second. Brad stuck with tea and Jerry had already had his quota of beer.

"Sorry your Chiquitita couldn't make it, Jerry," Brad said to his partner.

"Mother-in-law trouble," Jerry explained, disappointed.

"*Chiquitita?*" Vivi asked.

"My name for Maria Carmen. It's a long story," Brad told her.

"I know, like Flyin'."

He laughed, then glancing out of the steamed-up window, said, surprised, "Well, Jerusalem, my friend, just look who the wind swept in instead."

Everyone turned to look as Dr. Ralph Sandowski walked in. He spotted them, looked surprised and walked over to their table, carrying a long narrow leather case.

"Talk about coincidence," he said, sounding astonished. "I had to pick up something round the corner from here, thought I'd stop in and get a bite."

"You picked a good place. Why don't you join us?" Brad got to his feet, as did Alex and Jerry as well as Flyin', who stared suspiciously at Sandowski. The doctor knew everybody except Alex, and Brad introduced him. He also told him exactly *who* Alex was.

"I'm sorry," the doctor said. "It's a tragedy. You have my sympathy." He took the empty chair meant for Jerry's wife and placed the long, worn leather case on the floor next to him.

Brad glanced at Jerry. The case looked very much like it held a shotgun.

Jerry said to Alex, "We had a long chat today with Dr. Ralph, about the kind of person we should be looking for in this case. In *your* case," he added, apologetically.

Vivi's eyes met JC's. They were both thinking Dr. Ralph was really rather nice, being so kind to poor Alex.

"I wanted to try to help the detective," Alex said, shrugging his shoulders. "But I find I have nothing to offer."

"I'm afraid I had little to offer also," Dr. Ralph said. "Only some guidelines on the mental makeup of the type of person they could be looking for. Like you, I'm no cop, no trained police detective. I think all we can do now, my friend, is leave it to them. I'm sure the detectives will come up with the answer."

"If we don't the mayor will have our jobs," Jerry said, as more plates of food followed the Peking duck. Long, peppery steamed Chinese green beans with sesame oil; beef braised with broccoli, and at Vivi's special request, her old childhood favorite, sweet-and-sour chicken, which here, ceased to be boring. More jasmine rice. More tea. More wine.

Vivi's phone rang. She fished for it in her bag. "Hope it's not the hospital," she said, excusing herself and walking to the door to take the call.

It was Fen, of course, dying to know how things were going.

"Is my Intruder there?" she asked.

"Shit, Fenny!" Vivi exclaimed.

"Kindly do not use that word, especially so loudly in my ear," Fen said sharply. "All I asked was is he there?"

"You mean Alex, I guess?"

"Am I talking about the Pope? Of course I mean Alex. My *Intruder*. And what I want to know is, do *you* want to 'look after' him?"

"No. I do not want to 'look after' him."

"Well, that certainly makes a change. How's the date going then?"

"My *date* was not with Alex, he came along because he wanted to meet the detectives. My actual *date* was with Brad Merlin."

"Hmm, how appropriate. Vivian was Merlin's lover, you know, in mythology."

"Oh, Fen, is that *really* true?" Vivi was remembering the pangs she had felt earlier. "I mean, when you think you're going to care about someone, I mean you know, *care*, is that when you get those pangs? Or is that merely sexual attraction, the kind you can find anywhere?"

"Dear girl, there are pangs and there are *pangs*. Only you can tell the difference. Just make sure you know what you're doing this time. And anyhow, how is JC getting along with my Intruder?"

Vivi glanced over her shoulder at the table. From where she was standing just outside the door, she could see JC in earnest conversation with Dr. Ralph. She reminded herself again to call him *Ralph*.

"I don't think there's much doing there," she said. "Gotta go, we're eating. Love you."

She hung up and went and sat back at the table.

"Fen sends her love to her 'Intruder,'" she said to Alex, so then of course Alex had to tell the story of how he had met her the night of the storm.

The last of the tea was drunk, fortune cookies opened. JC's said new plans would lead to happiness, and Vivi's said that work and a good heart made a good soul. None of the men opened theirs, so JC snatched them up and ate the cookies while reading out the messages, none of which said anybody was going to get rich quick or meet the person of their dreams.

"Tell Charlie Lew to get better fortune-tellers," she said gloomily to Brad.

"You shouldn't even bother reading them," Dr. Ralph said. "They're worse than reading your daily horoscope in the newspapers."

"Oh, but I *do*," JC confessed, making them laugh.

"What about you, *Doctor* Vivian?" Brad asked.

Vivi shrugged. "I pretty well know my day-to-day, I don't need the newspaper to tell me what will happen."

"They might have told you you'd get to meet Alex," JC said.

Vivi always thought JC was a believer in love; in an earlier era, she would have been a "flower child," all long hair and beads and free love.

Brad called for the bill. Tonight was on him, he told them, handing Charlie back the black plastic folder along with his credit card. Then, looking at Dr. Ralph, he said casually, "By the way, sir, that case you're carrying, I'm thinking it could contain a shotgun."

"Ah. Well. Yes. Yes, indeed it is a gun. One of a pair of Purdeys I own. I bought them in London a few years ago, though they date from the seventies. A perfect pair, custom hand-scrolled silver engraving, double trigger mechanism, line-up dead straight. I'm no great shot but with these guns it's hard to miss."

"And what is it you shoot?" Jerry leaned back in his chair, wondering about a permit.

"Don't worry, I have a permit," Dr. Ralph said. "I picked it up from the gunsmith who cleaned them for me, and I'm licensed to carry it in my car."

Brad saw the doctor missed nothing, but it was a long way from an iridescent Murano glass paperweight he used in his office like worry beads, and a pair of expensive retro-Purdey shotguns that could shoot someone dead.

"So what exactly do you hunt, sir?" he asked. "Just curious, y'know, not being a huntin' type myself."

"With the Purdeys, just game in season, I like to go to England for the pheasant, Scotland for the grouse. Best shoot in the world, there. Locally, I have a cabin in the woods. Not that great but I get some deer, not with a Purdey of course, with a rifle. I like it there. Before the snow hits, there's all the peace and quiet a man could want."

"How wonderful." JC leaned across the table and touched his hand. "I don't know about the shooting but the idea of a cabin in the woods sounds wonderful, all that crisp clean air, the piney smell of the forest."

Vivi wondered suspiciously why her sister was suddenly getting all carried away with nature. Could JC be *coming on* to Dr. Ralph?

"Then if you like it so much you'll have to come for a weekend." Dr. Ralph took a card from the breast pocket of his jacket, handed it to JC. "Call me tomorrow, about the job."

Vivi stared at him, astonished. First he gave JC a job, now he was inviting her for a weekend.

Brad signed the check, pushed back his chair, slid a bunch of bills into Charlie's discreet hand, more into the two young red-jacketed waiters', and summoned Flyin'. The restaurant was still crowded, the aromas still enticing.

"We'll be back," he told Charlie, who bowed again as he held the door, and said he hoped so.

Dr. Ralph was hauling his vintage leather shotgun case by its worn strap.

"You okay with that?" Jerry asked.

"I'll be fine, thanks. I'm parked in a lot close by."

"My car's back at the hospital," Vivi said.

"I'll drive you back there," Alex offered quickly.

"Or I can," Dr. Ralph said.

Brad asked Alex, casually, what car he drove.

"Range Rover. Always liked that car. Even if I did crash it into Fenny Dexter's tree."

"And you, Doctor, what do you drive?" Jerry was curious about the medic with his expensive Purdey guns and his cabin in the woods and his antique shop. Where the hell did the man get his money anyway? Could he make that much being a world-renowned psychotherapist?

"Same," Dr. Ralph said. "Always found it fast and reliable."

"Yeah, well, take care of the Purdeys, sir," Brad said. He turned to look at Vivi. "Wanna go on somewhere?"

Vivi's eyes lit up, she'd thought the "date" was over. "You mean like a club? I have work early tomorrow though," she said.

"Just a drink at a place I know. There's somebody I'd like you to meet."

"Okay. Sure." Vivi felt that little pang "downstairs" again. Was she really *flirting* with Brad under her eyelashes?

It was agreed Alex would drive JC back to the hospital where she would pick up Vivi's car, and Dr. Ralph took off alone, toting his expensive guns.

As they watched him go, Brad's eyes met Jerry's. "So what d'ya think? Coincidence?" he asked, quietly so Vivi could not hear.

"I don't believe in coincidences," Jerry said. "I'll bet he knew where Vivian was going tonight and he came along."

"A man who fights for what he wants," Brad said, thoughtfully, then he asked Jerry to check Sandowski's gun license, get a bit more background on those expensive Purdeys.

"Will do," Jerry said, disappearing into the crowd, heading back home to mother-in-law from hell and a crying baby and a wife he adored. He'd missed her tonight.

Vivi and Brad watched Alex and JC set off arm in arm for the parking lot, she frozen-footed of course in her flat bejeweled summer sandals and bare brown legs with her orangy faux-rabbit jacket; he tall and elegant in chinos and loafers and a black peacoat. They saw Alex give JC his cashmere scarf which she flung round her neck, shivering as they walked away.

"That leaves just us." Brad smiled down at Vivi who was smiling up at him.

"And Flyin'," she reminded him.

"The three of us have a date," Brad said, tucking her arm in his as they walked to his car.

If Veronica was surprised to see Brad walk in with a girl on his arm, she disguised it well, and merely said, "How y' doin', Merlin," giving Vivi a cool nod. After his harsh treatment at the hands of his ex-wife, Veronica was protective. Not exactly *motherly*; she had never been that, but she counted Brad as one of her friends and that meant for life. No woman was gonna fuck him over again, if Veronica had anything to do with it.

She slammed a shot glass of Maker's onto the zinc counter, slammed a foaming Kirin next to it, then proceeded to wipe things up with the always immaculate white cloth, studiously ignoring Vivi.

Brad put his hand over Veronica's, stopping her in mid-wipe. "I'm doin' good, Veronica. And so is Dr. Vivian Dexter, to whom I am introducing you, since you didn't have time to ask."

Veronica threw Vivi an upward glance, then went back to her wiping. "A doctor, huh. For real? Or one of them PhDs who go round calling themselves a doc, then when you get a broken leg they wouldn't know how to fix it, even if you were dyin.'"

Vivi got the message: somehow Veronica counted Brad her property. "A doctor for real," she said, giving Veronica a sweet smile, which she ignored but which Brad certainly noticed.

He loved that smile, he loved Vivi's cushiony lips painted a pale lustrous rose. It had been a long time since he had wanted to kiss a woman this much, and he definitely, right now, wanted to kiss the doctor. He'd bet she would not permit that. Not on a first date. If you could call tonight's merry multiple get-together a "first date." Vivi wasn't that kind of girl.

"A real doctor," Vivi was telling Veronica. "Emergency room. Someone shoots you, you come see me."

Veronica stopped wiping and looked assessingly at her. "Nah," she said, after a long minute, "you're too young. Probably still in med school or something." She looked at Brad. "You check her out?"

Brad grinned. "Saw her in action just the other day," he assured her. "It's just that she has that girly look, the pink cheeks and those innocent golden eyes . . ."

Veronica peered intently into Vivi's eyes. Vivi blinked. Veronica said, "Those eyes are brown, Merlin. You're letting yourself get carried away."

"Oh, I do hope so," Vivi heard herself saying, blushing at the same time. "I mean a man like Brad, a detective, all that stress and trouble looking for murderers, you know . . . well as a doctor, I think he needs to de-stress."

"Over a drink with a pretty woman," Brad agreed. "Now, stop it," he ordered Veronica, "and get Dr. Vivian a glass of whatever she wants." He held up a warning finger. "Remember, she's in charge of the emergency department, you never know when you might need her."

"Yeah, like next time a customer wants to shoot the barkeep." But Veronica was smiling, running her hand through her platinum wig, hitching up her bosom prior to asking Dr. Vivian exactly what it was she would like.

"Oh, a vodka tonic, two olives please, if you have them that is," Vivi added.

Veronica gave her a "whaddaya think" look and said of course she had olives. Blue cheese or plain?

Vivi took the plain, noted that the vodka Veronica poured was a good one, Belvedere, that the olives were from a jar and the drink generous.

"You're forgettin' all about poor Flyin' now you have a woman," Veronica said, throwing a biscuit in the poodle's direction.

Brad looked at the dog sitting next to Vivi, who was running her fingers through the rough fur, and darn it if the dog wasn't gazing adoringly up at her, the way it had once gazed up at his ex. He felt Veronica's eyes on him. She nodded knowingly in the dog's direction.

"Looks like Flyin's got the future all worked out," she commented, returning to polishing glasses with a new white cloth. "A bit previous, I'd say."

"I wouldn't." Brad hitched his bar stool closer to Vivi's and rested a casual arm along the back. She turned to smile at him and suddenly his past life raced before his eyes, then disappeared forever. He *was* looking at his future.

He watched Vivi sip her drink. She picked out the two olives and ate them. "Hungry?" he asked. His arm was around her, his hand resting on her shoulder now. He'd forgotten they had just eaten Chinese.

Vivi took another sip, more of a gulp this time, remembered JC's words of wisdom that morning: *Go for what you want, girl. It always works with a man.*

"I think I might want to be kissed," she heard herself saying . . . could it really be *her*? But she so did want to kiss this man, why shouldn't she tell him? "JC was right," she added.

Brad looked perplexed. "About the kiss?"

"Maybe."

He got up, took her hand in his, helped her down, waved goodnight to Veronica who was now busy at the far end of the bar. There was no need to call Flyin', the dog was already at his heels.

"Where are we going?" Vivi asked, breathless with love, or lust, or perhaps both.

"My place," he said.

"Ooh, why?"

"Because your sister is at *your* place. My place, we can be alone. If that's what you want."

It was. Vivi knew it.

Within minutes they were parking on an alley in Chinatown, and Brad was opening his red lacquer front door. Flyin' was first in. Vivi followed, then Brad who closed the door behind him. He switched on the lamps, switched on the gas logs in the green-tiled fireplace, switched on the music . . . not Neil Diamond, old Roxy Music, a favorite: soft, sexy, sentimental.

Vivi took in the dark-beamed room, the slightly battered taupe microfiber sofa—awful but certainly better than her own black leather one—the obviously unused kitchen, the fifty-five-inch TV, the overflowing bookshelves, the hi-fi. She smelled the sweet smell of incense wafting in from the tiny temple at the end of the street, looked at the dent in the sofa where the dog obviously slept even though there was a perfectly nice brown velveteen dog bed in front of the fire. This was no bachelor pad; this was a place where a man lived alone.

"Nice," she said, turning to Brad.

He put his arms round, held her close. Vivi liked that. Liked the breadth of him, the strength of him, the pressure of his muscled arms, liked the smell of him, some aftershave, some fresh air, some bourbon . . .

"I'm glad you don't smoke," she said. "It's bad for you." And then she was kissing him, and all she wanted was for life to go on like this, exactly the way it was at this moment, with that urgent feeling "downstairs" and the pressure of his lips on hers, his hand hard on her lower back, pressing her closer, his body against hers . . .

She shouldn't be doing this. It was against the rules. She turned her face away, pushed him back.

"What happened?" Brad said, astonished.

"I just remembered, this is a first date."

She sounded so prim and virtuous he laughed.

"You're right, it is," he agreed. "What I'm wondering is how does a guy get a second date with you?"

"He calls me." Vivi smiled, all sexual danger averted. Brad would never know, at least not for a while, how close she had come to saying "take me I'm yours" in true slut style.

"Got to work tomorrow," she told Brad, knowing it was purely a delaying tactic because she so wanted to stay, so wanted him.

"And I've got to work too, I guess," he answered, though for once his mind was definitely not on work.

He held her hand. It reminded her of the first boy who ever took her to the movies; she'd thought she would faint then, simply from the touch of his hand on hers.

She said, "You know that Vivian and Merlin were lovers. In mythology, that is."

"I had heard that." Brad sounded thoughtful.

"Just saying." Despite herself, she was smiling. Her eyes locked with his and she said, "Kiss me some more. Please." She was always a polite girl.

And of course Brad did just that and Vivi so badly wanted to touch him, and be touched by him, she wanted his lips "downstairs," she wanted to use her mouth on him, feel the smooth texture of him, breathe him in, exactly the way he was doing now with her.

Her last thought before she sank into the delicious oblivion of sex when all time stopped, was that she was glad she had worn the Victoria's Secret black panties and matching demi-bra, and that if he stopped kissing her, stopped stroking her, she would simply die, or maybe she was dying now of sheer pleasure.

Hours and much lovemaking later, filmed in a sweet sweat and still held in Brad's muscled arms, she said, "Thank you," making him laugh. Then she remembered she had to be at work the next morning. No! *This* morning.

"Isn't this where we started out?" Brad asked as she grabbed her clothes and headed for his shower, almost tripping over the dog, who sat guard near the sofa from which they had not strayed.

Vivi threw him a smile over her naked shoulder. She sure hoped it wasn't where it would end.

Later, outside her apartment when they were sitting in the black Ford pickup, they turned to look at each other. Their eyes locked. They did not kiss. They did not need to.

Brad got out and went to open the car door. Her face was clean of makeup and her long brown hair blew in the wind. She put up a hand to touch his cheek, her fingers lingered on his mouth. Then, "Goodnight," she said and turned and hurried down the steps to her apartment.

Brad waited till he heard her door slam. He rubbed a thoughtful hand across his chin, remembering the taste of her mouth. She was something, his Dr. Vivian. Something wonderful.

31

JC was waiting up for Vivi, watching a late-night vampire movie on TV. Well, not *that* late: it was only two thirty, but anyway she wanted to talk to her sister about the antiques job.

She heard Vivi's footsteps on the stairs, heard her trip on the third step down, the one that was a bit worn at the edge. She heard her say, "Oh darn." It was *so* Vivi not to have said "oh shit" like anybody else would. Vivi had always been too good for her own good.

"What are you doing, still up?" Vivi asked her as she came through the door, looking, JC noticed, pink-cheeked and shiny-eyed, like a woman who'd just been kissed.

"Did the Merlin kiss you then?" she asked, uncoiling herself from the obnoxious black leather sofa and making room for her sister.

"JC!" Vivi looked shocked. "It was a first date! Not only *that*, it wasn't even a *real* date, you know it turned out to be a free-for-all, everybody welcome."

Vivi flung her bag on the floor and sat next to her sister, easing off

213

the red suede platforms that had nearly brought her downfall on the stairs. "These shoes are killing me."

"They're supposed to. That's how you look good in them. Men mistake the pained expression on your face for passion."

Vivi threw her a long irate look, then they both burst out laughing.

"By the way," JC said, "there's a message for you from the hospital. They want you to take over the night shift tomorrow instead."

"Jesus, that means midnight to eight." Vivi shuddered. "The graveyard shift they call it, and they mean it. We get more shootings and stabbings and domestic violence and drunks then than at any other time."

She hated the thought of the night shift, especially because now it might disrupt any future plans she was hoping for with Brad.

"Still, it means I can sleep late tomorrow," she said.

"It's already tomorrow." JC gave her a wary glance. "So what's with you and Alex, anyway?"

Vivi stared back at her, then getting what JC was after, replied, "Alex is okay, I mean I like him a lot."

"Hmm, me too. We had a good time together. Before he took me back to the hospital to pick up your car, we went for drinks in some dive in North Beach, kinda sleazy, a lotta loud music, fun. But you know what? I believe Alex is half in love with Fen, he told me he phoned her, and he never stopped talking about her, and how great she is."

"She calls him her 'Intruder.'" Vivi yawned. "And he calls her 'Fen.' How about that! Our aunt's gotten herself a new nephew."

"Hmmm, I sure hope that's what it is." JC looked a bit doubtful.

Vivi threw her an exasperated glance. "You've seen too many movies, JC. Anyway, what did the two of you talk about besides Fen?"

"About his fiancée, of course. She's the reason he came here, but now he realizes there's absolutely nothing he can do. Julia—that was her name—is dead and it's up to your detective and to my psycho-guy analyst, to sort it out and find who killed her. As well as all the others." JC stopped talking and looked at her sister. "Oh, Vivi," she said, "Alex cried. I mean, real for God's sake tears. He said he's over losing her, but he feels this need to avenge her. He told me she was such a good woman, so gentle, so happy."

"Like Elaine," Vivi said, thinking of the girl still in the coma, her desperate parents still hovering at her bedside. She shook off the somber thoughts and tried to remember her evening with Brad.

JC uncrossed her legs and got up. "Tea?"

"Thanks." Vivi yawned again, remembering what had happened between them, thinking of those pangs "downstairs" when she'd looked into Brad's eyes and kissed him, and what had happened. She reminded herself about the French "fiancé" and that she was supposed to be in the process of "moving on"; concentrating on work and not, as Fen had warned her, of taking care of yet another man. Somehow though, she did not get the feeling Brad Merlin needed taking care of. There was a steel core to his soft heart, she knew it was true because he'd adopted that strange poodle that looked as though it knew all the secrets in the world. That dog had checked out everyone at the table and found some wanting, possibly Alex, certainly Dr. Ralph. *Ralph!* Which reminded her.

"What were you doing flirting with Dr. Ralph?" she demanded.

JC was making the tea, which involved *almost*-boiling water (she was too impatient to wait for it actually to come to a boil) and a single tea bag dredged between two mugs, which left a brownish trail across the white-tiled counter.

She turned to look at her sister, amazed Vivi didn't get it. "That's what you do when you want something from a man," she explained.

"You flirt a little, let him know you think he's terrific—which actually, Dr. Ralph is. I mean, he's quite a celebrated therapist, maybe I can even get some free therapy thrown in with the job at the antiques store. Anyway, I think he's kind of cute."

"He's too old for you," Vivi protested. "He's even too old for me," she added, thinking about it.

JC brought over the tea, slopping some on the floor on the way and dusting over the drops with her bare toes. The nails were painted silver. "So maybe I'll try Alex instead," she said, with a wicked grin at her sister. "And of course, there's always Merlin."

"Shut up, JC!" Vivi got up. She did not want the tea. She did not want her sister interfering in her life. She did not want to look after JC, but knew she had to because that's the way it had always been, since they were small girls, and that was the way it would always be, forever and ever, amen.

"I know you didn't mean that," she said.

JC thought there was a note of hopefulness in Vivi's voice and took pity on her sister. "Just joking," she said.

Vivi hoped so.

• • •

Much later, the man stopped at a gas station. He checked his mobile for messages; filled up the tank then went into the restroom. He was coming out again when he saw a young woman lounging outside the ladies', looking desperately at the trucks driving past, obviously in need of a lift, of a quick-money trick in the truck's cab; women like this frequented these places.

"Wanna lift?" he asked. He was acting on impulse again, though he knew it was wrong. She swiveled her head and her long hair swung over her face in the breeze. She checked him out, top-to-toe.

She knew what she was doing and so did he. Women like this made their living from men like him. He told himself this was not exactly random behavior; he was choosing her now. Carefully.

"Nice car," were the first words she spoke to him as she got in. And the last. There was the quick hard needle jab in her arm, her eyes opened wide and she let out an exhausted-sounding oooh . . . and that was that.

He pushed her down in the seat, covered her with a blanket, saw she was carrying a purse, flung it into the back with the other one, Elaine's, that he'd been meaning to dispose of.

He drove until he was in deep countryside, flat land dotted here and there with isolated farms, drove until the last farm was well behind him, slid the big car between some trees, where he parked.

He got out, lifted up the rear door, took out his hooded mask, slipped off his jacket, put on the black turtleneck, black track pants, the boots with the rubber soles from which he had painstakingly scraped off the identifying tread with a sharp knife. He strapped his other knife, the one that meant business, in the sheath around his calf. He took out the camera and the tripod. His routine was in prog ress.

The wind was up. It whistled in the trees, sent a shower of brittle dead leaves over him. He lifted his masked head, stood, sniffing the air, like a hunter. Then he went to get his prey.

The next morning, promptly at eleven and without any nagging from Vivi about did she know what time it was, JC showed up at Verily Antiques on smart Jackson Square, an area that in the rough, tough, gold-rush days used to be known as the Barbary Coast. Then it was the haunt of sailors, now it was home to the city's financial institutions in their towering skyscrapers.

Verily Antiques, though, was in an old building. Its wood-framed window was painted an ashy-green, the color of September trees, JC thought approvingly. There was a single item on display behind the plate-glass window, so you knew it had to be expensive: just a low, gate-legged round table fashioned from some exotic-looking burled wood. The table rested on a pale fringed rug that JC guessed came from Persia, when it was still Persia that is, and when artists hand-knotted such works of art to be walked on by velvet-slippered, chiffon-draped harem women, whose light footsteps left no trace.

She was still admiring it when someone said, "It's silk, of course. That rug."

JC turned, startled, and found Dr. Ralph standing next to her.

"Oh," she exclaimed. "Yes, of course, it must be, it's so sleek and soft-looking."

"It dates from the eighteen hundreds and is a perfect example of its kind. Notice the subtlety of the colors, the softness of the blues, the pale corals, the luster of the cream."

JC was gazing at the doctor, wide-eyed. "But how do you know all this?"

"Come on inside," he said, "take a look around and I'll tell you about the stock. You'll need to know everything if you're going to be able to sell it for me, because my customers certainly know what they want and a lot of them know exactly what they are looking at."

He held open the door and JC walked into a wonderland of soft rugs, damask silken drapes with golden cords knotted around them and chairs like thrones. There was a long slender walnut dining table—JC knew it was walnut with that particular mellow sheen because her aunt had once had something like it, only smaller. This one came though, with a set of eight lattice-back chairs.

"Authentic English, not Massachusetts copies," Ralph told her. "And here, on the wall, you'll find some fine examples of early nineteenth-century American landscape artists. Not that I'm in the art gallery business but people bring things in to sell and I buy them, or more usually take them on commission."

Drawn by their flamboyant colors, JC stopped in front of a display of framed butterflies, pinned behind glass, looking as perfect as when they were alive.

"Someone brought these in the other day," Ralph told her, running a finger over a frame to remove a line of dust. "Had it been just the one, I would probably not be able to sell it, but since it's a collection," he shrugged, "people go for 'instant' collections."

"It saves them the time and trouble of doing it themselves, I guess." JC turned her smile on him. He really was nice-looking . . . not exactly *good-looking* but . . . well, kind of nice, with his long narrow face, his broad forehead. His hair was thinning a bit, age, she supposed, though she had no real idea what age he might be. Anyhow, he looked lean and fit and he was very intelligent, and for her that made a change.

"Do I get the job?" she asked, unable to wait. "I promise to dress appropriately," she added, making him laugh.

"Let's go get coffee, talk about money," he suggested. "And please, don't call me Dr. Ralph. Here, in my store, I'm Ralph."

Over coffee at Café Amici where the barista drew a heart on the foam of JC's cappuccino, giving her a lingering look that said he appreciated her, it was decided JC would begin work the following week. She said she was visiting her aunt in Big Sur that weekend and could not begin any earlier. A modest salary was settled on. It wasn't lavish but JC figured she was considered a learner and when she got more experience could ask for a raise.

"Dr. Ralph," she said. *Oh fuck*, she was like Vivi calling him Doctor. "*Ralph*," she amended, taking a sip of her cappuccino, which left a line of sweet foam along her upper lip. She licked it off and smiled at him from under her lashes.

He did not smile back. Instead he said, quite seriously, "If you're still interested, you should come visit my cabin in the forest. I can make you as good a cup of coffee as this."

Surprised, JC met his gaze. "*Strings* usually go along with an invitation like that," she said warily.

He nodded, agreeing. "In my business, as a therapist, I've found that to be the case only if the person involved *wants* 'strings.' Otherwise it's perfectly reasonable for a man and a woman—admittedly a beautiful woman—to have a friendship. Companions, you might say. Besides," he pushed his horn-rims further up his nose, "I'm helping you find yourself."

JC smiled, pleased. Just what she needed: free therapy.

Dr. Ralph pushed back his chair, said she must excuse him, he was needed at the hospital. He took a key from the pocket of his tweed jacket—a very good tweed jacket, JC could not help but notice, but then she always noticed those things, like the silk Persian rug. The key was attached to a silver Tiffany key ring in the shape of a heart. JC knew it was Tiffany because she'd seen it there on one of her strolls through the store. Still, she thought a heart an odd choice for a man, and certainly for a shop key.

"I'll take care of it," she promised, putting it in her enormous green leather tote, where it immediately got lost in the tangle of stuff she kept in there on a permanent basis.

"We're closed Mondays," Ralph told her. "So, let's say Tuesday through Saturday, eleven till five. And I'm leaving tomorrow for China, be back in a week, so you'll be on your own. Okay?"

"Okay. *Ralph*." JC beamed as he walked out of the café without a backward glance. She was employed. She was earning money. She was in charge. She might even consider that weekend in the woods, though she would never shoot deer. Pleased, she turned her attention to the cute barista with the hair to his shoulders and a black tee who was heading her way with a cup of espresso.

"On the house," he said, as JC smiled angelically up at him.

33

Vivi did not hear from Brad all that day and she did not call him because, as she reminded herself, after all it was only a first date. But she was restless when she showed up for her shift that evening. She parked in the garage, noting again it was almost empty. She was still wary after her scary episode with the footsteps on the stairs that had turned out only to be Dr. Ralph. The same Ralph who was now involved with her sister. Odd, Vivi thought, gloomily, how life went: JC getting lucky with the job with Ralph, plus an invitation to dinner from Alex tonight, though Vivi wasn't at all sure that JC hadn't issued that invitation herself.

"So, what about you and Dr. Ralph?" Vivi had asked, but JC had simply grinned and said she was starting work Tuesday, though the doc was away and she wouldn't be seeing him till he got back. She fumbled in her cavernous handbag and brought out a key on a silver Tiffany heart key ring, waving it triumphantly.

"He's gone to China, left me in charge," she said gleefully. "Eleven till five, Tuesday through Saturday."

"The poor man doesn't know what he's letting himself in for," Vivi had told her, as JC dialed Alex's number and set up her date.

Vivi wished *she* had a date, but Brad had not called and she was worried she had behaved like a slut on a first date.

At the hospital, she took off her coat and hung it in her locker, took off the black pants and sweater she had worn just in case Brad called and asked her out for coffee, or even the next morning, for breakfast. She put on the faded burgundy scrubs and her scuffed white clogs. Her toes still hurt from the red platforms and she winced as she strode to the emergency department, transformed in minutes from a worried woman moodily remembering a man's lovemaking to the efficient, ever-alert doctor. At least she was in full control of that part of her life.

The emergency department was extra busy that night. Gurneys lined the halls with the victims of accidents or violence, or simply the ill. The emergency team would take care of them all, some just had to wait.

It was late when the woman wearing a blood-stained faux-leopard coat walked in under her own steam. She was clutching a plastic supermarket bag. Her face was swollen, black-and-blue marks were turning purple, one eye was shut and blood leaked from a scalp wound half hidden under a mass of tiny braids that stuck like corkscrews from her head.

"Domestic violence, I'll bet," Vivi said to a coworker. God knows they had seen examples of it often enough. Vivi took the girl's arm, guided her into a curtained-off cubicle, had her remove her coat and lie down on the paper-draped gurney while she assessed the damage.

The woman looked silently up at her through swollen purple eyelids.

"You have a broken nose," Vivi said after a minute. "Amongst other things."

"Shit."

Others on the team came in now taking the woman's pulse; her temperature; removing her high-heeled shoes; checking her legs, her arms for breaks, other wounds. She still clutched the plastic supermarket bag which she refused to give up.

"So what happened?" Vivi asked, inspecting the scalp wound. Pretty bad but she had seen worse.

"The bastard attacked me."

"What bastard was that?" Vivi began to clean the scalp wound and the young woman let out a shriek of pain. Vivi sent someone to fetch the cop she'd noticed interviewing an injured gang member earlier. Domestic violence needed to be reported. A nurse was unfastening the woman's pants and she sat up and shoved her away.

"Hey, hey, take it easy," the nurse said.

The cop arrived, took in the scene and her bruises and broken nose. "What ya hiding in that bag anyway?" he asked, but the woman only cursed him and Vivi waved him away.

She pushed the woman gently back against the gurney, told her it would be okay, she would fix her up good as new. Of course she was lying but it was one of those untruths that made a victim's life easier and she was all for that. Temporarily, of course. Soon enough this woman would face herself in the mirror and she'd still be ranting on about the "bastard" who'd done it and to whom, Vivi had no doubt, she would return. They always did.

"I ain't givin' it up," the woman muttered, still clutching the plastic bag to her chest, but she was weary and wounded and had no strength left to protest when Vivi finally removed it from her clutches and took a look inside.

"Why, it's only a ski cap," Vivi said, surprised; she'd half expected to find a weapon and was glad the cop was still there.

"There's something inside it," the woman blurted through her rapidly swelling lips.

"He wanted my money," she said, seeming unable to stop talking now she had started. "I'd hidden it in that cap. I'd earned that fuckin' money, a thousand dollars the trick paid me. *Me!* You wanna bet I never seen a thousand dollars before in one whole fuckin' lump? And that guy who'd picked me up in his car just took it out and counted it off in hundred-dollar bills. For a whole night he told me. So I said yeah baby, let's go and then the fucker puts this wool cap over my eyes so I can't see and drives me to some freaky house and I just know he's gonna kill me and when I got out of the car I start screaming . . . screaming my freakin' head off . . . I thought if I'm gonna die I'm going noisy so the neighbors'll hear . . . So then he shoved me back in the car, told me to shut up or he'd surely kill me and I sat there with the cap still pulled over my face so I can't see him and with his thousand still in my coat pocket . . . sure I'm gonna die . . . sure . . . sure . . ."

She began to sob, gripping Vivi's latex-gloved hand. Vivi was thinking how many times she'd heard a similar story, how often it came through the ER doors, how sad she was for women like this who didn't stand a chance in life's uncertain lottery. "It's okay, you'll be okay," she said soothingly.

"That trick's a freakin' madman," the woman yelled. "Fuckin' freakin' crazy . . . he was gonna kill me . . ."

Vivi realized the cap had been used as a mask so the woman could not identify her attacker nor see where he was taking her. As she took the cap from the bag a pile of hundred-dollar bills fell out; the "thousand dollars" the victim was talking about. There was also a piece of paper. A green Post-it, on which was printed carefully the words, *Please Don't Tell.*

Vivi's knees threatened to buckle; she gripped the edge of the gurney, reminded herself that she was a doctor on duty, it was her job to take care of these people, not faint on them. She looked at the pathetic young woman lying there, beaten to a pulp, realizing she might easily have been looking at a corpse. It had been that close.

Making sure the woman would be okay in the hands of her team, she handed the cap and money and the Post-it to the cop, and then she got on her mobile and called Brad.

34

Jerusalem Guiterrez was arranging the collection of knives on Brad's desk, spreading them out so they could see the details of each one.

He said, "They're all chef's knives, fileting knives to be exact, some eight inches, others nine. Approx the size our killer used. According to forensics, any one of these might have done the deed."

Brad was all work, all concentration. He studied the knives, each one formed from a single piece of steel shaped into a handle, diminishing into a thin wafer intended for the delicate slicing of filet mignon, not a young woman's throat. Looking at those knives turned his stomach; it was inconceivable any man should kneel over a drugged victim and kill her in such a brutal, sadistic manner and gain some perverted sense of sexual satisfaction.

"God knows, sex has a lot to answer for," he said to Jerry who stood, arms folded across his chest, also studying the knives.

"Could have been something else, a flick blade, of course, or a pocket knife. This knife is the kind the bastard's wife might have used for cutting up their Sunday chicken, feeding the kids."

Brad held up a hand. "I don't want to think of this pervert with a wife and kids."

"That's what Doc Sandowski told us could be the case," Jerry reminded him. "Serial killers don't always come under the category of 'single,' and they're not always found in bars picking up young women, normal style."

"Sandowski also said that the man *knew* the women he killed, maybe not on a personal level, but he knew who they were, he'd *watched* them."

"Fuckin' voyeur," Jerry said. "Watching them and all the while planning on killing them."

"Which means he had access to them. And yet they were all from different walks of life, different jobs, nice young women, earning their living. Two were engaged, one only moved to San Francisco six months ago, all led normal lives."

"He picked 'em out, Sandowski told us. He was obsessed with them."

Brad hefted an eight-inch fileting knife, testing its weight, thinking of the young women sliced by exactly this, their throats cut like pieces of meat. He was thinking of Elaine, lying mute, still in a coma in a hospital bed, and who might never be able to tell them what happened, about who the man was, how he had done it. And their only firm clues were Elaine's name badge, the tripod, and the opinion of a top psychiatrist that the man might be married, might even have kids of his own. But then surely the wife would know something?

In Brad's experience the wives *always* knew something was wrong. They watched TV, read the newspapers, knew what nights their man was home and the nights he wasn't, knew what time he came back, knew for fuck's sake that they were living with a freak, a weirdo, and yet they all clung to their claim they knew nothing. *Somebody knew something.* This jigsaw puzzle was missing a few pieces and it was up to him to find them.

Phones were ringing all over the place. Jerry picked up one: Brad answered his mobile.

"Oh, hi, Vivi," he said, coming back to the real world with a jolt. "I meant to call you." But then he stopped and listened instead. When she'd finished he said, "Be right there." He looked at Jerry who was already grabbing his jacket; the cop at the hospital had called at the same time. In seconds, they were on their way.

Brad didn't even bother with the parking lot: he simply screeched to a halt outside Emergency, flashed his police blue and red, and he and Jerry ran inside.

In Emergency, Dr. Vivian in her burgundy scrubs, hair pulled back, was standing by the gurney. A cop stood on the other side. The woman on the gurney turned her swollen eyes on Brad and moaned.

"Shit, not more cops," she whispered through lips still bleeding where her teeth had penetrated when the pimp hit her. "I shouldna came here, I shouldna done it, now they'll say I stole the money, they'll put me in jail for soliciting as well . . . no, no, no I'm not gonna say nothin' . . ."

She turned her head away from Brad, who'd gone to stand next to her. Jerry was on her other side. There was no escape and the woman knew it.

"Don't you worry, hon," Jerry told her calmly. "We'll get the bastard that did this to you. It'll be him in jail not you, girl. So why not tell us what it was all about anyway?"

"Let's start with your name," Brad suggested.

But she closed her eyes, shutting him out. Brad noted her wrecked

231

face, thought she'd be lucky if she got plastic surgery to fix that nose, lucky if she could even see properly again.

"It's okay, ma'am," he told her. "We're on your side in this one, all you have to do is help us out a little bit, and we'll get it taken care of for you. And Dr. Vivian here will make sure you're okay, so no worries in that department." He glanced at Dr. Vivian, who threw him a look back with a tiny shrug of the shoulder that meant she surely hoped so.

"Lawanda, that's my name," the woman said, eyes still closed. "Lawanda Willis. Used to be Lawanda Lavinia Miller, back when I was a kid. A nice kid, y'know, skipping class and fetching a fix for my mom . . . all the kids I knew used to do that. Anyways, that was then . . ."

"So what's now?" Jerry pulled up a chair and took a seat next to the gurney. "Like *exactly* what happened last night?"

"I was out and about in North Beach, my usual routine; a car stops, I asks what he wants, promise him the world in a quick ten minutes . . . but he tells me to get in . . ."

"You remember what kind of car that was?" Brad asked.

Lawanda frowned, giving a little gasp as the stitches in her head pulled painfully. "An SUV, big, black; with black leather seats, had that kinda new-car smell, y'know. And the man smelled nice too, like lemonade, I remember thinkin' when he was counting out that thousand. He was wearing a wool cap pulled down low and dark glasses, but y'know guys don't always want you to see who they are . . . I remember the car now, we were at his house, in the garage, and he had the cap over my face, only different from his, mine was the mask. I was leanin' back against the trunk, my hands behind me . . . I could feel the chrome letters under my fingers . . . funny thing to remember at a time like that when I thought I was gonna meet my maker, but my fingers spelled out 'Range Rover.' Just goes to show schoolin' pays after all . . ."

Brad's eyes met Jerry's. They had their vehicle.

Lawanda Willis went through her story one more time, about the trick counting out the thousand bucks, taking her to a house, about how she became scared, it wasn't normal, he wasn't acting normal, he'd blindfolded her and everything . . . About how she'd run away through the park, the thousand still in her pocket, the black ski cap that had been her mask shoved in on top of it.

"I got back home, gave my pimp a hundred, said it's all I'd gotten. It didn't work. He found the rest, beat the shit out of me and I ran away. All over again," she added bitterly.

The detectives had Lawanda's address now, and already had an APB out on the pimp. They sent the black ski cap to forensics for traces of hair, of saliva, of sweat, other than Lawanda's. They would trace stores that sold this kind of black woolen cap. They had the leopard coat, where the thousand dollars the killer had counted out had been stashed, sent over too. Lawanda had told them the vehicle smelled like a "new car." They would check local dealers for recent sales of Range Rovers. They would check on the cologne he wore that smelled like lemonade. And they had another Post-it with that terrible message, this one meant for Lawanda.

Brad knew the outline of the jigsaw was always the hardest part, but now they had it. All they had to do was fill in the middle. But then, he also knew there was always that one piece that didn't make sense. One piece that simply did not fit.

He was aware of Vivi in the background keeping an eye on her patient. At last he was able to talk to her.

He walked over, took her hand between his, patted it gently, looking at her. He thought she looked like hell, all smudged shadowed eyes, tight mouth, hair scraped back, pale in her scrubs and white coat.

"Vivi, I'm sorry you had to see this," he said.

She shrugged it off. "It's my job."

"I know, I understand. You see everything here. Anyway, I want to thank you, for catching it, for calling me."

There was a defeated look in her eyes as she asked, "Did it help?"

"Yes," he replied. "Oh, yes. It helped."

They stood, awkward in the sudden silence between them.

"Will you call?" Vivi asked, just as Brad said, "I'll call."

"I know you're busy now," Vivi answered.

He smiled, shrugging off his concerns, thinking now of her, of the woman he wanted to see again, who he wanted to know better. He said, "I might even be here to take you for coffee when you get off work."

"Eight o'clock," she replied quickly. "And make that breakfast."

"It's a date."

"Our second," she said.

They were both smiling as he waved and walked away.

35

B rad and Jerry were on their way to Veronica's when Jerry said, "What kinda vehicle did that guy Alex say he drove anyway?"

Brad swung him a surprised glance. "You mean Vivi's friend?"

"Dr. Vivian's aunt's 'Intruder,' if I got it right. Came outta nowhere." Jerry shrugged. "Just a thought."

Brad thought about it now. "He drives a new black Range Rover, smacked it up on the aunt's tree at the top of her driveway."

"And his girlfriend—his *fiancée*—was one of the victims." Jerry looked across at Brad, who was just turning on Mission. "Coincidence?" He shrugged. "Just another thought."

Brad sighed. He'd never even thought of going there. "He seemed like a decent guy," he said, still doubtful.

"He shows up here, to find the fiancée's killer, he says—and oops there goes another one. Another dead girl in San Francisco."

"Jesus," Brad muttered. It didn't sound right, yet somehow it all fell together. He thought about JC walking off with Alex the previous night, arm in arm; about Alex lending her his scarf, the two looking as if they'd known each other forever. And what about the stormy night at the aunt's anyway? Alex had simply shown up injured; he'd charmed her, spun her a story, spent the night there.

"So we'll check Alex out," he said grimly. "And I'll have to warn Vivi to keep her sister away from him, without her knowing what I'm really thinking."

"Can't have JC upsetting the applecart," Jerry agreed. "And we can't give Alex fair warning. I'll get onto it right way, check his background, his movements."

"He runs a private security company out of L.A.," Brad said. "The man knows how to cover his movements."

"We'll see about that," Jerry said.

They parked under the swinging pink neon sign that spelled out Veronica's name, flickering on and off like it was Vegas.

It was late and there was only one other couple in the bar, holding hands across the table in one of the patched red vinyl booths while Veronica flicked a feather duster over her gin bottles.

She threw them a look over her fluffy white angora shoulder. "I'm already closed," she said.

Brad and Jerry swung onto their usual stools while Flyin' took up her normal waiting position next to them, eyes fixed hopefully on Veronica, who sighed and said, "If it were not for that friggin' dog I'd throw you out. A girl has to get some sleep y'know."

"And what would you do with *them*?" Jerry jerked a thumb in the direction of the love-smitten couple, a silver-haired Romeo and a blond older Juliet.

"Tell 'em to get a room of course." Veronica disappeared into the kitchen and came back with a plate of chopped chicken which she handed to Brad. "For Flyin', poor little bitch, I'll bet she's had no dinner tonight."

Brad hung his head in shame. "You're right. And thank you."

"Meanwhile, what about us?" Jerry asked plaintively.

"Kitchen's closed." Veronica wiped the counter firmly in front of them. "Lucky if you get a drink."

"Thanks, I'll have a Bud Platinum, in the bottle please," Brad said. "And I'm sure Jerry will join me."

"What happened to the bourbon and tequila?" Veronica was surprised.

"Too much on our minds," Jerry replied, as Veronica took the beer from the fridge and placed the icy blue bottles in front of them. Then, relenting just a little, she shoved a bowl of peanuts over.

"Don't like to see a man drink without a bit of nutrition," she told them. "Gotta keep you guys thinking. After all, it's you we need when it comes to the crunch."

Brad tipped back his head, the iced beer flowed down his throat, chilled as a mountain stream. Somehow it cleared away the hospital disinfectant smells, cleared his head for a moment of the sight of Lawanda's smashed face, of Dr. Vivian Dexter in her professional capacity, taking charge, though he could have sworn she looked ready to faint when she saw that Post-it with its grim message.

Thinking again of what Jerry had suggested about Alex Patcevich, he said to Veronica, "Let me ask you something, hon, knowing you as the fount of all wisdom that you are. What if you had met someone . . ."

"A man," Veronica interrupted, still dusting.

"A man. You met him through somebody you know is okay."

"A woman." Veronica knew the score.

"You accept him on her say-so, yet it seems she has only known him for a day or two, though he'd met her aunt, who'd vouched for him."

"How did he meet the aunt?" Veronica leaned her elbows on the counter, interested now. Her white angora bosom shed fluff, making Jerry sneeze. "Wuss," she commented.

"It was a dark and stormy night," Jerry began.

Veronica rolled her eyes.

"The guy crashed into a tree at the top of the aunt's drive near Big Sur. She was alone, she was scared, then it turns out the guy was okay, or seemed okay anyhow."

"Until now," Veronica said. "So what happened to make you change your minds?"

"He has the right car, he had the right fiancée who turned up dead, and he's always in the right place at the right time."

Veronica went back to her dusting. "Elementary, my dear Watson, as Robert Downey Jr. always says in those movies. I'd check him out."

"Yeah, except Brad's not Sherlock and I'm not Watson," Jerry said, just as Brad's phone rang.

Brad did not recognize the number but clicked on anyway. "Detective Merlin here."

He heard a chuckle at the other end. "And Dr. Sandowski here."

"Doc? What can I do for you?" Brad glanced surprised at his watch. "Isn't this a bit late for you?"

"Late for *you*, my friend. Not for me. I'm calling from Hong Kong. I'm attending a symposium here, be back next weekend. Meanwhile, I've been thinking over our discussion the other night, reference the man you are seeking."

"The killer," Brad said.

"He's been on my mind and I've been wondering if maybe I've

not been steering you in the wrong direction. I'm not infallible you know, psychiatry is not a science, there are various different ways to think of this."

"I'm interested," Brad said. And so, he noticed, was Jerry who was calling for another Bud, as well as Veronica whose ear was practically in his phone.

"I led you to believe he could be a businessman, well-to-do maybe. Confident certainly. Maybe even good-looking. After all, there have been killers who, when you look at them, you ask yourself why they need to rape a woman and kill her, when with their looks, they could easily have gone into any bar and picked up some pretty girl and . . . well, you know the rest."

"Yes, sir." Brad rolled his eyes at Jerry. Bored, Veronica went to clear the table as the romantic older Romeo and Juliet departed, too lost in each other's eyes to even wave goodbye. She turned off the lights, turned the door sign to "Closed," locked it and returned to the pool of light over the bar where Brad sat listening.

Sandowski was saying, "I'm thinking the other way now, thinking of how a man like this would pick out his next woman, thinking what if he *is* a blue-collar guy, working somewhere where he meets these women by chance, then stalks them. Someplace like a garage. A man like that would have access to women but would never ask them out, never get a date with them. Anyhow I would guess he is married."

"Then the wife knows?" Brad said.

"No. Oh no, she does not know. She might *suspect*, but she puts that out of her head. She has her family to think of, her good standing in the community, she's not going to be the wife of a rapist killer. Besides, he treats her right, doesn't beat her up, gives her housekeeping money, keeps a roof over her head."

"Dr. Sandowski, what can I say?" Brad wiped a hand wearily across his brow. Their whole construct of a single, confident businessman killer had just been wiped out.

"Just wanted to give you my thoughts and wish you well. You're doing important work for the community, Detective. I hope I've been some help."

"I'm sure you have, Doc. And thanks for taking the time to call."

Brad clicked off his phone, his eyes met Jerry's. "What the fuck," he said, shrugging. "We're still checking out Alex."

36

Fen almost was *not* surprised when Alex called; he had been so much on her mind, or at least in the back of it, she thought he must have felt it. Silly, of course, but then she was feeling silly. *Foolish* was more like it, thinking romantically about a much younger man, a man more suitable for Vivi than herself. But now here he was on the phone telling her he'd been thinking about her too.

"You are on my mind, Fen Dexter," he said.

Fen knew he was waiting for an answer. She should not encourage him but she had not felt this way about a man in years, and fool that she was, she said, "I've been thinking about you too."

It was a step forward in what was definitely the wrong direction but she couldn't help herself. Now the silence on the other end of the phone was deafening. Fen twisted a strand of hair nervously round her finger, like a love-struck schoolgirl. Even her nieces would not have behaved this way.

"I want to see you again," Alex was saying, and Fen's heart was jumping all over the place.

"Well, why not," she heard herself reply. "Come over for dinner, I'll cook something. What would you like?"

"You," Alex said.

Oh my God. This could not be true, it could not be happening. She must remember her years, her dignity . . . Instead she said, "This evening, at six. I'll be waiting."

"And I'll be there."

Fen told herself there was no need for explanations. Alex wanted to see her and she wanted to see him, it was as simple as that. They liked each other, each enjoyed the other's company. She liked to cook. She would make him a great meal. And she would wear her Paris underwear. God, why was she even considering underwear? Showed her body had a mind of its own! She would definitely not wear stilettos; ballet flats would do, and a simple straight skirt and a pink cashmere sweater she had been saving for a special occasion but which she'd thought was too young for her. She should really give it to Vivi, though it was more JC's style. JC could carry it off better. What was she *thinking*! She was fifty-eight years old!

Fuck it. Sex was still an option at any age and anyway who said Alex even *wanted* to have sex with her.

Fen reminded herself again Alex was simply coming by to talk to her. Probably about Vivi or his poor murdered fiancée. She'd almost forgotten about that. She hoped he was not in fact going to talk about that; it was too scary and far too intimate. Anyway, she would dash out to the shops, dream up some delicious food, put in another bottle of Champagne to chill and stop thinking like a fool. Everything was normal. Everything was okay. Wasn't it?

. . .

He was on her doorstep promptly at six, bearing flowers, pink peonies beautifully wrapped in silvery tissue and a bottle of Perrier-Jouët.

"I'm better prepared than last time you opened the door to me," he said, standing there, clutching the bouquet and the wine.

"And a lot drier," Fen replied, remembering how he'd looked, soaked and bleeding in the middle of the storm.

Hector rumbled over to check who it was. He quit his rumbling and wagged his tail when he saw it was Alex. "It's always a good sign when the dog likes you," Fen told him.

"Actually, I'm more interested in what the dog's owner thinks of me," he said.

Fen put his gifts carefully on the kitchen table and turned to look at him. It was still there, that connection between them, in his eyes, in hers. She said, "This dog's owner is very happy to see you again."

She took a careful step back, giving him a smile over her shoulder as she led him into the sitting room where a bottle of rosé wine and two glasses awaited.

"I thought you might enjoy the rosé, even though it's winter," she said, settling into the sofa while he took the seat opposite. "Besides, it matches my sweater."

"Wonderful."

She knew he was watching her as she poured. Her hand shook.

"Allow me." He reached across, took the cold bottle from her shaky hand, filled their glasses, took one, held it out to her, lifted his in a toast.

"To us," he said.

Fen cast her eyes down, took a gulp, almost choked . . . *This could not be happening to her, it was not happening to her* . . .

"Why did you come back?" she said, meeting his gaze again. "Really? *Why?*"

"I told you I'd never met a woman like you. I meant it. I need to know you."

Fen's heart skipped a couple more beats. She could tell from his look Alex meant what he was saying.

"I've got caviar all ready for us," she said quickly. "I mashed hard-boiled egg yolks with crème fraîche, and I made the blinis myself . . . after, there's fettuccini, I'll grate fresh Parmesan into it . . . I didn't make salad, you don't seem like a salad man . . . but for a surprise I made a rice pudding, a real *man's* pudding . . . just Arborio cooked slowly with cream and nutmeg and a little butter and I have a choice of coffees . . ."

Alex came over and sat next to her. He took her in his arms. "I don't want food," he said. "I want you."

· · ·

Fen had made love on a sofa before, but not this one. She had slept with a man before, but not in this bed. She had made love many times, she knew the magic of sex with a new person, a new body on hers, a new mouth demanding hers, new hands seeking her . . . but not this one. The younger one.

The next morning, she was alone though, in that bed, not quite believing the way her body felt, the new bruises of love and the re-membered shimmer of delight. She knew the first time you made love with a man you were attracted to was always special, the newness of his body, his caresses, his tongue, his hands. But now the man was not there. Instead there was a single pink peony on the pillow where his head had rested. A note was attached to it.

I could not forget you the first time I met you. Now I will never forget you.

Fen sank back, the note clutched to her lips. Silly schoolgirl that she was again, she took the pillow where his head had rested, clutched it to her face seeking his smell. Then she opened her eyes and looked down at her naked body in the full cold gray light of a winter morning.

Her thighs were still good, as long and as lean as when she was a dancer; her breasts were small without that downward pull, but her belly was too soft and her hands looked old and worn from all the gardening and her skin was winter pale. With a wry smile she remembered Leonard Cohen's song, *"Dear Heather with your legs all white in the winter . . ."* Leonard Cohen was a man who knew his women well, and appreciated them winter-white or otherwise. Perhaps Alex was the same, perhaps Alex hadn't noticed her defects in the lamplight. Or perhaps Alex hadn't cared.

She closed her eyes again. It was all a dream, all candlelight and wine, smoke and mirrors, a thing of the moment, a young man's fantasy come true for just one night. She could accept that. Well, *maybe* she could accept that. Oh Lord, no! She would *have* to accept that. All she could do was keep the memory forever.

With a quick dart of shock she remembered thinking earlier that Alex would be good for Vivi, but thank God Vivi was not interested; she was keen on Detective Merlin. And JC was dating the rich therapist. No, Alex wasn't taken, but that didn't mean she could have him.

He belonged in his own world, dedicated to his search for the killer of his fiancée, to his business, his life, while she belonged here in her own small private world. She and Hector.

She rolled over and looked at the dog who was on his feet staring at her and, Fen guessed, about to burst. Life would go on. Though not exactly the way it had been before.

• • •

A week passed. Fen eyed the phone, wishing it to ring. It did not, so again she took Hector out for a long walk. The poor dog must be exhausted with all the walks she took to avoid waiting for the call that never came.

She had not seen Alex since their night together. She kept the flowers with the note he'd sent her in her top dresser drawer along with a few other old treasures, like Vivi's first ballet shoes, JC's first demo tape, faded photos of their parents, and the photos of herself when she was a girl.

He had gone from her life as surely as the sun set each evening and he would not be back. Of course it hurt; she felt betrayed, because if Alex had felt nothing for her at least he might have respected her dignity. He'd charmed her into bed as though she was some girl, so hot for him she didn't care. There was no future with him, she knew that now. She would never hear from Alex again. So be it.

Fen whistled for the dog who was wandering too near the edge of the cliff.

Hector came at the gallop, tongue lolling. She knew she should not, but Fen still wished she could speak to Alex.

37

Brad was not waiting for Vivi outside the hospital at eight the next morning, but Flyin' was, and there was a note attached to her red leather collar. Smiling, Vivi patted the dog, who flattened her head skittishly. Vivi wasn't sure, but she thought Flyin' might be jealous. She took the note from the collar and read it.

Back in five, please will you wait? Brad.

Of course she would. The dog leaned companionably against her leg. How sweet, Vivi thought: maybe she likes me after all, then she remembered she was wearing black pants and Flyin' was probably shedding all over them. But then she also remembered poodles didn't shed, or did they? God, she couldn't even think straight anymore. She considered not waiting for Brad; she looked like hell, and felt worse.

She drooped, exhausted. She was at the end of her rope. Too

much had happened in the past few days; too many broken people, too many killings, too many patients to take care of when all she wanted was for somebody to take care of her. Last night had done her in and now she was supposed to have some sort of breakfast date with Brad. She should never have agreed to it. Wait a minute though, wasn't it *she* who had suggested it? Anyhow, it was a mistake. No man would ever want to look at her the way she was. All she had done in preparation was wash her face; no makeup, not even lip gloss, not so much as a hint of perfume. Her hair was wrecked, her black pants probably had dog hairs and she had forgotten to change out of the friggin' white clogs. Her camo-green quilted jacket was three years old and she was draped in JC's cashmere scarf. No. JC did not have a cashmere scarf. Of course, it was Alex's, JC must have kept it when he lent it to her, leaving the Chinese restaurant. Vivi thought JC didn't seem that keen on Alex, but with her sister you never knew exactly what she was feeling. Hadn't she just told Vivi how to get a man to do things for you: flatter him, tell him he's wonderful and he'll become a pussycat was about the sum of it.

The dog leapt up suddenly, causing Vivi to lose her balance, and then Brad was there. His arms were around her, steadying her, and he was saying, "Hey, baby, you look tired. I bet you haven't eaten since last night."

It was true, Vivi had not had so much as a Snickers bar. She relaxed against him, grateful for his burly presence. It was so comforting to be in his arms. He smelled of the fresh wind and clean skin and a hint of aftershave, though his jaw was already blueing again. His hair was spiked from running his hands through it and his blue eyes held a smile.

With his arm around her shoulder they walked together to his car and Vivi let Brad look after her. She let him put her in the front seat,

snap her seat belt around her, close the door. He put Flyin' in back, then he drove her to Chinatown and his favorite dim sum place.

She flopped gratefully into a hard little chair at a plastic-topped table, while Brad brought her tea and delicious small nibbles.

Sitting opposite, he looked very serious. "You can't go on like this," he said. "Burning the candle at both ends."

"I've only burned one end," she objected. "I haven't had a chance to light the other yet."

"There's still time," he said, making her smile, and wonder what he meant.

"Let's go." He picked up the take-out box of pork *sui mai* for Flyin', who was waiting patiently outside as always, while suffering the indignity of pats on her soft pinkish poodle head from passing strangers. She leapt up when Brad appeared, giving Vivi a glance that Vivi thought was calculating, before leading the way to Brad's pickup.

In minutes they were at his home. Brad closed the door behind them, lit the fire, switched on a lamp, drew the curtains. He removed Vivi's coat and hung it up. Vivi sank into the sofa. Brad lifted up her feet so she could stretch out. The poodle sprawled on the floor, its eyes watchfully on her.

"I'm making coffee, okay?" Brad said.

"Great." Vivi closed her eyes.

Minutes later there was a mug of coffee in her hand and Brad was sitting next to her. He took her feet and put them across his lap, massaging her ankles.

"I have something I must tell you," he said in a serious voice that made Vivi wake up and take notice. "It's about Alex."

"What about him?"

"We need to ask him some questions, about where exactly he was

the night his fiancée died, where he was the day Elaine was abducted."

Vivi shot upright, spilling her coffee. The dog backed nervously away. "You can't be serious. Alex could never do anything like that, and why would he? A man like him, good-looking, successful, charming . . ."

"He's a man who can attract any woman. Men like that have also been known to have *problems* with women. Sexual problems. Men like that have been known to be serial killers. We have nothing concrete to go on, I'm just giving you a heads-up on where the situation might be taking us."

Vivi's first thought was of her aunt. Fen adored Alex. Then she thought of JC and Alex walking arm in arm the other night, Alex's scarf around JC's neck; JC in her silly summer sandals, all long brown legs and long blond hair and innocence, because damn it her sister was an innocent. JC thought the world loved her, good or bad.

She said, "JC has a date with Alex tonight."

"Call her and tell her to cancel it," Brad said.

38

For once JC woke with the birds. Or she would have had there been any birds. In her view seagulls did not count; they were simply accessories to the shore.

She got out of bed—Vivi's bed, of course, she was not about to sleep on any more sofas if she could avoid it   and padded barefoot to the window. She twitched the curtain aside and took a look at the day. It was not promising. Gray, windy, and she would bet, cold. Shit. She let the curtain drop, thinking as she did so that she must tell Vivi to shop at Pottery Barn. They had much better curtain panels than this flimsy silk that wasn't real silk, and which anyhow JC would bet had belonged to the previous tenant of this subterranean apartment. What was Vivi thinking? I mean, couldn't the woman get herself somewhere *decent* to live? Nearer the hospital, in better shape and with a bathtub without rust stains and a stand-alone shower where you didn't skid on the curved bit of the tub. JC hated

251

shower curtains. They reminded her of the movie *Psycho*, which always sent a chill through her.

She went to the kitchen and looked gloomily at the immaculate counter with the old-fashioned press coffeemaker. JC couldn't stand homemade coffee; somehow it tasted different. It was all in the head, as no doubt her own "psycho"—her analyst that is—would tell her. Free therapy went along with the job in Dr. Ralph's antiques store. She smiled, remembering the doctor telling her he was "straightening her out." Vivi should be pleased about that.

She went and sat on the edge of the bed, contemplating her silver toe polish and feeling very alone. It was okay for Vivi; she had her work. It meant everything to her, always had. JC envied her that. Heaving a sigh, she reminded herself that she now had a job; she would start next week, she would be in sole charge of an antique store with its treasure trove of valuable furniture and paintings. It came to her in a flash. Of course, that's what she should do today; go to the store, familiarize herself with the stock; make notes about dates and provenance and prices; generally prepare herself so that come Tuesday she could show up a "professional," a woman who knew what she was talking about to her customers who, Dr. Ralph had told her, usually knew what they were looking at and talking about.

She leapt from the bed, excited at the thought of being alone in the store, and her new job. She was halfway across the floor heading for the shower when it occurred to her that Vivi would be coming home soon from her night shift. She would need a good rest.

Nice girl that she was, she quickly stripped the bed, put on fresh sheets and smoothed the white cotton duvet over the top. She plumped the pillows and for good measure, gave the whole thing a spritz of her new favorite eau de parfum, Balanciaga's Paris. Next, she tidied up the bedside tables, put the water glasses in the dishwasher, plumped the orange Target cushions—quite nice really—on the uncomfortable black leather sofa; and wiped off the coffee table. Then she went and took a shower, making sure to clean up the bathroom after herself.

Feeling virtuous, she got dressed in her usual jeans and a green cashmere sweater of Vivi's she found in the top drawer of the bureau, a place most women usually kept their underwear not their sweaters, but that was just Vivi. The polo neck felt soft against her skin. With her blond hair pulled back against the tug of the wind, JC felt wonderfully warm as she strode up the treacherous steps from the basement apartment and down the street, heading for the nearest BART subway station.

Half an hour later, she was standing outside the store, admiring the table in the window and the way a single curtain of heavy blue silk was pulled to one side, the better to display it, as well as the Persian carpet with its soft blues and apricots and creams. Dr. Ralph had shown her the single blue glass bead in the fringe, that showed that someone, long ago, had made this rug and put his identity right there in order that people like her might know his artistry.

She searched in the bottom of her bag for the key on its silver Tiffany heart, opened the door and walked into her new domain. Eyes closed, she breathed in the scent of the past, of luxury, of faded silk, of wood hundreds of years old. Odd, how she had lived all these years and never known such a world existed, especially since her aunt had a house full of treasures that somehow had simply never registered. They were just there, and like Fen, you never expected them to change.

She had just closed the door behind her, slipping on the latch when her phone rang. It was Vivi.

"Hey," JC said, "what's up, Doc?"

"JC," Vivi said, "I want you to cancel your date with Alex tonight."

"What? *Why?*" JC set her bag down on the antique table, then snatched it up again afraid she had made a scratch. She put it down on the floor.

"Nothing important," Vivi said, too casually JC thought. "It'll just be better if you do. Until things are sorted out."

"Vivi, what are you talking about? What *things*?" She slipped off her coat and flung it down next to her bag.

"It's only that Brad is, well he's kind of keeping an eye on Alex about the killings. He wants you to be safe, that's all. It's only for a while, a day or two . . ."

JC suddenly got what Vivi meant. She said, "You can tell your Detective Merlin to fuck off, to stay out of my life, to stay out of Alex's life. I'll do exactly what I want and so will he. Oh, and by the way, you can tell him from me also that he's no great mythological wizard, he can't even get this one straight. My God, Vivi, are you nuts too?"

Steaming, she slammed her phone down on the antique table, then looked down at it, stunned. Oh God, now she had *really* scratched it. What was it you were supposed to do about scratches on wood? Fen had once told her something about a walnut half and rubbing it into the spot. Meanwhile, she spat on her fingers, rubbed at the scratch, then peered hopefully at it. Two unexpected fat tears spilled onto the table. Jesus! Two hundred years or so of loving care and in seconds she had wrecked it.

She plumped down into the grand rose silk damask throne chair, resting her hands along the arms that ended in carved lions' heads, straightening her back, lifting her neck, holding her chin up, like a princess. She should get back to yoga, get into meditation, it helped you deal with situations like this.

How could they even *think* Alex might have killed somebody? They had to be kidding! Of course she wasn't in love with him but she really liked Alex. Still, there was a niggling doubt at the back of her mind. What if they were right? What should she do? If ever she had needed advice, JC knew she needed it now.

She glanced round at Verily Antiques, at Dr. Ralph's beloved things. She'd bet he wouldn't be too happy to see any of them sell; she had sensed how much he cared, guessed he'd chosen everything personally over a long period of time. *Of course!* She should call Dr. Ralph, ask *his* advice. That man had an answer for everything.

She punched in his cell phone number.

"Dr. Sandowski," he said promptly.

All of a sudden JC remembered he was in Hong Kong. "Oh, shit, Dr. Ralph, I forgot there must be a time difference."

"It's JC, of course." Dr. Ralph knew immediately it was her, though she had not announced herself.

JC thought he sounded a bit distant, impatient even. "Of course it is," she replied quickly. "And Dr. Ralph . . . *Ralph*, I mean, I wouldn't be calling if it wasn't important. What time is it there, in Hong Kong, anyway?"

"I don't know," he said.

"Oh!" JC was taken aback. Why didn't the man just look at the clock? "You mean you don't *know* what time it is?"

He was definitely impatient. "The curtains are drawn, I'm working on my speech."

"There are clocks in hotel rooms," JC said, still surprised that an organized man like him could be unaware of the hour, even with the time difference and jet lag.

"I have an abiding dislike of clocks," he explained.

Sometimes Dr. Ralph was so pompous JC wondered if they could be friends. She said, "But you live your life by the clock. I mean, an hour here, an hour there, another patient here, another patient there."

"Exactly," he said calmly. "That's why I dislike them. In hotels, I put the clock under the bed."

OMG, the psychotherapist was nuts! "*Under the bed*," JC repeated, stunned.

"So I won't be disturbed by those flickering green digital numbers."

"Oh." She got it now. "It's the visual thing that disturbs you. I can understand that."

"I'm very glad you can," he said. "I don't like to be disturbed."

Did his voice have an edge to it, or was it just her guilt for calling him at whatever late hour it might be in Hong Kong?

"Actually, I'm calling for your advice," she said, and then she told him what was going down with Brad, and about Alex and her sister telling her not to see him.

"Dr. Ralph, please tell me it can't be true about Alex," she begged. "It's all too horrible."

There was a silence. JC thought obviously Dr. Ralph was thinking. She waited, hoping he was going to be on her side. What did she mean "*on her side*"? Was Alex a good guy? Or was he a killer? Could Dr. Ralph give her the answer?

At last he spoke. "JC," he said, "I cannot tell you if it is true, I can only repeat what the detective has said, that Alex needs to be looked into, and also his movements over those few days, and who exactly he is, what he is."

"But I *know* what Alex is! I know *who* he is. Fen knows who he is, she'll vouch for him."

"Fen?"

"My aunt. Oh of course, you don't know the story." JC gave him a rapid fill-in on Alex's stormy night in Big Sur. "I know what I'll do," she said at the end of it, "I'm going to take Alex back down there, to Big Sur, to talk to Fen, help get Vivi's detective off his back. I mean, oh, *Ralph* . . ." (she'd almost called him "Ralphie") "I *like* him."

There was a long pause. Oh God, now she had gone and hurt Ralph's feelings. "Listen," she said, suddenly inspired, "when you get back why don't we go to your cabin for a weekend, the fresh air is bound to get rid of your jet lag and my worries."

"Good," he said.

Another long silence.

"I'll be back in a couple of days," he said finally. "How are things at the shop?"

"Great, just great, I'm here dusting away, polishing, tidying, you know, all those things a girl like me is good at."

"You are better than that, JC, but thank you anyway. Have a nice day," he said, and abruptly he hung up.

A minute later, JC received a text from him. *We have a date at the cabin next weekend. Okay with you?*

JC's heart sank; she had committed herself. Not only committed, she had suggested it! Now, though, she did not want to go and didn't know how to get out of it.

39

Fen was driving back from Carmel where she'd enjoyed lunch with a couple of friends. For once she had not taken Hector with her; he would have had to wait in the car and she never liked that. She drove quickly, anxious to get back and let him out for a run.

Though it was still only November, Carmel had looked so Christmasy, all strung with colored lights, ornaments slung between the old buildings, a tinseled tree. Fen wondered if it was only her, or did Christmas seem to come earlier every year. Nevertheless, she'd been inspired to pick up some new multicolored lights. She had some already, of course, but somehow by the time she got them wrapped around the tree there always seemed to be one light missing so nothing lit up at all. Better to be safe than sorry was her thinking.

The girls had promised to be there Christmas Eve, when they would have oysters and she would make the traditional French fish soup. At midnight they would attend the carol service at the local church. They would roast the turkey together on Christmas Day with Fen's special stuffing: apple, sausage, sage and onion, slathered in brandy. She would use the last of the bottle she and the Intruder had drunk together, that famous night of the great storm.

She allowed herself to think about Alex again. About them. There was no going back, and there was certainly no going forward.

It was after three when she pulled into her driveway. Hector heard the crunch of her tires and was behind the door leaping with delight that she was back. She gave him a hug—my, he was a big dog. Kissing his graying muzzle she said, "Don't worry, Hector, my boy, we're getting old together, you and I. Alone here, in our tranquil retreat."

She took off her wine-colored overcoat, bought in Paris a decade or two ago. It had been expensive even then, but cashmere lasted.

She unraveled her scarf—orange, blue and yellow, loosely hand-knitted and bought at a charity sale for rescued animals, and every time she wore it she thought of other dogs like Hector who needed homes and a bit of money, and who gave the priceless return of love and loyalty for your small investment. She slipped off the pointy-toe boots that still killed her, put on green Hunter wellies, and a quilted weatherproof jacket, then followed Hector out the door. The poor dog deserved a walk after waiting all this time.

She took the path—well worn by her feet and Hector's—through the little copse, out onto the cliff beyond, and stood for a minute or two while Hector raced off his energy, gazing out over the Pacific, rolling smoothly, inevitably, in. There were no great hissing waves today; simply a deep calm that made you sense the dark fathoms that lay beneath the green surface shimmer.

She walked on, skirting the edge of the cliff, the sound of the sea in her ears, and Hector's barking.

Hector's barking?

She stopped, looked around. Where was Hector anyway? There he was, racing toward a man standing near the edge of the cliff, a hundred yards or so away.

"Hector!" she called. She was too far away to recognize the man, though she felt sure anyhow it was a stranger. No one here would dress in a suit for a walk on the cliffs.

The man obviously had not noticed them, but, watching, Fen saw him take two objects from under his arm, then fling first one, then another over the edge of the cliff. He turned to look at the dog coming at him. Fen saw him crouch, lean in to the dog, who barked joyfully; everyone was always glad to see Hector. And then she saw the man kick Hector in the throat.

She stood riveted to the spot. Her hand flew to her mouth.

"*Hector!*" she screamed.

The dog was lying on the ground. The man kicked him again, one shove and he would be over the cliff, but then the man spotted Fen and set off running . . .

Fen stumbled to the edge of the cliff and fell to her knees beside Hector.

She cradled the dog's big head in her arms, strangling on her own sobs. Hector's eyes were closed, he was limp, unmoving. Below the cliff the shimmering green tide rolled smoothly in, unknown depths where the secret of what the man had thrown there would remain hidden.

Fen found her mobile and called the vet. He would be there immediately. Then she called 911.

40

Fen rode in the back of the veterinary ambulance with Hector's head in her lap. An oxygen mask was strapped to his muzzle and she could hear him breathing, but so slowly she despaired.

"Please, give him more oxygen," she said to the nurse, sitting beside her in her vet-nurse's jolly outfit with its pattern of blue-and-pink cats and dogs.

"We're trying our best, Mrs. Dexter," the nurse said kindly. "And so is Hector."

Of course he was. Hector had always done his best. Fen held back her tears, she had to be strong, give that strength to Hector! "Never give in" had always been her motto in life; in fact sometimes she thought she should have it inscribed like a heraldic sign over her doorway, the way the gates to hell were supposed to say "Abandon Hope All Ye Who Enter Here." Which was where that bastard who'd kicked Hector would end up.

"I'll kill that bastard myself if I ever meet him," she said out loud.

The nurse looked at her, surprised. "I shouldn't worry, Mrs. Dexter," she said. "The cops'll get him, they're good at that sort of thing."

"I'm sure they are, but nobody's dog has ever been kicked to death by a stranger before." Fen stroked Hector's soft beigey fur which, when he was young, had been as golden as her own hair.

Then they were at the veterinary hospital and big Hector was rolled out on a gurney, Fen thought just the way patients must be in her niece's hospital, and just as much care was being given to her dog. He was so much more than "her dog." Hector was her friend. Her best beloved. Hector was a bona fide member of her family.

Fen and the vet knew each other well. She had been coming to him for Hector's shots and minor illnesses since he was a pup, and they occasionally met at social functions, a concert in Carmel, or at a dinner party. It was a small community and everyone cared. Now, he hugged her, said he would take care of Hector, insisted she go to the waiting room, have some coffee, he would keep her posted.

Fen put out her hand to stop the gurney as Hector was wheeled away. She looked at the familiar face, stroked the soft ridge of fur over his nose. He looked as though he was sleeping.

"Thank you," she said to the vet and the nurses. "I know you'll do your best." Then she went and sat on a bench outside in the fitful sunshine and called Vivi.

Vivi's phone did not ring; it had obviously been switched off so Fen could not even leave a message. Instead, she called JC, who picked up on the first ring.

"Fen, I was just going to call you," she said, surprised. "I need your help."

"No," Fen said, her mind still with Hector.

"*What?* You don't understand. I might be in trouble."

"It's Hector," Fen said, and despite herself the tears came. "I'm at the vet now. Hector's injured. Oh, JC, I don't know if he'll make it."

"Jesus!" JC groaned. Hector meant everything to her aunt. "Are *you* all right?" she asked, then, "What am I saying. *Of course,* you're not all right. I mean, tell me what happened."

"It was a man, a stranger. I knew that because he was in a suit and nobody goes for a walk on my cliffs in a suit. I saw him throwing something over the edge. Well, you know Hector, he went bounding up to say hello. I don't know if the man thought he was going to attack, anyhow he kicked Hector right in the throat . . . oh God, JC, my boy went down like a dead dog . . ."

JC was silent, trying to take in the horrifying picture of a man kicking Hector, of Hector terribly injured . . . of her aunt in tears . . . Fen *never* cried . . .

"I'm calling Vivi," she said finally. "We'll be there as soon as we can. Hold on, we'll be with you soon, we love you . . . and remember Hector is strong."

"JC, Hector is old," Fen said wearily. "But thank you. I'll see you later then."

• • •

When JC called Vivi's mobile there was no reply.

Since she knew that doctors almost never turned off their mobiles she guessed her sister must be involved in her romance with the detective. She did not have Brad's number but she got it from the precinct where she spoke with his partner, Jerusalem. Detectives did not turn off their mobiles, ever, and when she called Brad, he answered promptly.

JC thought it was better to explain the whole story to him so he could tell Vivi, rather than her going into it all over again on the phone. Besides, she wanted to ask the detective about the stranger her aunt had seen throwing something over the cliff, right before he'd kicked Hector in the throat.

"I'm telling you all this because this man must be caught," she said, trying not to cry. "My aunt said he was throwing something over the cliff, and whatever it was, it was important enough for him to attack the dog and then run off. Fen knew he was a stranger," she added, "because he was wearing a suit. I mean, who wears a suit to go for a walk on the cliffs? And what was he throwing over there that was so important anyway?"

"JC, you've missed your calling," Brad said. "You should be a detective. Of course I don't know what he was throwing over there, and perhaps I never will, but I promise you everything will be done to try to find whoever it was."

"And when you do, you'll arrest him?" JC said urgently. "You'd better, before Fen kills him."

"I understand," Brad said gently. "And don't worry, I'll tell Vivi. She'll call you right back."

JC was still at the store. She turned out the lights and collected her things. She was just locking the door behind her when Vivi called.

"I'll pick you up," Vivi said. "We'll drive down to Big Sur. Meet me back at the house, I'm calling Fen now."

JC said okay; then, because there was dread in her heart for her aunt, who was about to lose her beloved friend, and she was feeling very alone, she called Alex.

She didn't care anymore what the detectives thought about Alex, or didn't think about Alex. JC knew Fen cared about him and that was good enough for her. And she knew Alex cared about Fen. Fen had been a rock in the storm for Alex that night, and now he could be the rock for her.

41

Charlie Lew, immaculate in a black pinstripe suit of fine light-weight wool, with a black Sea Island cotton shirt and silver silk tie, was sitting in the back of one of his lesser-known and very small cafés, tucked behind a noodle factory at the very end of a dark and narrow cul-de-sac, watching a game of *pai gow*. The stakes were higher than usual and at least one player was betting his shirt. Charlie's face remained impassive. In fact there was no sign of excitement in the small back room which contained only a green baize table, six straight-back cane chairs and a dozen or so empty bottles of beer. An overhead lamp swung low directly over the game area leaving the corners of the room in shadow. Blue swirls of smoke curled under the lamp. The only sound was the slapping of cards and the occasional grunt of acknowledgement as somebody lost. Or won.

Charlie was not playing. He provided the premises, the dealer, and the security and received a percentage of the winnings. Charlie knew what he was doing.

He was not amused therefore, when his mobile buzzed urgently in the breast pocket of his shirt. It was not good chi to interrupt the flow of the game. He slid quietly from the room, emerging directly into the café behind the white-tile counter, where a young Asian in a Yankees baseball cap was shifting chicken broth around in a steel pan, stirring in the heads and feet to add flavor. There were no customers and Charlie felt free to check his text message.

It was from a sales clerk at the camera store. He told Charlie someone had just come in and bought exactly the same tripod the killer had used when videoing his victims.

Charlie was not normally excitable but this time the adrenaline flowed. This might be an important clue. He wondered if he should alert Brad first, or call the salesman back and tell him to keep the customer there until the police and Charlie arrived.

He speed-dialed the store's number and was told the customer had already left.

"Go after him," Charlie ordered. "Follow him immediately."

"Sir, it was a woman," the salesman said. "And she left five minutes ago."

Sweat beaded Charlie's upper lip as he exited the café heading for the store and called Brad Merlin on the phone. He stepped up his pace until he was almost running. People turned to look. Nobody had ever seen Charlie Lew run and they wondered if the law had finally caught up with him.

When Charlie got Brad on the phone, he gave him the story, said he was already on his way to the store. "Don't worry," he added, "our security cameras should have gotten her. That's why we have them."

. . .

Brad and Jerry met with a screech of brakes outside the camera shop, hurtling out of their separate vehicles. Watching them, Charlie thought they were exactly like cops from *CSI*, though he much preferred the old *Miami Vice* himself. In fact he had the complete set of videos and had based his own "look" on Don Johnson's.

Now he smoothed back his already smooth hair, mopped the sweat from his face, and said, all formal, "Welcome to my store, detectives."

"Oh quit that shit, Charlie," Brad said impatiently. "Where's the guy who sold the tripod?"

The young salesman was standing in the middle of the store, beaming with excitement.

"I got her," he told Brad confidently, because though he was a recent immigrant from China he had already watched a lot of detective shows and knew what was expected. He was young, maybe twenty-three. Brad knew that in this young guy's mind, tonight he would be a star in his own firmament in the Chinese community; the man who had helped catch the serial killer.

"Describe her," he said.

"Caucasian. Middle of ages. Hair brown, maybe gray. Glasses, heavy brims."

"Rims," Charlie corrected.

The salesman ignored him. This was *his* moment.

"No smile," he went on. "Middle tall, middle short. A fat skirt and ankles."

"You noticed her ankles?" Charlie protested. "You were supposed to be selling a customer a tripod!"

"Gray jacket, blue blouse under. No rings."

"No rings?" Brad said. "That was a good observation."

"Thank you." The young salesman beamed, while worried Charlie scanned his camera store for customers who might be distracted and put off by the detectives' presence.

"Perhaps we can speak in the rear end room," he whispered behind his hand to Brad, who shook his head.

"How did the woman pay?" Brad asked.

"Cash, sir, Detective. The lady pay cash. I keep it to one side, thinking maybe you need to test it for fingerprints."

"Good thinking," Brad told him. He asked his name and was told it was Keanu.

Jerry stared at him, surprised. "Like in Keanu Reeves?"

The young man looked bashful. "I take name of actor I like," he said. "It suits me better than my Chinese name, here in San Francisco. And the girls like it," he added.

They were definitely getting off track. Charlie was pacing nervously between the door and the counter, behind which the three other members of his staff stood watching what was going on. Brad put the money in a plastic bag.

"By the way, Keanu," he said casually, "what kind of purse was she carrying? Y'know, like a leather tote, or what?"

Keanu closed his eyes, thinking. "I know it," he said, a moment later. "It was a straw bag, a basket like women carry when they go grocery shopping, or maybe to the beach. Medium size. It had little beads on the front, sparkly beads. She put the tripod in there when she left."

Charlie interrupted. "The security video is ready for you to see," he said, looking excited.

And so he should, Brad thought, though by now he was doubting the female tripod buyer was their serial killer. Not with that straw bag with the beads on it . . . a woman like that wouldn't go round killing other women and getting her jollies off.

"Great minds think alike," Jerry said to him, knowing that Brad also did not believe the woman was the person they were looking for.

Brad shrugged, running his hand thoughtfully through his hair. "Maybe the killer sent her to buy it for him? It's a special small tripod, the same kind that would fit the small camera the killer must have used."

They stood around in the darkened back room while Charlie ran the video. Like most simple security videos it was not detailed enough though the woman could be seen both entering and exiting the store. Brad thought Keanu had done a good job: she looked exactly as he had described her. It was not possible to see her face, she was walking too fast and the camera caught only a blur. From her determined walk though, Brad guessed she was maybe in her early fifties, her gray hair pinned sharply back.

She was not who he was seeking but it was a step in the right direction. One more piece in the jigsaw.

42

The man was sitting in a Big Sur café overlooking the ocean. A glass of chilled white wine was on the table in front of him, along with a basket of warm sourdough bread. Olive oil was presented instead of butter, with an added slurp of balsamic vinegar, a rather outdated touch the man thought. He was not hungry but he had been awake for forty-eight hours straight and he needed to slow down, take stock. Things were not good.

He took a piece of bread from the basket and dipped it into the oil. As he lifted it to his mouth he observed that his hand shook. A thrill of pain shivered down his arm, like tiny needles. He put the bread down, reached instead for the wine, swallowing deeply.

He removed his Ray-Ban sunglasses, took the clean white handkerchief from his breast pocket and mopped his brow, surprised to find he was sweating. It was a chilly day and he had elected to sit outdoors, the only diner to do so. He contemplated taking off the jacket but since he was wearing a suit thought it might look a little conspicuous. And he never wanted to be that.

He drained the glass of wine, lifted a hand to catch the waiter's eye and ordered another, warning himself all the while not to drink too much; waiters were aware these days of drinking and driving: they kept an eye on their customers. And rightly so. One should not be reckless on the road.

But reckless was what he had become. He had lost control. *Allowed* himself to lose control, was more like the truth. His hand shook again as he lifted the glass to his lips. He sipped this time, savoring the Sonoma Chardonnay. He knew the Sonoma area well, knew the vineyard in fact; small, well tended, one of those places with a cute name and an even cuter label on the bottle. He guessed that's the way competition went in the wine market these days, it wasn't so much the quality of your wine as how eye-catching your label. Any gimmick in a storm. His thoughts returned to himself and his predicament.

Of course Jekyll and Hyde had always been used as the psychological image of the dual personality, though he considered himself much cleverer. He was educated, charming when needed; he wore good suits, drove a good car, made a good living. He had the kind of discreetly expensive home a man in his situation should have, and he attended all the correct museum openings, concerts and galas in the correct company. In between, over the years, he killed people. His easy charm and good reputation as a charitable man went a long way, and he never gave anyone a glimpse of what lay beneath.

Was his condition pathological? Of course it was, he didn't need a therapist to tell him that. It was who he was. And he enjoyed it. Except now, it was different. Now, he was out of control, he had become careless, he was no longer the voyeur choosing his women carefully, stalking them, videoing them as they walked down the street, went about their daily lives. Getting to know them made the ending so much more pleasurable.

But now there was Elaine, who for God's sake still would not die, and might at any time wake up and remember what happened. Then the hooker, where it had all gone wrong, and he'd made the triple-threat mistake of not only picking her up and paying her, but of driving her to his home. And now the latest, chanced at the gas station restroom, still out there, in the woods, her throat cut and maybe—because he had been unprepared and supremely careless, with his own DNA on her because he had not had a condom. Of course he had cleaned her up as best he could, but it brought back the memory of his younger sister, who was fifteen, and the night he had killed her. His first one.

His story to the cops was that the sister had gone missing. Later, they found her body in woods. He'd helped them search, of course, the poor agonized brother—he was thirteen and sexually preco-cious and the sister had lured him on in her low cut tank tops, and her long brown hair, sprawling on the sofa, laughing at him.

It had been his first great pleasure to slit her throat and fuck her. He'd lured her into the woods by telling her a boy she fancied was waiting for her. He also told the cops about that boy, and they had actually arrested him and checked him out. It was before DNA was used to accurately define the identity of the criminal, and they'd had no evidence and the boy was released. Nobody ever went to jail. His mother was dead, his army father long gone in some bar fight in Seoul, South Korea. Nobody cared.

After that first "pleasure" he had been "celibate" as he liked to call it, for a long time. He'd gone on to college, then university, gotten his degrees, met as a social equal for the first time with fellow students, and then with professors and businessmen. He took girls out, charmed them, dropped them. Like hot stones, he thought now. They were not for him. When he needed he would choose more carefully. And she would be of a certain type, look a certain way: the long soft brown hair like his sister's; the smooth white neck. She'd be petite with sparkling eyes and a wide smile. She would be a good, trusting girl—and of course she would trust him.

But now, like a crazed fool, he had blown it. He had gone mad with irresistible lust. Not for blood, he was no movie-actor-vampire, though he did love the smell of blood, but for the thrill of the chase, of the setup with the camera, of the helplessness of a naked woman spread out before him. The thrill of his power.

He suddenly became aware of the waiter asking him a question, remembered he was in the café, remembered kicking the dog and the stupid woman screaming at him, remembered he had had no sleep for two days and nights. Exhaustion swept over him and his hands shook as he accepted the bill in a plastic folder, inserted his credit card and handed it back to the waiter. He signed, left a decent tip, twenty percent was always appreciated, and walked out to the parking lot.

No need to check the gas gauge, he'd filled up the night before. It was a longish drive but he would be back in San Francisco that evening. Back home. Safe from the strange impulses that had taken over him. The next day he would begin work on his chosen victim again. Dr. Vivian. Now *she* was simply perfect.

43

B rad stared at the message on his iMac not wanting to believe it. He put a hand wearily over his eyes. Another woman was dead and he had failed to prevent it. The burden of responsibility bowed his broad shoulders. Who knew how many more before this madman stopped. If he ever would stop. Brad doubted it; this killer was on a roll and he was enjoying it.

He studied the information on the screen again. This was a different murder though. First and most importantly, there was no green Post-it message saying *Please Don't Tell.* Plus the woman was arranged differently, not with the usual meticulous care, arms spread, hands just so, legs apart. She had been raped but this time no condom had been used and there was semen. There would be DNA. If this was the same killer and not a copycat—something not unknown in multiple sex murder cases like this, just some other "crazy" wanting his fifteen minutes of fame—then their man had gotten careless.

Brad's guess was that this time he had acted on impulse. And impulses led to mistakes.

The woman had been found by the Highway Patrol south of San Francisco near Big Sur. They did not yet know her identity but probably would before too long, since her picture was already on TV and being circulated in the area. Nobody was wasting time. Fear was sweeping the city. It was like the era of the Boston Strangler when women stayed indoors or went out only in groups, trying never to be alone, locking their doors and windows carefully, always aware the killer might be somebody they knew.

Brad took the next incoming call, one of hundreds from would-be witnesses who thought they might have helpful information. This one was from the manager of a gas station on Route 1, a half-hour drive from where the body had been found.

"I have some information," the man told him, importantly, as they all did.

Brad immediately pressed the record button, and warned that he had done so.

"That's good," the caller said, "because you guys'll need this info on your books. I know the woman. What I mean is, I don't know her name, but I've seen her here at my gas station plenty of times, picking up truck drivers, if you get what I mean."

Brad put his feet on the desk, interested. "A hooker," he said.

"She'd hang out, y'know, till I'd have to ask her to move on. Regular customers don't like it, women like her loitering, checking out their husbands while they're filling the tank. She'd laugh at them, but she was older, looked as though she was having a hard time servicing the guys who'd pick her up and drive off."

Brad said, "Get to the point."

"The point is I saw her pick up this guy last night. Not a trucker, a regular guy driving a black Range Rover. He's, like, comin' out of the restroom and so is she. He gives her the eye and she gets in the car. Simple as that."

Brad was already putting on his jacket. "You have security cameras?"

"We do. You can bet it's all there."

"What's your name?"

"It's Hank, sir. Hank Brandolini." He gave Brad the address.

"We'll be with you in half an hour, Mr. Brandolini, and thanks for the information. I must ask you not to talk to the press," he added, and was reassured that of course Hank would not. Brad didn't believe him. Everybody wanted to be a celeb.

It was when he and Jerry were about to board the helicopter that he got the call from the sheriff's department. A handbag had been swept ashore in Carmel. The contents were soaked but the driver's license was encased in plastic. It belonged to Elaine Mary McCarthy.

A second call came immediately from a fellow officer. A security tape at San Francisco Airport had identified the number of a Range Rover parked there as belonging to Alex Patcevich. It was parked there the night his fiancée was killed, picked up two days later.

"It's our man all right," Brad said, as they strapped themselves in for the flight. "He was in that area yesterday. Vivi's aunt saw him throwing something over the cliff. I'm willing to guess they were the victims' handbags. Our predator has changed his method; he's not searching out his victim and stalking her first. He's behaving irrationally, picking up a woman like this one at the gas station on impulse. Our killer is disturbed, Jerry, and I'm wondering what happened to change him."

"He's not changed that much," Jerry said. "The fucker's still killin'."

Jerry was nervous. He needed his kids to calm his soul. He couldn't be without them for long and now he switched on his phone and summoned up a photograph of his baby son. "Growing up to look just like his pa," he said proudly, showing it to Brad.

"Then let's hope his pa turns out to be someone he can be proud of because he caught the serial killer of the decade," Brad said, sharply.

"Hey, just showin' ya the kid." Jerry put away his phone, huffed. "No need to go off on me."

"Shit, man, I'm sorry. It's just that I'm thinking of Vivi down there at Big Sur. Her aunt, Fen Dexter, lives in an isolated cottage on the cliffs. Our killer was right next door when Mrs. Dexter saw him throwing those handbags over the edge. The man kicked her dog in the throat. She said it went down like a ninepin, might not make it. He ran off but she was too distraught over her dog to think to look where he went or what he was driving. But you can bet your boots, Jerusalem, it was a black Range Rover."

Jerry snapped his fingers. "And I can also bet that's how close the aunt came to being sent over the edge of that cliff too. Shit, Brad, this is getting too close to home."

· · ·

The gas station manager, Hank, was waiting for them in his office, along with a couple of the local sheriffs and a couple of his deputies, already contacted by Brad. The five of them stood around while Hank replayed the security video for them.

Brad wished, as always, that security cameras took better pictures; they were always in jerk-time, fast movements, faces obscured. He had Hank run it again in slow-mo.

The black Range Rover parked in the shadows at the back of the station. It was impossible to see the number or identify the driver, but they saw the man get out and walk to the restrooms. He was wearing a black ski cap and Ray-Bans even though it was dark.

Brad had Hank stop the film while they studied him. The man was of medium height, slight build, and wearing a suit which looked out of place with the black ski cap pulled low over his forehead, and also obscured his facial features.

Hank ran the tape on and they watched the man stride toward the restroom, a long confident stride.

"Wait a minute," Brad called. "Stop it right there, Hank." He turned to Jerry and said, "Take a look at our man's shoes. Tell me what you see."

Jerry peered at the screen, saw the recognizable snaffle-bit buckle. "Jeez," he said after a moment, "I'm looking at Guccis."

He glanced up at Brad as they high-fived. "Dr. Sandowski got it right, Jer," Brad said. "Our killer is a man of means, he wears expensive shoes, he drives an expensive vehicle, and I'll bet he goes to expensive places for dinner. He's no garage mechanic. We're definitely looking at a man of the world."

He signaled Hank to run on the tape. And there she was, the redhead, emerging from the restroom in a denim skirt so short there was no point in trying to tug it down the way she was on camera. She looked up when she saw the man emerging from the gents' at the same time. In seconds she was walking with him to the Range Rover. She closed the door. And he drove off.

Hank switched off the tape. They stood silently, each thinking that they had just seen the last moments of the woman's life.

Brad organized for the tape to be sent at once to headquarters, while he and Jerry would go into Carmel to collect the handbag fished from the ocean.

"Did you notice Alex Patcevich wears Guccis?" Jerry asked, in the back of a police car en route to Carmel.

"I never saw him wear dark glasses at night," Brad said.

"You didn't see him stalking women at night either."

Brad was thinking about Vivi and her sister, about them alone with their aunt, about the dog kicked by the killer right there, on the cliff near her cottage.

He leaned over, tapped the driver on the shoulder, said, "You know where Cliff Cottage is, somewhere between Big Sur and Carmel?"

"Mrs. Dexter's place, y'mean? Sure I know it, sir. Everybody round here knows Mrs. Dexter. We're all sorry about her dog."

Brad thought news traveled fast in these parts. He told him to drive there first. He needed to see Vivi. He needed to see that the aunt was all right. He needed to ask her some questions. And he needed to see if Alex was there.

Vivi was glad when Alex offered to go with them to Big Sur. JC rode with him in his Range Rover while Vivi followed in her Jeep.

She had changed into jeans and a blue sweater with her camo-quilted jacket and flat black boots. Her sister of course was wearing Vivi's own green cashmere polo with her ripped jeans and towering red platforms. Total country wear, Vivi thought resignedly. There was no way to change JC.

She was so tired she wished she could just sleep, simply cut out the tragic events happening around her and remember the way things used to be not so very long ago. Somehow violence had invaded her life, not only at the hospital but also now closer to home.

They got there in record time. When they got out of their cars Alex pointed out the damaged tree he'd hit the night of the storm.

"Without that storm, without that tree, I would never have met your aunt," Vivi heard him say, but Vivi was thinking about Brad, about being in his arms only a few hours ago, about how safe she'd felt with him, how protected, cared for.

Fen heard the cars and hurried out to meet them. She enfolded both girls in her arms. Looking up, she saw Alex leaning against the car.

"Welcome back," she said quietly, then led the way indoors.

JC thought Fen looked tired. "How is Hector?" she asked.

"He's what they call 'holding his own.'"

Vivi recognized that consoling phrase; she hoped this time it was true.

"The man didn't succeed in breaking Hector's windpipe," Fen added. "And he didn't break his neck, though the way he kicked my poor dog, I felt sure he had. They've operated, patched him up, I suppose." She looked appealingly at Vivi, her doctor-niece. "You understand all that stuff, it's what you do every day."

"Not exactly, but I'll call the vet now, find out what the story is and if we can go and see Hector."

Fen's head drooped. She sank into a chair at the kitchen table. "I said goodbye to him," she said quietly. "Just in case. We've been friends for twelve years, you know. That's a long time."

The kettle was boiling and Vivi made a pot of tea, the *lapsang souchong* her aunt always used. Nothing ever changed here, yet now it had. She wondered if anything would ever be the same again.

Alex had been standing quietly, listening. Now he went and sat next to Fen. He took her hand and held it in both of his. "He'll be okay," he said.

Fen glanced searchingly at him. "How do you *know*?"

"Trust me, this time I know."

Vivi went into the other room to call the vet. If it was bad news she did not want her aunt to guess it from her end of the phone conversation, but then she was told Hector had rallied.

"He came through surgery well," the vet was saying. "He's an old boy but he's alert and ready to get out of here. In fact I think he'd be better off at home. Tell Mrs. Dexter to keep the plastic ruff on so he can't worry at the stitches and he'll be fine. A bit doped up so he's feeling no pain. He's all yours; just bring him back again day after tomorrow for a checkup."

"We thought he was dead," Vivi said, relieved.

"So did I when I first saw him, but hey, this is Fen Dexter's dog. He's not about to quit so easily. We'll drop him off in half an hour if you like."

Vivi thanked him and went to tell her aunt the good news.

Fen looked stunned for a moment, then of course she cried. "It's so silly," she sobbed. "I told myself I couldn't cry, I had to be strong for Hector when he needed me and now I'm bawling like a baby." Alex went and put his arms round her.

Watching them, Vivi thought how tender he was, taking care of Fen the way she must have taken care of him the night he'd shown up wounded on her doorstep.

"I'll fix some sandwiches," JC said, surprising Vivi because she'd imagined a sandwich was something JC thought you bought in a shop. But her sister was already rummaging in the refrigerator.

"I didn't know you had a sandwich talent," Vivi said.

"I worked in a sandwich bar in Napa when I was broke. In a couple of weeks any girl can learn to make a decent sandwich."

"I'll bet yours is special," Alex said to JC, but he was looking at Fen.

Then the vet van was there and Hector was being carried into the kitchen with a big plastic ruff round his neck, like a Victorian baby bonnet.

"I could swear he's smiling," Fen said, fussing over his cushion where the dog now lay, tail thumping slowly on the kitchen floor. She needed Vivi's medical opinion and to comfort her, Vivi took Hector's pulse. He licked her hand, grateful to be home, then sighed and lay back on his bed.

Tires crunched on the gravel. "Are you expecting someone?" JC asked, as a knock came at the door.

Fen shook her head. "Perhaps it's a neighbor anxious to see how Hector's doing."

But when Vivi answered the door Brad was standing there, looking at her, unsmiling, serious.

She had almost forgotten how big he was, how rugged, with his offbeat good looks. His wife must have been crazy to leave him for a free Hawaiian holiday. "Oh, it's you," she said, pleased. But this time Brad did not lean in to kiss her cheek.

"I'm sorry," he said, "but I'm here on business. I know Alex Patcevich is here. We need to talk to him."

"About what?" JC came to the door, standing next to Vivi.

Brad said, "This is my partner, Detective Jerusalem Guiterrez."

Jerry nodded a greeting. His face was as cool as Brad's.

Now Fen came to the door. "Why don't you ask these gentlemen in," she asked, surprised. "Whoever they are."

Brad gave a small bow. "I'm Detective Brad Merlin."

Vivi saw Fen's worried frown turn into a smile.

"Brad Merlin," Fen said warmly. "I've heard about you. Welcome to my home. I suppose you've come to see my niece, Vivian."

"In fact, no, ma'am. Not this time. Detective Guiterrez and I are here on business. We're here to ask Alex Patcevich some questions."

"And what kind of questions would those be?" Alex came forward. Now they were all huddled in the small doorway.

"Mr. Patcevich, you might prefer to speak in private," Brad suggested.

"You can ask everything you need to ask right here, in front of my friends," Alex replied.

"In fact, sir," Jerry said, "*we* would prefer to talk business in private with you."

Alex nodded and stepped outside. He turned to look at Fen, still standing in the doorway, looking stunned. "It'll be okay," he said with a smile. "Everything's okay."

But somehow Fen knew it was not.

45

Alex was silent on the drive to the local sheriff's station, alone in the backseat. No one else spoke either.

Brad watched him in the mirror. Alex was sitting, head down, shoulders slumped, a frown on his face. He looked like a man in trouble.

When they reached the station Alex walked in, between Brad and Jerry. They had not cuffed him because he had not been charged with any crime.

In the small room used for that purpose, Brad took his place behind the table and indicated that Alex should sit opposite. Jerry chose to stand to one side, in the "good cop" role, leaning against the wall, hands shoved in his jeans pockets, watching, listening.

"Mr. Patcevich," Brad began, "you will remember being interviewed at the time your fiancée was killed. We have it on record and I'm going to remind you of what you said then. We asked your whereabouts that day. You said that you were in Los Angeles all week, that you had planned on joining your girlfriend that weekend, in San Francisco. You were going to take a wine country tour."

"The Napa Valley," Alex agreed. "We'd booked into the Auberge."

"Mr. Patcevich, that hotel is in Sonoma County. Not Napa."

Alex shrugged. "Sorry, I forgot, I'm not sure about wine country, I've never been there."

"You bought a new car that week."

"Yes, I did. The Range Rover. The one you saw outside Mrs. Dexter's place just now. You may not know the story but Mrs. Dexter and I met the night of the great storm. I skidded off the road and hit her tree."

"I know," Brad said. "And was that the first time you had driven in the Range Rover to San Francisco?"

Alex waited just long enough before replying for Jerry to catch the hesitation.

"It was," Alex said finally. "When I got the news about my fiancée I was too distraught to drive. I flew instead. I stayed a few days, long enough to take care of things that needed to be taken care of, including talking to your guys." He looked Brad in the eye as he added, "I'm still trying to make sense of it all. You have no idea how often I ask myself why? Why *her*?" He flung out his hands. "I still have no answer."

"Then maybe you have an answer to this. Your Range Rover has recently been identified by its number, parked in the lot at the airport the night your fiancée was murdered. You were also caught on the security cameras, picking it up from there two days later. You were in San Francisco when she died, Mr. Patcevich, and I need you to tell us why."

Alex bowed his head, silent now.

"I'll go get coffee," Jerry said. He looked at Alex, asked, "You take sugar? Milk?"

Alex said nothing and Jerry shrugged.

Brad sat watching Alex, who seemed incapable of moving.

Jerry came back with the mugs of lukewarm coffee, boosted with sugar. He felt sure they were going to need it. He set one down in front of Alex, then Brad, and went back to his position against the wall, sipping and watching.

"Please try the coffee," Brad said to Alex, more gently now. After all, he had no real evidence against this man, nothing concrete to charge him with: he could only ask questions, get reactions, and hopefully answers. Alex had lied to the police and there had to be a reason why.

Alex ignored the coffee, he ignored Brad, ignored Jerry.

Brad said, "A vehicle, exactly like yours, was identified at a gas station not too far from here last night, when another woman was murdered."

Alex's head shot up and he stared at Brad.

Brad said, "The man was wearing brown suede Gucci loafers, identifiable by the snaffle. Exactly like the ones you are wearing now."

"It wasn't me." Alex spoke for the first time.

"I'm not saying it was."

"Okay, so I was in San Francisco when Julia was killed. I was going to surprise her with the trip to Napa, but then she was murdered and I knew I would be a suspect. Maybe it wasn't the right thing to do but I didn't want that. And I'll tell you *why*, Detective Merlin. Because I wanted to find the man that killed my fiancée and I wanted to kill him myself. I wanted revenge, and I still do. If you're looking for a future killer, you're looking at me." Alex slammed himself back in the small wooden chair.

Brad looked patiently back at him. The evidence was purely circumstantial. Alex had admitted to lying to the police and now he'd given a reason for doing so. The Range Rover and the man in the Guccis at the gas station could have been any man with a car like that and with shoes like that. They had no number plates from there, no viable security picture. They had no evidence of Alex buying a night-vision camera and a tripod, or even owning one. They had no valid reason to keep Alex there.

He said, "Thank you, Mr. Patcevich, for answering our questions. You understand why we had to ask them again, since you misled the sheriff the first time."

"I do. I admit it. And I am sorry." Alex was on his feet now.

Brad said, "We'll have someone drive you back to Mrs. Dexter's."

He watched Alex stride out of the room as though he couldn't wait to get away. He didn't blame him. It couldn't be a good feeling being suspected of some of the most heinous crimes of the decade.

JC couldn't believe it and neither could Fen when Alex simply walked back into the house, told them he had to leave immediately for L.A., without saying one word about what had gone down at the sheriff's station. Then he drove off without so much as a see you soon, call you, or even a thank you.

It was so not like the Alex she thought she knew, Fen was worried.

She said to Vivi, "Can't you at least ask that detective what's going on?"

"I could, but I know he won't tell me. He was here on business, not to visit me."

JC came back inside and closed the door behind her. "*Alex* was the detective's 'business.'" She slumped onto a chair, elbows on the table, head in her hands. "They think it's *him*," she said.

"It'll be okay, you'll see," Vivi said, trying to sound encouraging while inside she was sick with worry.

Fen went to the sink and began to wash the teacups. For once she did not know what to say. They suspected Alex of being the killer. Of course it was not true, but how could he prove that. He could have killed *her* easily that night when she was alone in the storm. But then, she was not this killer's type: he murdered women with long brown hair, young and vulnerable, not too-smart-for-her-own-good older women like her.

Hector snored suddenly, making them laugh, breaking the tension. JC went and lay down next to him. "You're okay, Hector," she said gently. "The killer didn't get you." Then she thought of something. She sat up and looked at Vivi and her aunt. "But it wasn't Alex who kicked Hector. He couldn't have. He was in San Francisco."

Fen stacked the cups on the drainer and dried her hands. "How do you know that, JC? For certain, I mean."

"Because he told me so." JC hung her head, realizing of course that she had no proof at all, it was only what Alex had said. He could have been in San Francisco, or here, or anywhere.

Fen went and sat on the floor next to her in front of the fire, and Vivi came and joined them.

"Look, my darlings," Fen said, knowing she had to be strong, she had to be sure, even though her life was unraveling bit by bit. "We can't allow this to interrupt your lives. What happens with Alex is something *he* has to deal with. Something is wrong but his story must play itself out, and Detective Merlin will make sure he has the right answer."

"The right piece in the jigsaw," Vivi murmured, thinking of Brad saying that for him, solving crimes was like a jigsaw, putting all the pieces together to make a whole picture. Then, and only then, could he know what he was dealing with and exactly what to do.

She looked at her sister, all sad blue eyes and long blond hair. She said, "We have to get back to town. I'm working tonight. Besides, shouldn't you be at Dr. Ralph's antique shop, checking your stock, or something?"

They had just said goodbye and driven off when Vivi's phone buzzed. She was plugged in to Bluetooth and answered it.

It was Brad. His voice was low and urgent. He told her he was worried about her and did not want her to go anywhere alone, especially not the hospital parking garage.

"But why ever not?" Vivi asked, surprised. "Nobody cares about me."

"I do," Brad said. "And I want you to promise me."

Suddenly nervous, Vivi promised. She very much wanted to ask about Alex but knew Brad would not tell her. Instead, she said, "When will I see you?"

Brad's voice softened. "I can take some time off tomorrow. How about you?"

"I'll swap shifts," Vivi said, with a smile on her face. "I could cook you a proper dinner."

"My place or yours?"

"Mine. JC's off to Dr. Ralph's cabin for a couple of days."

"She is?"

Brad sounded surprised and, looking at JC, Vivi realized so was her sister; she had obviously forgotten she'd committed to the "date" and was equally obviously regretting it. She told Brad to be at her place at six-thirty, then with a sideways look at JC's stony face said, "It'll do you good to get away for a while."

"No it won't," JC said. "How can it, when I've just heard Alex might be a murderer."

"He was only *questioned*," Vivi reminded her, but still she knew what JC meant. Things did not look good for Alex.

"So okay," she said, trying her best to sound cheerful, "you'll go to Dr. Ralph's, get a bit of free therapy."

"I sure could use it," JC said.

In San Francisco, later that evening, Vivi just made it to the hospital in time for her shift. She circled the parking garage and quickly found a space on the third floor. It wasn't until she got out of the Jeep and locked it that she remembered she had promised Brad never to be alone there. She looked nervously over her shoulder. This was ridiculous; now he had gotten her scared when she was perfectly safe. This was a *hospital* for God's sake!

Nevertheless, she checked out the other cars as she walked warily by, keeping to the center of the aisle so no one could jump out at her. It was silly she knew, but still she was apprehensive remembering the footsteps that had turned out after all to be only Dr. Ralph.

She was almost at the elevator when she heard the squeal of tires and a car sped round the corner directly toward her. *Her heart jumped. She skipped quickly to one side. Should she make a run for it? Stairs? Or elevator? The car was behind her now, and she was running . . .*

Someone called her name. *"Vivi!"*

She sagged against the wall with relief; it was Dr. Ralph. "Oh my God, it's *you* again!" she said. "I thought you were in Hong Kong."

"Got back early." He leaned over and held the door open. "Get in for a minute, Vivi, I need to talk to you."

Vivi hesitated; she was late for work, there was no time to talk, and anyway what could be so urgent that he needed to talk in the parking garage? Did Dr. Ralph want to tell her he was in love with her sister? He seemed like a man smitten; he'd done so much for JC, giving her the job, a weekend at the cabin, and everything. She checked her watch.

"Sorry, but I'm already late." She gave him a little wave as she hurried to the elevator. "We can talk later. Why don't you call me?"

"*Please*, Vivi." The Range Rover slid closer, almost blocking her access. "I must talk to you, about your sister."

Vivi stopped. He opened the door for her and she smiled hesitantly. "I know you want to talk about JC, but I'm really sorry, I can't. Not now. Why don't you call me later? I really have to go now."

With a ping the elevator stopped at Vivi's floor; people surged out and she stepped in and with a final little wave, pressed the button. The doors closed. How sweet, she was thinking, JC had a "beau." At least that's what Fen would have called Dr. Ralph.

47

Two days later, JC was packing for her visit to the cabin in the woods, a procedure that involved dumping a collection of rather unexotic cotton underwear (unexotic that is for such a would-be glamour girl given the money) in the same beat-up travel bag with which she had arrived the night of the storm. Then, she had simply dumped the contents into Vivi's bureau drawers, shoving her sister's stuff to one side to make room.

"Not that I have much, as you can see," she said disconsolately now, to Vivi, who was sitting on the bed, watching, fascinated.

"As of next Tuesday you'll be earning money, but knowing you, you'll go right out and spend it." Vivi picked out a blue knit top that belonged to her. "I haven't even worn this," she objected.

JC gave one of those one-shoulder I-don't-care shrugs. "You never did learn how to share, even as a kid," she said. "Anyhow, that color doesn't suit you."

Vivi held up the top, frowning. "Are you sure?"

"Certain sure. You're better in pinks and reds, maybe olive green, sort of camo-color, you know."

"I suppose that's why you're taking my jacket."

The quilted khaki jacket lay across the bed and now JC put it on, hugging round her body. "Mmm, cozy," she murmured. "After all, Vivi, you wouldn't want me to catch cold out there in those dripping-wet woods."

"The woods are not dripping, the sun is currently shining and there's a nice breeze."

"Quite the little weather forecaster, aren't you! All I know is it's gonna be *cold* and I'm taking my thermals and I wish I had a woolly vest to go with them, like in the old days. I mean, spending a weekend in a cabin has to be a bit like stepping back in time, wouldn't you think?"

"What I think is that *this* is *Dr. Ralph*'s cabin, therefore it will have every modern convenience including efficient central heating and electric blankets."

"I might rather have one of those nice cozy hot water bottles with its little knitted jacket to keep me warm." JC eyed her sister doubtfully. "You don't suppose Dr. Ralph intends for me to share his bed, do you? I mean he's not, like, into Sex and Romance is he?"

Vivi thought Dr. Ralph might well be into both of those things, and said so. "When I bumped into him a couple of nights ago, in the hospital parking garage, he wanted to talk to me. About *you*, he said."

"Jesus!" Alarmed, JC sank onto the bed, a sweater clasped to her chest, eyes bugging. "I mean, Vivi, I haven't ever thought of him like that, well only in a teasing way, you know, a little meaningless flirting."

"Maybe not so meaningless to him. Men can take these things

seriously. You are a beautiful girl and he's a man getting to the age where he's looking for the right woman."

"Oh God!" JC flung herself backwards and lay staring up at the ceiling. "I should cancel this," she said. "The only reason I'm going is because of what happened with Alex. I need to take my mind off things."

"That is not true. You accepted Ralph's offer before Alex, and anyhow, you can't just back out now."

"Why didn't Ralph call me, anyway?" JC sat up again, looking accusingly at her sister. "You said you saw him a couple of nights ago, but I thought he was still in Hong Kong. He even texted me from there to remind me of our date this weekend."

"I guess he just wanted to make sure you wouldn't let him down. And you're not letting him down, so that's that." Vivi tossed the camo jacket over to JC. "You can borrow this anyway. I won't be needing it. I'm staying home, cooking dinner for Brad Merlin."

"Aah, the *Merlin*." JC's glance was sorrowful. "Lucky you. *I'm* forced to go and rough it up in the friggin' woods. I never was an outdoorsy girl."

"You'll enjoy it." Vivi helped her sister cram the rest of her things, including two of her own sweaters, into the duffel.

JC zipped up the bag reluctantly. "I'll take your car," she said, looking at Vivi. "It's less likely to break down than mine, and it means I don't have to drive with him. If I get fed up or he gets sexy I can head right back home."

"Not too early, I hope," Vivi reminded her. "I have a date and I don't want any unexpected interruptions."

Two hours later, she waved JC off and set out for the Italian market where she bought Parma ham, sliced so wafer-thin it needed little sheets of wax paper between each slice, so they would not stick together in one un-unravelable lump, and meant they could be arranged by her, slice by exquisite rosy-pink slice across her square white china plates, with a generous spoonful of fig compote. After that, they would have fresh, handmade linguini (not handmade by her—also bought from the Italian store). She would serve it merely bathed in a hint of olive oil with roasted garlic, and dredged with fresh Parmesan, the pale kind Vivi liked best and knew came from the spring crop. With it, she would serve the easiest and best salmon dish ever. It was not only labor-saving but also life-saving to a busy hostess. First, she would arrange salmon fillets on a bed of melted butter in an ovenproof dish (enough butter so it came up the sides of the fish); then paint grainy Moutarde de Meaux on top of the salmon, thick enough to cover. More butter poured over the top of that. Twenty to half an hour in a three-hundred-degree oven, *et voila!* The softest, most delicate yet spicy salmon and without an ounce of effort. She thought it better not to tell her guest exactly how much butter had gone into its making, though.

For dessert, a delicious pear tarte, made in France, for heaven's sake, from Trader Joe's; a couple of bottles of Fen's Chardonnay, plus a bottle of light red which Brad might prefer; a baguette, and that was it. No salad, no veggies; Vivi couldn't be bothered. This was to be a romantic dinner . . . no fussing in the kitchen, no dishes . . . *love* would go along with dessert and coffee and kisses. She hoped.

Rushing back home to make her preparations and set the table and change into something sexy, Vivi thanked her aunt silently for teaching her how to put a meal on the table a man would like. She could always trust Fen.

48

The drive was taking longer than JC had expected. She tried calling Dr. Ralph from her cell phone to tell him she would be late but there was no reception. Anyway he was probably out shopping, setting up dinner for the two of them, just the way Vivi was for the detective. The difference was that Vivi and the detective had a "thing" going. True, it was in its first stages, but still a definite "thing," while she and Ralph were just friends.

She slumped behind the wheel, thinking not about Ralph, but about Alex. He had simply disappeared from their lives as easily as he had come into them. Especially Fen's. And as easily as he had come into those other women's lives, she supposed, thinking with a shudder of the murders. She must ask Dr. Ralph about Alex, let him tell her who the true man really was.

She made a left off the highway, down a narrow lane edged with brambles covered in frost. Behind them a mist rose slowly from the fields. No birds sang and JC did not pass another car, which she

303

thought was just as well since the lane was so narrow she might have ended up in the ditch.

The Jeep did not have GPS, though it did have a compass so at least she knew she was heading northwest, which was generally the right direction, and of course she had the directions Ralph had faxed her.

She took another left, drove for a mile and a half, as per instructions, squealing to a halt at what was supposed to be the proper turning; an unpaved country lane that meandered through dense Hansel-and-Gretel-looking woods. Worried now, JC wondered if it could be correct. To a dedicated city girl it looked like it led to the middle of nowhere. Obviously she had made a mistake; she should have taken a right instead of a left. She checked the directions again. No, this *was* the correct turning.

Vivi's old Jeep was tougher than JC had thought, it took the bumps like a pro, though she bounced about, almost hitting her head on the roof. Fuck. She had definitely not bargained for "the outback." She would have turned round had there been room but once you were on that road through the woods there was no turning back. The mist was getting thicker. She guessed they would not be dining out under the stars tonight. She also hoped she could find her way back after dinner because she was definitely *not* stopping the night out here. Now, though, she would just have to keep on going and pray she was on course and would get there sometime soon.

• • •

Brad knew he was going to be late for his dinner with Vivi. It was only five but she had said to be there at six-thirty, and he and Jerry were still going over the security video from the gas station. Something was bothering them and neither could put a finger on it. Was the man in the ski cap and Ray-Bans really Alex? The Guccis were the same and he was the right height and build, though the man in the suit did not look as broad-shouldered. Alex was obviously a guy who worked out and that was reflected in his stance, in the way he held his shoulders, the slight bulge of his biceps under a jacket. Besides, Brad would bet Alex never wore a suit.

He felt Jerry's eyes on him. "What d'ya think?"

"I think we got the wrong man."

"Then I think we should talk to Dr. Sandowski again. Get *him* to rethink, because we sure need his help."

Brad called Sandowski's cell, got no reply, called his office. The prissy secretary answered. "Sorry," she said, "but Dr. Sandowski is still in Hong Kong."

"I didn't know he was traveling," Brad said.

"Why, yes, Detective, the doctor left a couple of days ago. He's at the Grand Hyatt if you need to get in touch, though he doesn't like to be bothered when he's on these trips."

Brad understood. Nevertheless, he called the Hong Kong Grand Hyatt, asked for Dr. Sandowski, and was told he was not registered there. And no, he had not been there in several months, no there was no medical seminar going on, and yes, he always stayed with them when he was in Hong Kong.

Brad didn't like to be surprised. He got the sudden feeling he had put his faith in the wrong man.

"Something's weird here," he said to Jerry. "We need to check out the manifests of all San Francisco flights departing for Hong Kong, even those with stopovers, as well as out of L.A. two days ago. Our doctor has not been seen in Hong Kong. So? Where exactly has he been these last few days? And what has he been doing?"

"Jesus. You thinkin' what I'm thinkin'?"

"I'm thinking the doctor has not been telling the truth. He's disappeared for days on end, everyone thinking he's off on business, at a seminar in Hong Kong. And now I'm wondering exactly where he is."

• • •

Brad sat at his desk, twiddling a pen up and down between his fingers, thinking. He did not like to be fooled, and fooled he had definitely been. "Get someone onto AmEx," he said to Jerry. "I'll bet Platinum is the doctor's card of choice. We'll start from there. He might just have left a paper trail."

He glanced at his watch. He could be wrong; he might get the all-clear and find Sandowski was simply off on a fling with some woman he wanted kept secret. He might even still make his dinner with Vivi. He put down the pen and crossed his fingers. Then he got up and took Flyin' for a walk round the block.

"It was easy," Jerry greeted him when he walked back in. "Our doc had dinner at a bistro near Big Sur last night. He paid with American Express Platinum, left a twenty-percent tip and signed it, right there." He indicated the printout on Brad's desk. "In his own name."

"The night after the hooker was killed," Brad said. "By a guy who wears Guccis and drives a black Range Rover."

"He also wears a suit," Jerry added.

Brad got on the phone, called the doctor's secretary back. "Tell me something," he said. "Did you recently purchase a camera tripod for the doctor?"

"Why, yes, of course," she answered. "The doctor always trusts me with tasks like that. I got it from the Chinese camera store."

"Thanks, that's all I wanted to know." Brad put down the phone and looked at Jerry. "He's our man," he said.

He knew they had to find Sandowski before he killed anyone else. And he had to cancel on Vivi.

She answered on the first ring. "Hey," she said, happily, "it's you."

"It's me," he agreed.

She caught the hesitation in his voice immediately. "So," she said, "what's up then?"

Brad knew she thought he was going to cancel because she already sounded pissed off. He said, "I think we might have identified our killer. He's out there somewhere and now we have to get out and find him before he does it again. I'm sorry, Vivi, but I can't make dinner."

"How come you don't know where he is anyway?" Vivi was too close to tears of disappointment to keep it from Brad, but this time he did not apologize, or attempt to console her. He was just doing his job.

"We don't know, because he was supposed to be in Hong Kong. Turns out he never even went there. He's not at his house and nobody knows where he is."

"*Oh my God!*" Vivi said.

"I'm sorry, Vivi, I know you've worked hard on this dinner, I was looking forward to it, maybe some other time."

"*No!*" Vivi said. Then again. "*Oh my God!* I know *who* you're talking about. It's Dr. Ralph isn't it? Oh my God, Brad, I know where he is. *And JC is with him.*"

49

Ralph Sandowski had always been a meticulous man, even in the crimes he committed. Everything had to be in its place. He left no evidence around his home for his housekeeper to find, though he did throw the black track pants and black cotton polo-neck in the wash for her to deal with. Unless of course there was blood, then he would destroy the garments himself, either burning them along with garden clippings, or tossing them in a city Dumpster, well hidden in plastic bags. He hated that part of things because with it came a form of reality he did not want to face. Once it was over, the killing done, the sexual gratification that filled him with a sense of power achieved, he felt nothing. He did not care for women anyway. He drew them easily, with a smile and his credentials and his pleasant manner. Until lately, when he had diverged from his set script. He had behaved impulsively; he had left a chink in the armor he had so carefully constructed: that of the random killer, though the truth was he had chosen his victims with great care.

Now, he must take even greater care.

He was at the cabin in the room he called his den. The fire was lit against the cold, making the room cheerful, with its two red leather club chairs drawn up to it and a basket of rosy apples on the low wooden table where he had also placed his knife in its Mexican leather sheath, alongside the small camera and the new tripod, and two new black woolen ski masks. One was quite frivolous, with a pompon on top. *Girly*, he'd thought, smiling when he bought it. The salesgirl had smiled too, fluffing up the pompon and saying, "She's gonna like this one, sir."

"You bet she will," he'd replied.

Now, he took one ski cap and the camera and the tripod, carried them into his bedroom and set them on the bed ready for use. He strapped the leather sheath to his leg, lower down this time, by his calf, then looked for a long time at the knife, waiting on the table. Its cold steel glinted in the firelight. No one knew how many times he had used that knife over the years, how many places, how many women, all of them young, voluptuous, pink-cheeked innocents. Until recently that is, when he'd made his impulsive mistake. But he did not want to think of the hooker at the gas station, did not want to remember losing control. He put the knife safely in its sheath on his calf. It felt good there.

The pain shot suddenly down his left arm again, so fierce this time it made him cry out. He sank into the wing chair, gripping his arm with his right hand, forcing himself to take deep breaths. But now the pain shot up the back of his neck. His chest cramped as it sometimes did when he had heartburn. Telling himself bread always gave him heartburn and he should not have eaten that croissant for breakfast at the coffee shop that morning, he waited for the spasm to pass. He had an appointment on Monday with the cardiologist, he would take the tests, get this straightened out. God, though, he couldn't breathe.

He staggered to the door, dragged it open and stood gulping in air. He knew it couldn't be a heart attack because he got checked out regularly every year. He took those dammed stress tests that always left him gasping, until his pulse slowed and he was always given a clean bill of health.

There, now it was doing exactly that. He was okay now, just breathing a bit heavy that's all. Right. He should get on with his preparations. First thing was to check his rifle, a task he enjoyed.

He opened a bottle of wine, not a Bordeaux, a good heavy wine was not for casual drinking, this was merely an inexpensive California Merlot. He took a few sips, contemplating what was to come, then he got on with his task. Everything was all right again. Now.

50

The Jeep chugged uncertainly up the hill through thickets of encroaching bare-branched trees that scratched at the windows and cast a deep shade. JC switched on her lights, focusing her high beams on the half-graveled lane. Shit, Dr. Ralph might have warned her about this. She would have said "thanks but no thanks." What if she was lost? Really and truly lost. My God, she was really losing it, gruesome Hans Christian Andersen—or was it Grimm's—fairy tales were turning into reality. She had always hated those damned "fairy tales" anyway; they were creepy and scared the life out of her as a kid. Now, they were doing it all over again.

Plus she was hungry and wishing she'd thought to bring a sandwich for the journey, the way Fen always used to when they were small.

JC smiled, thinking of Fen, and then, as though she was her goodluck charm, emerged suddenly into a clearing at the top of the hill. Perched at the very top was the most charming cabin. Exactly like

one from a "good" fairy story, all chunky logs with a chimney stuck on one side and there too, in the open doorway stood Dr. Ralph in a ski cap and dark glasses. Dr. Ralph also had a gun tucked under his arm. *Jesus!* He was really serious about hunting, and she did not want to kill any deer.

"Welcome, welcome," he called, smiling. Then noticing her shocked face said, "Oops, sorry, I was just cleaning the Purdeys, didn't mean to alarm you."

"Oh, the famous Purdeys." JC remembered them from the dinner at the Chinese restaurant. "I never knew what a Purdey was till I met you," she said, as he propped the shotgun against the door and hurried to the car to help her out.

"Then now I have the opportunity to teach you all about them."

He pulled her bag from the back, pretending to drop it from the weight. "Whatever have you got in here?" he demanded. "Diving boots."

JC laughed as she gave him a hug; not that she wanted to get too close, nor did she want him to get ideas, but it seemed the right thing to do, hug a friend, kiss both cheeks. Anyhow, he smelled good, sort of like lemonade.

"Too cold for swimming," Ralph said. "Though we do have a beautiful natural pool in the woods, complete with a little waterfall that's delightful in summer. We can take a walk later, if you like, and I can show you."

JC looked back at the narrow road leading through the dense thicket of trees. Almost a forest, she thought. She looked at the neatly shaved fields surrounding the fairy-tale cabin on top of its hill. She hoped it had electricity.

"You're shivering," Ralph said. "Quick, come on in, let's get you

warmed up. I have the fire going, and you can tell me what you would like to drink."

His arm rested lightly over her shoulders as they walked together into the cozy room with the glowing fire and the bowl of rosy apples, the open bottle of wine and two glasses.

"Here, let me take your coat." He put his hands on her shoulders but JC hugged Vivi's camo-coat closer, still chilled. "I'll just keep it on for now," she said, semi-apologetically because he was so obviously concerned for her comfort.

"Then let me pour you some coffee. It's fresh, I made it ten minutes ago. Brazilian dark roast, and there's hot milk too, if you like. Maybe a glass of wine as well?"

JC sank into one of the red leather wingback chairs in front of the fire, still clutching the coat around her. Her feet were numb and she was definitely unhappy but she smiled at him as he fussed with the coffee. He was wearing his ski cap and she thought he must be feeling the chill in his bones too. Plus he still had on the tinted Ray Bans, even though they were indoors.

She wished she had never come. What on earth were they going to talk about for an entire day? *And* night, because there was no way she could drive that friggin' road in the dark and God help her if the car broke down and she was stranded in the middle of those gloomy woods with no cell phone reception. There was no way out of this. She guessed they would just have to talk antiques, then maybe she might get him to give her a bit of the free analysis she obviously needed badly.

"Maybe I'll take that glass of wine," she said wearily. It had been a long drive for nothing. Closing her eyes, she wished she was at Fen's.

"JC?"

Her eyes popped open. Dr. Ralph was bending over her.

"Your wine," he said, smiling.

She could not see his eyes behind the dark lenses.

He stepped back, waiting till she took a drink, then he said, "Why not let me show you your room? Perhaps after that, we can go for a walk? Get the blood pumping in your veins after that long drive? I really want to show you my own private waterfall, it's so beautiful."

"Right," JC agreed. So okay, she would play the role of the good guest, she would drink the wine—not even a *good* wine, she thought, surprised, I mean you'd have thought the doctor might have splurged a little. Oh well, perhaps at dinner he'd go for the better stuff. Meanwhile, good guest that she was, she would look at her room though she was definitely not going to unpack. She wasn't staying long enough for that, even if she had warmed up a little. She would go for that walk in his bloody woods. *Her! The city chick! Walking in woods!* She should have stayed home, except Vivi was having the Merlin over for dinner and she hadn't wanted to cramp her style.

Go, Vivi, she thought, as she quickly dumped her bag in the very small, very dark back room that was to be hers and obediently followed Dr. Ralph to the cabin door, waiting while he unlocked the glass-fronted gun cabinet and took out what looked to JC like a very powerful rifle.

"Oh God," she exclaimed, shocked. "Don't tell me you intend to shoot something with that thing!"

Dr. Ralph relocked the cabinet then turned and gave her a long silent look. "Oh, no, my dear JC," he said finally. "I do not intend to kill anything with this, unless, of course, a wandering bear crosses our path. No, no, you see I'm really not that kind of hunter."

"So what kind of hunter are you then?"

"Why don't we go and find out?"

Ralph's eyes behind the dark glasses held JC's, then suddenly the sharp crack of a shot came from down the hill. He swung round, the rifle at his shoulder, a bullet already in the chamber. *Ready*, JC thought, with a sudden terrified shiver, *to kill*.

"Someone's on my property." Ralph crunched off through the gravel toward the woods. "Come on, JC, I don't want to leave you behind, let's find out what's up. Poachers, I'll bet."

JC did not want to go with him. He was scary. She did not want to know about poachers. She did not want any part of this cabin in the woods and rifle shots coming from nowhere and guns and more guns. Ralph had changed in an instant from the smooth, charming doctor who understood your problems, to a cold stranger. She didn't know this man. She was afraid of him. *She wanted out of there.*

She tried quickly to think of an excuse and how to escape. "Hmm, I think I'll just go back inside and get a hat," she called. "It's so cold out here." She would grab her bag, make a run for the car and just drive off. She didn't care what he thought. It was creepy as hell here.

Inside, the fire flickered cozily and the apples gleamed rosily

Oh God, *why* was she scared? It was ridiculous. The man was a doctor, a psychiatrist, he would probably tell her exactly what was wrong with her if she asked him, only now she didn't want to ask him.

She ran to her room to get her bag, passing his room on the way. She stopped at his door and stood, staring at his bed. On it was a black woolen ski cap. A small camera. A tripod. And a green Post-it pad.

Jesus! Oh Jesus! Fear exploded in JC's head. *Everything she'd ever heard from Brad Merlin and Vivi rushed through her mind: the way the murderer killed his victims, the way he photographed them; the green Post-it notes that said Please Don't Tell* . . .

JC wanted to scream but did not. Nor could she telephone; there was no reception. Her trembling fingers found the car keys still in her pocket. She could escape while Ralph checked the shot from the woods, she might make it back down the hill . . . unless he shot her first! But no, Dr. Ralph had different plans for her. She knew it now.

Her heart was beating so fast she doubted she could make it out of the door, never mind down the hill, but it was her only hope. She saw him still scanning the woods, rifle at his shoulder, and realized she would never make it to the car. She would have to hide in the woods, they were her only answer, her only hope. She was out that door and running.

Trees closed round her, she stumbled over roots, through brambles, thorns tugged at the camo-coat that at least gave her some sort of protection since it was the same color as the landscape. *Thank you Vivi, oh thank you Vivi . . . will I ever see you again . . .*

JC stopped, out of breath, heard him crashing through the thick shrubbery, heard him curse, then a rifle shot . . .

"Don't think you can get away, JC."

His voice came from close by, cutting through the freezing air.

"I know every inch of these woods," he called. "You'll only tire yourself out when we could be having a nice glass of wine in front of the fire, talking about things. You know I have a lot to say to you, JC. You're not exactly my ideal woman, in a way of speaking, but I really care about you. You have an independent spirit that I like, so why not let's call a truce? Come back with me to the cabin and let's talk, before you catch your death of cold."

JC crouched into a groove worn into the hill; it wasn't deep enough to be a cave but at least it gave her some cover. She sat perfectly still. If she moved he might hear. Too afraid for tears or to even breathe too loudly, she waited for her end to come.

Oh Vivi, oh Fen, she thought. *I'll never see you again.*

The tears froze on her face.

51

In Big Sur, the weather was calm but cold. Fen was in her kitchen brewing up a *coq au vin*. She was a classic old-fashioned French cook and she wasn't about to change to any avant-garde deconstructive cuisine with drizzles and discombobulated olives and strawberries reshaped to look like—guess what—olives and strawberries. In her house olives came the way they grew on trees or in a bottle of good oil, like the one she was using now to sizzle the chicken parts while stirring the *mirepoix* (now there was a French word from her long-ago cooking classes at Cordon Bleu in Paris) which meant a mixture of chopped onions, garlic, celery and Roma tomatoes, to which she was about to add a definitely not classical-cooking-school slug of brandy, letting the alcohol flare and burn off before adding her chicken and a bottle of decent wine. Not the *best* wine; that would be a waste, but certainly the decent kind one might drink of an evening, like the one coming up, spent alone. Of course, not exactly *alone*: she was with Hector, who looked angelic in his ruff and was sniffing the cooking smells appreciatively. Hector was not allowed to eat chicken but Fen had a good beef bone the butcher had saved for him and later he would be gnawing happily while she was drinking happily, and probably gnawing on her own chicken bones.

She paused before turning the chicken, glancing out the window at the mist curling in from the ocean. Earlier it had been sunny, a bright, cheerful kind of day. Now though, the fog brought a hint of eternity with it, a half-hidden glimpse of the familiar, made unfamiliar. Without any reason, Fen was suddenly unnerved. She strode to the French doors and flung them open, remembering the storm and the roar of the wind and the rain pounding on her roof like bullets, not so long ago.

Hector came, as he always did, to stand next to her, sniffing the cold air before turning back, preferring the warm kitchen and its good smells. Fen suddenly wished her girls were with her. She wished they all three were in the kitchen, stirring the pots on the stove, snacking on olives and cheese, choosing a wine to drink with the chicken dish.

JC thought about Alex, being questioned by the cops. She had not heard from him since and guessed she never would.

Feeling very alone, she called Vivi on her mobile, surprised when she answered on the first ring.

"Is it you, JC!" Vivi exclaimed when she answered.

Surprised, Fen replied, "No, darling, it's me, Fen." But Vivi sounded upset. "What's the matter?" she said. "Where is JC anyway?"

"Oh, Fen, I wish I could tell you where but I can't. It's not possible, not yet."

Visions of JC in the hospital rushed into Fen's mind. "My God, girl, what are you talking about? Whatever's going on with JC? And *why* can't you tell me? Is she hurt?"

Sensing something was wrong, Hector got up and came to her. She pushed her hand distractedly through his thick golden fur. "Vivi, tell me where JC is," she said. "*Right now. This is your aunt* speaking."

"Later, Fen, I promise," Vivi said. And hung up.

Stunned, Fen held the phone away from her. *Vivi had cut her off.* Immediately she punched in JC's number. The line was dead.

Oh God, what had happened? What was JC up to now? Fen went to the stove and turned off the flame under the *coq au vin.* It didn't seem important anymore.

• • •

Vivi was already back on her phone, trying JC's number for maybe the thirtieth time. Of course there was no reply. Brad had told her there was no reception in that area. She thought of Brad in the helicopter, on his way to Ralph Sandowski's place, and her sister.

JC had taken Vivi's Jeep so now she had to call a taxi to take her back to the hospital. She would wait there, wait to see if her sister, who was at the mercy of a serial killer, was still alive. If she was injured Brad would bring her there. Vivi would look after her. *She would not let JC die.*

• • •

The helicopter droned over the dense canopy of trees where the last of the leaves fluttered to the ground. Yellowed clouds filled with the promise of snow pushed down on them and a gray mist swirled up from the damp ground. From where he sat in the bubble, Brad could see the three helicopters following: one of them was a medevac. Jerry was in one of the others with a SWAT team. There had not been a break in the forested landscape in five minutes yet they were

321

close, Brad knew, to Sandowski's cabin. He could see the narrow road snaking up the hill through the trees, then suddenly, like a mirage, there it was at the top in a clearing. The undergrowth had been cut back in a wide swath all around and the pilot searched for a landing spot, wanting to leave room for the others.

"We got it, sir," he called out over the roar of the rotors and then they were descending, landing with a bump on the rough terrain.

Brad heard the rifle shot as he jumped out. He reached for his AK-47, warning the pilot to keep down. The other two copters fluttered to a landing nearby. The medevac hovered above. Brad gestured a warning to Jerry, who held up his hands to keep the other men back, then came in a crouching run toward him.

"What's going on?" Jerry demanded, already out of breath.

"Rifle shot. Came from the woods, right there." Brad pointed with his gun at the trees nearest the cabin. "Not too far away either, but our guy wasn't shooting at the copter. I'll bet he was shooting at JC."

The SWAT team and their hostage experts swarmed to the trees, forming a human cordon, rifles at their shoulders, fingers already on triggers. The canine unit with its German shepherd waited silently. Brad and Jerry took a stance at the center.

A leaf fluttered loudly from a tree. A small creature rustled the grass. Tension crackled like lightning jabs. Everyone knew their job, knew the importance of getting JC out alive.

Then, through a megaphone that sent his voice slinging through the trees, Brad asked the doctor to surrender.

• • •

Deep in the woods, his own rifle at the ready, and a smile on his face, Dr. Ralph listened.

Let them beg. He wasn't coming out of there until JC was dead. The stupid bitch had upset his entire world, never mind his plans for her and her bitch sister, Vivi. God how he hated them.

"Dr. Sandowski." It was Brad on the megaphone now. "I'm asking you to give yourself up. Let us negotiate. Just let the girl go and you will get fair treatment. There's nothing to be gained now by a meaningless tragedy."

Sandowski was listening, not to Brad though, not the stupid know-it-all detective who believed all crime was a jigsaw puzzle simply waiting to be solved. Nobody would ever have solved this one had it not been for JC's stupidity and, he had to admit, his own carelessness. He had always worked in the dark. Always alone. Just himself in his watch cap and his glasses, with his knife strapped to his calf, ready. Now though, he planned to catch JC before those stupid bastards could even know where he was, or where *she* was. He would spread JC's arms and legs on the bed of leaves that would form her shroud; he would slit each wrist with that so beautiful sharp knife, watch the blood ooze, watch JC's eyes go dark with shock. Only then would he slit her throat.

If these cops thought anything was different they had another think coming. Now, all he had to do was find her. He lifted his head, sniffing the air like a dog. He could almost smell her fear. He knew she was not far away.

. . .

JC held herself so still, in her tiny cavelike space; she thought her cramped muscles would surely give way under the strain. Thorny brambles bit into her legs, scratched her face. She only hoped they would hide her until Brad got here. She'd heard his voice over the megaphone and knew help was at hand, but *oh God, oh God,* he might not be in time. Dr. Ralph was going to kill her, as surely as he had killed the others.

"I know you're there, JC," she heard Sandowski call out. He sounded closer. "Remember, I know these woods like the back of my hand, I know where you, are, I can *smell* you, JC, I *smell* your fear."

. . .

The canine unit's German shepherd strained at his leash. Its officer had been afraid to let the dog go, afraid of disturbing their quarry, afraid he might shoot. Now though, Brad gave the signal for the dog to be freed and it plowed through the trees with them following. The SWAT team lined up closer to the woods, cutting off all escape routes, AK-47s at their shoulders.

. . .

Dr. Ralph *heard* JC. He heard her exhale, a sigh of misplaced relief, thinking help was at hand. He smiled. Now he knew exactly where she was hiding, in the shallow aperture that almost became a cave. He pushed through the vegetation, holding his rifle high over his head, like a marine in combat. And then he saw her. And JC saw him.

JC screamed. A long, high scream that cut through the silence of the forest to the waiting men, who came crashing through the trees, led by the dog.

. . .

Fuck it, Dr. Ralph thought, taking all the time in the world and getting JC squarely in his sights. She was flattened against the bank of earth behind her, arms spread, looking like a silent-movie star in peril. Her eyes met his as he crouched and took aim.

As he did so a pain shot down his left arm sharp as the bullet he had not yet fired. It hit his chest like fire, traveled up his neck like a lightning bolt. He could not breathe. He still had his finger on the trigger though.

• • •

Ten feet away, Brad took aim. The AK-47 was a powerful weapon, but he did not shoot to kill. He wanted this fucker alive. The bullets raked Sandowski's legs and he fell face-forward, his own rifle still aimed at JC. He was still looking at her when he pulled the trigger.

52

Sandowski was sprawled, facedown, on the ground. His blood soaked the carpet of dead leaves.

A few feet away JC lay in an untidy heap, legs scrunched under her, arms over her head. She was bleeding from a wound in her side.

Jesus . . . oh God . . . Brad ran toward her. Jerry was yelling for medics and the SWAT team crowded forward, guns still shouldered.

The German shepherd stood proudly over JC, its lips curled in a warning growl as Brad came closer. The trainer called it off.

Brad knelt over her. He took her arm and lowered it gently from her face. Her eyes opened and she looked at him. "It hurts like hell," she said, putting a hand over the hole in her side from which blood oozed. "Now I've messed up Vivi's camo-coat," she added with a flicker of her old grin. "She'll kill me."

"Nobody's gonna kill you, JC," Brad said, as the medics bearing collapsible orange stretchers lumbered toward them and began quickly to assess her injuries.

Jerry stood, AK-47 drooping from his hand, looking down at the killer, as other medics slid a stretcher under him. Sandowski's eyes were shut and his face had a greenish pallor. The medics were attempting to stem the blood pouring from his shattered legs where Brad had sprayed him with bullets. Jerry knew Brad could have aimed higher, taken him out immediately, but he'd so badly wanted Sandowski alive, so badly wanted him to pay for his terrible deeds in a court of law in front of twelve good men and true. They both wanted Sandowski to know the fear his victims had known.

One of the medics glanced up. "It's his heart, sir, as well as the bullet wounds. This man is in cardio shock. He may not make it."

Brad's eyes met Jerry's. "Get the bastard to the emergency room," Brad barked. "Right now."

Sandowski was loaded onto the orange stretcher and carried through the woods to the waiting medevac. On a stretcher behind him came JC, so pale her lips looked bloodless, her pupils dilated with shock and the pain medication and the epinephrine they had shot into her.

"You'll be okay," Brad said into her ear, as they carried her past. "You're all right, JC. He's gone now. And Vivi will be waiting for you. I'm radioing her now to say you're on your way."

JC's smile was, Brad thought, the smile of a true innocent. A happy young woman who had always treated life as though it was a game to play. And now the game had been turned on her. JC was very lucky to be alive.

• • •

As soon as they were gone, Brad got on his radio and called Vivi at the hospital.

"JC's okay," he said, before she could ask. "She took a bullet in her left side. The medics say it hasn't punctured anything important, but she'll need your loving care."

"Oh, God, oooh God . . ." Vivi's voice was faint with relief.

"Sandowski is also on his way. He's been shot in the legs. Seems like he might also have a cardiac condition. I'm not suggesting you give him your loving care, but do your best to keep him alive. I want him to face his judgment day. Alone. In court."

53

Vivi was waiting in the emergency department for the medevac to touch down. Cops swarmed round the place, but the media who had somehow already heard the news had been kept outside, where TV cameras and newspersons were already giving an unoffi cial version of what had happened. They knew the serial killer had been caught, that he was being brought to the hospital. What they did not yet know was his name, or who he was.

Vivi's team were silent: the young interns and the wonderful nurses with whom she had worked for years, all knowing who was coming, all as apprehensive as she was. A call warned them the medevac was arriving.

Vivi tucked her hair under the plastic cap, she scrubbed her hands one more time before pulling on the thin surgical gloves.

They wheeled JC in first and Vivi went to her. The team were already cutting off JC's clothing, taking her pulse and her blood pressure, inserting lines, placing an oxygen mask over her face.

"JC, it's me, Vivi," she said, looking not at her sister's face but at the neat round hole in her side. "Lift her up," she commanded. "We need to see where the bullet exited." Now she saw it. Blood still trickled from the wound but at least Vivi knew there was no bullet lodged in JC's abdomen. She cleaned the wound then quickly sent her sister up to surgery where they would repair the damage.

As she watched her go, she heard the wheels of the second gurney screeching fast toward her.

The man on the gurney did not look like the Dr. Ralph Vivi knew. His eyes were closed, his face bloodless, exactly like the masks used in Venice at Carnevale; a grotesque face, the mouth twisted into a mockery of a grin. His hands were clenched into fists. His legs were swathed in bloody gauze.

Vivi's own hands clenched into fists as she stuffed them in the pockets of her white doctor coat, standing there, unmoving, staring down at the man who had tried to kill her sister. The man who had brutally murdered many other young women. The man who had put the lovely young girl, Elaine, still here in the hospital, in a coma, cutting her throat and leaving her for dead. This man was a monster and now she was supposed to help him.

Silent, her team stood watching. For once nobody moved to help the patient in distress. For once there was no sound in the emergency department.

Vivi closed her eyes. She reminded herself of the Hippocratic Oath, the oath every medical doctor in the world learned and promised to keep. The oath that told her she was there to help mankind. Not to pass judgment.

He was a man in pain, a man on the edge of life. And she was a doctor. It was her job, her *duty* to try to save him.

She pulled herself up taller, took her hands from her pockets and began calling out orders. The team sprang into action. In seconds they had Sandowski hooked up to machines that read his pulse, his heartbeat, his blood pressure. Others cleaned the leg wounds, stemming the blood flow.

One glance had told Vivi she was looking at a cardiac victim. The monitor flickered wildly as Sandowski fought to breathe. She bent over him to affix the oxygen mask and his eyes shot open.

Vivi's horrified eyes looked into his. And then he spoke.

In a rough whisper he said, *"It should have been you, bitch."*

Shocked, Vivi took a step back. *Dear God, she could almost have thought the man was laughing at her.*

Getting her nerves together, she had him rushed immediately to cardio. Then she went into the nurses' room and cried. Not for herself, and certainly not for him, but because she was first and foremost a doctor, and for a moment she had almost betrayed herself, and that oath, her promise always to do her best to save a life.

• • •

Dr Ralph Sandowski succumbed to a second major cardiovascular attack exactly one hour later. He died without another word, as stealthily as he had lived. Gone, when the nursing staff's back was turned for just one instant. Everyone at the hospital had done their duty. Everyone was thankful. Some even said they were glad.

• • •

A short while later, the police chief held a news conference outside the hospital. He explained the situation, told the shocked media that the serial killer was a man well known to many of them, gave them Sandowski's name and the details of exactly what had happened at his cabin where he had held the sister of one of the doctors hostage.

"That this emergency room doctor, Dr. Vivian Dexter, looked after this terrible man when he was brought wounded and dying to this hospital is a testimony to her character," he added. "And to the job our emergency room doctors and personnel do every day for this great city of ours.

"It's also a proud testimony to the perseverance of my detectives, Brad Merlin and Jerusalem Guiterrez, who sifted through a myriad of false trails and details that would have confounded many others. It's thanks only to their determination to find this killer that he was in fact caught and brought to his final justice. Dr. Sandowski died an hour ago. I do not believe he will rest in peace. Thank you, ladies and gentlemen. And now perhaps we can get back to the land of the living."

· · ·

Brad burst like a tornado through the doors of Emergency. He was still wearing the Kevlar bulletproof vest. Dirt clung to the knees of his pants where he had thrown himself down to take aim. His new shoes were caked in mud and his springy hair was dark with sweat. Every head turned to look at him but Brad didn't even notice. All he saw was Vivi in her bloodstained scrubs and her plastic shower cap, eyes dark pools in her pale face. The officers still on duty stood respectfully to one side as he strode toward her.

"You can't come in here," Vivi said. "Not like that, I mean."

But Brad already had his arms around her.

"I'm on duty," Vivi told him, her head nestled into his neck where she could smell the sweetness of his skin and the sharpness of his sweat, feel the *life* of him, feel the strength of his arms holding her. She didn't care who was watching, didn't care what she should or should not be doing right here in the ER. She wanted to take him home right that minute; she needed to revive under his caresses, the touch of his hands.

The terrible events of the day faded into the background; as did her fear and self-doubts that she would be able to carry out her work as a doctor; and her hatred of the insane man on the gurney hissing his curse at her even as he was dying.

"It was terrible," she whispered in Brad's ear. "So bad, I can't even tell you."

"Later, you will. We'll talk about it later, baby. God, I need to be alone with you." He held her away, looking into her eyes. "Haven't you done enough for one day? Can't you just leave, come home with me now?"

Vivi shook her head. "I'm waiting for JC to come round from the anesthetic. She just had surgery to repair three broken ribs and a broken ulna, a bone in her left arm. And Fen is on her way, she took a commuter flight from Monterey."

"Then you'll come to me later? Whenever you're free? I'll go back to the precinct, wrap up some paperwork, get a drink with Jorry. But I promise I'll have the fire lit and the candles, I'll have Chinese takeout and a hot bath waiting."

Vivi laughed. "You know, you're perfect," she whispered, kissing his ear. "Just *perfect*."

"Just doing my best," he said, and then he gave her a long deep kiss that drew cheers from the watching outpatients and staff and the other cops.

"Eightish, then," Vivi called after him as he strode away, with that good long-legged lope and his big feet. God, she loved a big man. This big man, anyway.

54

When Brad and Jerry walked into Veronica's an hour or so later, she was behind the bar, elbows on the counter, head tilted back, watching the evening news replay of the police chief's speech.

She didn't bother to turn round. "The conquering heroes," she said, switching off the sound. "Ask me how I know."

"Yeah, so how do you know?" Brad hitched himself onto his usual seat; Jerry took the one next to him, and Flyin' sat waiting for her handout.

"I know because only a cop would have feet as big as yours, Brad Merlin. You bring your own sound effects."

"Maybe you should get yourself a pair of those Guccis," Jerry told Brad, accepting the shot of Patrón.

"They wouldn't have 'em in my size."

Veronica deposited the Maker's Mark in front of Brad. "Listen, if Arnie Schwarzenegger wears them, trust me they'll have your size. Anyhow, this is on the house."

"Thanks, Veronica."

The two men saluted her with their glasses, drained them, then gulped the ice-cold Bud.

"Listen, seriously now," Veronica said, propping her leopard-print bosoms on the bar, looking from one man to the other. "I'm saying a personal thank-you. In fact, I think every woman in California is saying a personal thank-you to you two guys. Because of you we can go to bed tonight without wondering if some monster is gonna climb in the window. Jesus, detectives, I think I'm seriously in love with you."

Brad leaned over and patted her hand. "Thanks, hon. I'm in love with you too, but I'm already taken."

Veronica heaved a mock sigh that sent her boobs a-jiggling, then went back to wiping glasses. "Story of my life," she said.

"Y'know somethin'?" Jerry slugged back the icy beer, enjoying every second of it. "I don't *know* the story of your life, Veronica. *Nobody* knows the story of your life."

"And nobody ever will. 'Cept here I am, and here I stay and tonight anything you want is on the house. In fact, listen up everybody." She waved a hand to silence the couple of dozen customers. The cute new barmaid with her long brown hair also stopped midway to delivering the special chicken dumpling soup, balancing three bowls precariously as she turned to look.

"Listen up, folks," Veronica said again. "Tonight is my party. We're honoring San Francisco's finest. Drinks all round and a toast to these two detectives, without whom more of us might not even be here."

A cheer went up, people crowded the bar to shake hands. "See, I told you, you were stars," Veronica said, throwing Flyin' a burger intended for the folks in a booth in the back. "More where that came from," she told the dog, who made short work of it.

"Sorry, Veronica." Brad untangled himself from the bar stool and the sea of people. "But I've got a date."

Veronica leveled a look at him which said she regretted that, for her own sake, but was glad for him. "Always had a soft spot for you, Merlin," she said softly. "I'll bet it's Vivi, isn't it? Your Dr. Vivian?"

Brad nodded. "She's the one."

Veronica pulled a couple more beers, always careful to keep the foaming head on them. "Lucky girl," she commented, giving Brad a wry smile.

"Lucky man, you mean," Brad added, as his phone buzzed.

It was Vivi. "I'm calling to tell you that Elaine came out of her coma," she said quietly. "If I were not a doctor, I could almost call this a miracle. She can speak, only a whisper yet, but her parents were there, and she recognized them. Her first words were, 'Hello mom.'"

"Luck," Brad said, "comes in many guises. Elaine finally got lucky."

Then he and Jerry swung back out the door, Jerry on his way finally to spend time with his wife, avoid his mother-in law from hell, see his kids and hold his baby boy. While Brad and Flyin' headed back to his place and his date with Vivi.

Worried frantic though she was, Fen had dressed carefully in her smart little navy Chanel suit, the classic one with its cream braiding and the gold chains on the inside hem of the jacket to weigh it down. It was a source of pride that it still fit like the day she had bought it, in the seventies, from the Chanel boutique in avenue Montaigne in Paris, though perhaps her butt had looked better in it then. Sort of *higher*. She sighed, checking herself in the long mirror. Getting older had its downfalls, one of which was her rear end.

She'd brushed her bobbed silver hair behind her ears, with a fringe that hid the new wrinkles on her brow. Maybe too girlish? Too Anna Wintour and *Vogue*? One could only do one's best.

The black suede boots were not exactly correct with the suit either but for her, comfort always came first. She also wore her blue peacoat because the wind had a winter edge to it.

She had left Hector in the care of the nice lady who came to clean the cottage once a week, and who adored him. It meant Fen could give all her time to worrying about her nieces, *both* of them, though Vivi had assured her JC was all right.

"She'll be fine," Vivi had told her just a few hours ago.

"Not without me, she won't," Fen had replied, already planning her flight.

Now, she was in a taxi, toting her ancient Vuitton bag (so ancient it was chic, unlike the vulgar piles of new luggage one saw the nouveau-riche and rock stars toting. A little "shabby" was always better). She also held a sheaf of dreadful puce-colored gladioli bought in haste en route from the airport for her poor broken girl. *Gladioli!* Stiff, horrible flowers that should be banned from all florists, doomed forever to adorn the graves of dead ancestors because they were certainly not a cheerful blossom for a wounded patient. Still, the roses had been tired and the chrysanthemums even worse, so the puce gladioli were better, Fen supposed, than nothing.

When the taxi dropped her outside Emergency, she stood for a moment, looking at the hospital where her niece worked, where she gave her dedication, her hard-earned knowledge and experience to help those in need. Fen was very proud of Vivi.

A woman pushed through the doors, a small child by the hand, a baby in her arms. She saw Fen, how worried she looked, and threw her a smile.

"Don't worry, sweetheart," she called, "they'll take good care of you in there."

Fen smiled back. "Wait a minute," she said, thrusting the gladioli into the surprised woman's arms. "My niece works here," she explained. "She's an emergency doctor."

"Then you're a lucky woman." The stranger clutched her baby and the flowers, thanked Fen and went smiling, on her way.

It was in fact Fen's first time ever in an emergency room. She stood by the doors, looking round at the sick and the wounded drooping on their plastic chairs, at the injured on gurneys lined up waiting for attention. She took in the air of controlled chaos, the superb calm of the nurses on duty, the calls for doctors coming over the intercom, the crying children, the blank faces and inert limbs of the mentally lost, and the brisk tenderness of the doctors as they leaned over those gurneys being wheeled into small rooms, partitioned with curtains for privacy. This was Vivi's world, and Fen suddenly admired her choice. It was not an easy life. People in need depended on these doctors, these nurses, they trusted their diagnoses, their decisions, their quickness to help and their knowledge.

It was for sure nobody ever came to Emergency looking their best, and somehow everyone except Fen looked as though they had thrown on their clothes in a hurry. She wished she had brought flowers for all of them. Now, she did not even have flowers for her own girl.

She heard someone speak her name, and turned to look.

"Mrs. Dexter?"

It was that big detective, Merlin, her niece was so fond of. "Fond of" might not be the correct term, she thought, holding out her hand to shake his.

"Vivi told me she was expecting you," Brad said.

Fen smiled as she looked up—a long way up—into his nice blue eyes. *Kind* eyes, she thought. Gentle. Even though the man looked as though he'd been pulled through a hedge backwards, pants and shoes covered in mud and wearing a strange type of vest.

"I'm surprised they let you in here, looking like that," she said, disapprovingly.

Brad laughed. "You'll have to excuse me, ma'am, I came straight from duty. I just had to see Vivi."

"Of course you did." Fen liked his honesty. "And I can bet Vivi was glad to see you."

Brad hesitated, wondering exactly how much to tell her, then decided to keep it brief and let Vivi fill in the gaps. "JC has been through a tough time," he said finally. "Right now, she needs her family, not me."

"Come closer, please." Fen beckoned him. He stepped toward her. "Now bend your head, I want to kiss you," she told him. Smiling, Brad bent and offered his cheek for her kiss.

"That's my thank-you, for taking care of my girls," Fen said. "I have the feeling we'll be seeing more of each other."

"I trust your feeling is right, ma'am," Brad said as she waved him goodbye.

"Fen, *there* you are!"

Vivi bore down on her, almost running into her arms. "I'm so glad you came."

"Of course I came." Fen stepped back and took a look at her.

Vivi had thought to put on a clean white doctor coat so as not to scare her, and she had taken off the plastic cap and run her hands through her hair, repinning it in a bun at her nape. She'd thought she looked okay.

"You look terrible," Fen said.

They stood, staring at each other. "Oh, Fen, it was scary," Vivi whispered. "It's so awful I can't even bear to think about it, about what could have happened. You've no idea what JC went through . . . I mean that madman almost . . ."

"Well, he didn't," Fen said firmly. "Thanks partly to that nice detective of yours. And thanks also to JC's own bravery and presence of mind. We always think of your sister as flighty and irresponsible, but let me tell you, Vivi, from what Brad told me, she came through this time. And she will in future. And let me ask you to remember something. You *will* get past this day, past all the bad things that happened. You'll get beyond the madman because you can never give in to evil. I'm not saying 'goodness' is easy to maintain, but most of us try for that goal. And you, Dr. Vivian, are succeeding. Now, take me to see my other girl, why don't you?"

JC lay in a narrow hospital bed, propped up with pillows. Her left arm was in a cast and her ribs were strapped up. Drips snaked from her arms and monitors told her medical story. She heard them coming and swiveled her big round blue eyes toward them.

"So, I'm okay," she said with a big grin that wobbled a bit at the edges. "I mean, like, it's just a couple of ribs and stuff, though this bloody arm is a nuisance. I'll never get a job, now, will I, Fen?"

Fen bent and gently kissed her. She stroked the long blond hair that was JC's signature and which now hung in strings round her face, that in fact did not have a single bruise on it.

"I covered my head with my arms," JC explained. "Vanity won over fear."

"Make no mistake it was the 'fear' that saved you," Fen said, pulling a chair up to the bed. "But as you know I'm all in favor of a bit of vanity. It keeps a woman young."

"I *am* young," JC reminded her.

"Young enough to enjoy Paris, I'll bet."

JC's face lit up. "You mean it?" she asked, thrilled.

Fen said, "When you get out of here, you're coming to stay with me at the cottage. Then, when you're well enough, I thought it would be fun, you and me, Paris in the spring . . . ?"

"But what about Vivi? We can't leave her out."

"Oh yes we can," Fen said. "Your sister already has a man. No need to go to Paris looking for one."

JC grinned at her. "Not like us, you mean," she said, and they both burst out laughing, which hurt JC's ribs so much she had to stop.

"I gave your flowers away," Fen told her. "Gladioli. I couldn't stand them."

"Nor can I," JC agreed.

Standing next to them Vivi glanced at her watch. "I have to leave," she said. "I'll look back in later though."

"Don't worry about me," Fen said. "I've booked into the hotel. I'll stay here with your sister for a while. It's time you went to see your guy."

"Give Brad my love," JC said, suddenly serious. "And my thanks."

JC was a very lucky girl, and she knew it. Then, looking past her aunt she saw Alex hurrying toward her, a bunch of roses in his hand and a worried expression on his face.

"Well, well," Fen murmured, getting quickly to her feet.

Alex stopped at the foot of the bed, looking anguished at JC. "I saw it on TV," he said. "I couldn't believe it. I *could not believe* it was happening to you. I should have realized it was him, I should have been the one to kill him . . ."

"No you should not," Fen said quickly. "You can never give yourself over to someone else's evil. It's exactly what they want you to do."

"Sort of like 'recruiting' you for the devil," JC said with a shiver.

Alex handed her the roses, gave her a quick kiss on the cheek and turned to look at Fen. "Are you all right? I was so worried about you . . ."

Her eyes linked with his. She was lost in his gaze. There was nothing she could do about it.

"Oh, you two are in love!" JC's voice seemed to come from a long distance, and then Fen was held in Alex's arms, and darn it if she wasn't crying again. And she *never* cried.

"You always cry when you're happy," JC said. And her pleased laughter made everyone all right.

56

Vivi almost flew home. Her old Jeep rattled and clunked up the steep San Francisco hills as she dodged trolley cars and stalled impatiently at red lights. Every minute lost was a minute less with Brad. Luck was with her though; there was a parking spot right outside her door.

She ran down those area steps and inside, flinging off her clothes as she went, leaving a trail all the way to the bathroom. For once the water pressure behaved and she lounged in the deep, rusty old tub amid a swirl of French bath oil—almond, which did wonders for the skin, and lavender mixed with vanilla, the two scents that she'd heard from Fen, the expert, were supposed to drive men crazy with desire. She wasn't taking any chances.

She stood under the shower and washed her long hair, letting the warm water rinse away the sweat of fear. She rubbed in a little of the Moroccan oil that gave it shine and because she was running out of time, left it to dry naturally while she painted her toenails silver, using JC's polish, and then her fingers a ladylike pink, though she was certainly not in a "ladylike" mood.

Victoria's Secret always came through when a girl needed a pair of silky panties; these were blush-pink like her nail polish and nothing as unsubtle as a thong. They were like the French knickers platinum blondes always seemed to wear in thirties movies, and the matching bra managed to look like a mere wisp of a thing while doing something magical to her breasts.

She put on black silk stockings, the expensive Wolford kind that stayed up without help and which she had bought long ago with the Frenchman in mind (with *who*? Who *was* that Frenchman? She did not even remember!) A pair of JC's heels, black suede, peep toe—was that correct with the stockings and all? She doubted it but liked the sexy way it looked and made her feel.

She sat in front of the mirror and stroked on Laura Mercier's Caramel tinted moisturizer, NARS Orgasm blusher (she'd had to be brave to ask for it by name at Bloomie's) black eyeliner and mascara, then Chanel's Deauville lipstick. Her hair had dried dead straight for once instead of in little kinks and she ran the brush through it and let it fall free around her shoulders.

A spray of Tom Ford's Jasmin Rouge in all the places that counted—and she meant *all*—then into the little black dress (her only dress-up dress), the fake diamond ear studs that looked really real, the diamond brooch from her aunt that was real, albeit small; a couple of antique (well, forties, that made them antique didn't it) Bakelite bangles, a black clutch, and she was ready.

She looked in the mirror. Tonight, she was not a doctor. Tonight she was a woman.

She went to the window and took a look outside. It was raining, of course. Her raincoat was all of seven years old but it almost looked like a Burberry trench. She threw it on, hurried to the Jeep and pulled out, heading toward those hills and the traffic and the sound of a joyous San Francisco night, leaving behind the stress, the terror, the worry, the "woman in charge." Tonight, she was Brad Merlin's girl.

· · ·

Brad opened the red lacquer door before Vivi even had time to knock. He was barefoot, in jeans and a white T-shirt. His hair was still wet from the shower and he was looking at her like he could eat her up. Which she sincerely hoped he would, later.

He had a bottle of Champagne in one hand and Flyin' by the collar in the other as he leaned in to kiss her, putting his arm round her, drawing her in out of the rain.

Flyin' rubbed her woolly head against Vivi's legs in greeting, while Brad kissed her again. And kissed her. And kissed her some more. "You smell wonderful," he murmured, his eyes still closed, breathing her in.

Vivi threw off her coat and let it slip to the floor, putting her arms round his neck. "Where do we begin?" she asked.

Brad opened his eyes again and smiled. "Well, I have Chinese food all ready for you. There's the beef with broccoli, that sweet-and-sour you always like, though I can never figure out why; there's Peking duck; there's jasmine rice . . ."

"I think I'll begin with you." Vivi was already unzipping her dress. "After all, I can't let all this effort go to waste, can I?"

"I'd never allow it," Brad promised, as she stepped out of the little black dress and stood there in her French panties and little bra, her black stockings and her heels. "Jesus," he said, awed, "I thought I had a date with a doctor."

"Not tonight, you don't," Vivi said, with the wonderful sense of freedom that at last she had finally achieved her goal. She was a doctor. But she was also a woman.

57

The hospital had done its best to make a happy Christmas. Paper chains and tinsel were looped around walls and over doors, baubles dangled from the ceilings and trees shimmered with lights. They had really gone to town on the children's ward of course, with presents piled up under a silver tree and nurses wearing Rudolph antlers.

Vivi loved it all; loved where she worked, loved her colleagues, loved her nurses, loved her job. It went without saying that she loved Brad. It had taken her all of five minutes to agree to move in with him and, next to taking her doctor's oath, it was the best thing she had ever done. Happiness did not come better than this.

She had talked to JC about Fen and Alex; they were so obviously besotted with each other, worse almost than she and Brad, they had wondered, worriedly, about the "older woman/younger man" situation, whether it might cause trouble in the future.

"I don't see why," Vivi said. "Look at all the older *men* with younger women." And that was it. She and JC had high-fived and silently wished them luck.

Now though, before she met Brad and drove to Big Sur for the holidays, Vivi was on her way to see Elaine, the serial killer's last victim. Vivi still could not bring herself to say his name, she had written it out of her mind so completely she could not even remember how he had looked.

She'd visited Elaine every day since they'd brought her into her emergency room, watched over her silent coma, wondering if she would ever come out of it. And then, quite suddenly, Elaine had simply opened her eyes and looked around. She looked at Vivi standing there and actually smiled at her.

Elaine had gone on from there, getting better day by day with her parents there to witness every one of them. Her voice was coming slowly back, husky, low, but she could speak. Now, when she saw Vivi clutching a red-wrapped parcel, she smiled and said, "Hi, you."

"Hi yourself." Vivi stepped into the room, walked to the bed, took Elaine's thin pale hand and squeezed it. "Just wanted to say Merry Christmas."

"Then why aren't you wearing your Rudolph antlers?"

"I left that to the other doctors," Vivi said and Elaine giggled, a sound that was music to Vivi's ears.

"This is for you," Vivi said, handing her the parcel.

"Oh, but I don't have one for you."

"Oh yes you do. You are *here*, aren't you!"

Elaine stared solemnly at her. She had once been a pretty girl. Vivi hoped one day she would be again, when her wounds had faded and her soul repaired itself.

"You saved my life," Elaine whispered hoarsely.

"Not just me, there were the nurses and the surgeons, a lot of us took care of you."

"I know it was you, though, Dr. Vivian. You were the one." She hesitated then said, "Do you mind if I kiss you?"

Vivi laughed. "I've always been a kind of kissy person," she agreed, putting her arms gently around the girl, feeling her lips soft on her cheek. She said, "Now, here's your Christmas present. Open it later, when they come round to sing carols. You'll love it."

Vivi knew she would, it was a nightie from Nordstrom, pale pink and girly. Exactly what Elaine needed to help her feel a whole woman again.

She waved goodbye and hurried back through the endless corridors to the exit where she knew Brad would be waiting for her. And Flyin' of course. There were three of them in this family.

58

Somehow Christmas had crept up on Fen. It was a good thing she'd bought new lights in November, now the glowing tree was lit and decorated and filling the entire cottage with its fresh piney smell, mingling happily with the mouth-watering aroma of the turkey she had risen at five to get into the oven, in time for late-afternoon Christmas lunch. That would be lunch for herself, her girls as well as Brad and Alex. Add two dogs, Hector and Flyin' who was accompanying her master as always. Brad had been given a generous couple of days off, as had Vivi.

JC, of course, was already there—and of course, she was still in bed. Giving her the benefit of the doubt, Fen assumed it was because she was still recuperating. Broken ribs seemed to take a lot out of a girl, though certainly not her appetite. JC was eating Fen out of house and home. In fact, she called down now to ask if the turkey was ready yet, and if so could she have a bit.

"Just to taste," she added, appearing at the top of the stairs wrapped in Fen's blue cashmere robe. "While we're at it," she added hopefully, "maybe we could open just one of our presents, y'know, like, just to check what we got."

Fen sighed. "JC, when will you ever learn the rules and grammar, and never to say '*like*' in front of your aunt."

"You're not my aunt anymore, you're really my mom," JC said suddenly.

Fen's eyes filled with tears.

In all the years the girls had been hers they had used the title "aunt." She had never asked for, never expected the privilege of being "mom."

"That's the best Christmas present in the world, to be your mom," she said. "What's more, I didn't even have to open it."

"It's true, though. You are our mom." JC's big blue eyes appreciated her. "Vivi says so, and so do I. It's official."

"So be it, then." Fen honestly didn't know whether to laugh or cry. This was the biggest thing that had ever happened to her. Except for Alex of course.

"So? Is he coming then?" JC was all innocence.

"You mean Alex?" Fen asked, equally innocently. "How would I know?"

"Well, because you asked him, I suppose."

Fen sighed and turned back to the giblets simmering in the big All-Clad pan on the stove, with a bunch of thyme and rosemary and a bay leaf.

"Can't a woman have any secrets?"

"Not when the woman is as transparent as you." JC was laughing at her. "And as goofily in love as Alex. And as smart—*experienced* let's call it—as me. I know love when I see it."

"Oh, JC, do you? Do you really?"

JC hobbled over and put her arms round Fen. "You bet I do," she whispered. "You bet I do, Mom."

"Where is Hector?" Fen asked, pulling back. "I haven't seen him all morning."

"On my bed, of course." JC looked hungrily at the stove. "Are you doing your famous roast potatoes?"

"Of course I am, parboiled first. As well as sweet potatoes, without, I can tell you, any of those marshmallows on top, because the potatoes are absolutely sweet enough as they are. *And* mashed, because men always go for those."

"But I love marshmallows." JC looked aggrieved.

"There's green beans," Fen gave JC a keen eye, remembering her childhood aversion to vegetables. "Which you will eat, or you will not get dessert."

"What is for dessert then?" JC was a chocolate ice cream fan, though any dessert would do in a pinch.

"You guessed it," Fen said, smiling at her because JC always seemed able to make her smile. "And you can have English Christmas pudding with brandy butter and vanilla custard sauce."

"I'll take both, thank you very much."

"Meanwhile you will go and take a shower and get dressed. Your family will be here soon."

"*You* are my family," JC said, throwing loving arms round her neck.

Watching her go, Fen thought about what she'd said about her and Alex. Was it love? Alex still had the dark memories of his fiancée to deal with, and she had to get on with her own life. The trip to Paris was meant to help with that.

Of course Vivi had moved in with Brad. Fen remembered the old days when *she* was a girl, having to sneak around to be with a man,

357

sometimes even marrying him if it was the only way to be together. Nowadays, young people took no chances; they simply gave marriage a test drive before taking their vows. Fen guessed it was not a bad way to go. Besides, those two loved each other, no doubt about it. You only had to see the way they looked at one another, the way each caught the other's glance, the small exchanged intimate smiles. Vivi had finally found what she was looking for.

Fen went and pushed the logs around in the grate. It was a fine, cold blue Christmas Day, with a wind that smelled of the sea and of applewood smoke and of cooking turkey. Seven red stockings adorned with Santa faces hung from the mantel. Five for people, two for dogs. Fen adored Christmas, adored the run-up to it, the secret shopping, the wrapping, the cooking. Her family.

Hector came and flung himself in front of the glowing fire, looking up at her. She bent to caress his grizzled muzzle.

"Another year, Hector, you and I. In our sanctuary. *Alone together*. How happy is that?" And Fen thanked the Lord for her blessings and for Alex and bent her head and kissed her dog.

Acknowledgments

As always, I must thank my "team" at St Martin's: Jen Enderlin, whose fertile mind sees possibilities around every corner; Sally Richardson, who oversees those possibilities; and Geraldine Van Dusen, who haunts me with copyedits and queries And of course my friend, and simply the best agent, Anne Sibbald and her team at Janklow & Nesbit Associates, who when we are not talking about kitties (her gorgeous little leopard-like Ocicats and my Siamese and glossy black rescue) are talking food and books and the future. Many, many thanks.

And of course, to Richard and my family (this book is dedicated to my daughter, Anabelle, and her husband, Eric) and friends. Who could ask for more?